# "Night," Xavier said, pulling on his coat.

She didn't mean to stare, but he made the act of putting on his jacket a spectator sport. He was definitely the finest man ever to step foot in Moose Falls. Maybe in all of Alaska, if she was being honest.

"Good night," True said, battling the urge to ask him to stick around a bit longer. It was a foreign feeling considering she was always eager to get home to Jaylen and relieve her sitter. Her brother would be asleep by now, but just being at home with him was always satisfying.

"Just a sec. I forgot something," Xavier murmured, moving toward her and not stopping until their bodies were mere inches away from each other. He looked down at her and cupped her chin in his hand. She noticed little caramel flecks in his eyes as he dipped his head down. "I've been wanting to do this since the day we met." True had a few seconds to step away from the incoming kiss, but there wasn't a single question in her mind that she wanted this to happen.

# FALLING FOR
# ALASKA

# ALSO BY BELLE CALHOUNE

**The Mistletoe, Maine Series**

*No Ordinary Christmas*
*Summer on Blackberry Beach*
*Falling in Love on Sweetwater Lane*

# FALLING FOR
# ALASKA

## BELLE CALHOUNE

FOREVER
New York  Boston

Forever
Hachette Book Group
1290 Avenue of the Americas, New York, NY 10104
read-forever.com
twitter.com/readforeverpub

First Edition: March 2024

Forever is an imprint of Grand Central Publishing. The Forever name and logo are trademarks of Hachette Book Group, Inc.

The publisher is not responsible for websites (or their content) that are not owned by the publisher.

The Hachette Speakers Bureau provides a wide range of authors for speaking events. To find out more, go to hachettespeakersbureau.com or email HachetteSpeakers@hbgusa.com.

Forever books may be purchased in bulk for business, educational, or promotional use. For information, please contact your local bookseller or the Hachette Book Group Special Markets Department at special.markets@hbgusa.com.

ISBNs: 9781538758205 (mass market), 9781538758212 (ebook)

Printed in the United States of America

OPM

10 9 8 7 6 5 4 3 2 1

*For my parents, who shared a beautiful love story
that inspires me every day.*

# PROLOGUE

Xavier Stone didn't like to cry. He didn't like the way it made his eyes sting or how his stomach twisted with every sob. Even worse, he hated to see his mom and brothers cry. Ever since they had left Moose Falls, his family unit had been falling apart at the seams. Packing up their belongings and leaving Alaska for Arizona had been terrible. The heat here was unbearable and nothing like what they were used to back home. He couldn't wear any of his favorite sweaters here or his thick corduroys. Mama told them it almost never snows in Arizona. There wouldn't be any sledding or snowboarding or dogsledding. Tears pricked his eyes, but he blinked them away.

*Crying is for babies.* His father's voice buzzed in his ear, reminding him to always be tough.

He couldn't cry. Wouldn't cry. At ten years old he was the oldest, and it was his job to stay strong. Xavier was the man of the house now. They'd left their father behind in Moose Falls, and from what he'd overheard, his parents were getting a divorce. Things had been bad for a long time now, with fights and shouting and slammed doors. Those moments had always scared him and his brothers, exploding like fireworks in the night sky—noisy and unpredictable. They could have been having the best time of their lives right before the trouble started, when everything would suddenly go haywire.

Over time Xavier had learned to expect the explosions. He would clench his fists at his sides during the happy moments—Christmas morning, birthdays, Easter—because he'd learned not to trust the calm. And even though his father's outbursts scared him, Xavier loved him with a fierceness that always confused him. He hadn't wanted to leave his father behind, but he was angry at him for breaking their family apart. Xavier couldn't stop thinking about him standing in the doorway with tears in his eyes as they had driven away, his deep baritone voice calling out their names. *Daisy! Don't leave me.* Xavier knew it would be a long time before those cries would stop ringing in his ears. If ever.

His mother, Daisy Stone, was beautiful. Everyone said so. With her long, curly hair, toffee-colored skin, and big brown eyes, she was someone people always looked at. Whether they were at the supermarket or the bowling alley or church, folks always gravitated toward her grace and beauty.

She was at the center of their family. Everyone revolved around her the way the earth revolved around the sun. He thought of her as a living, breathing magnet. Grandpa Joe said she was pure sunshine and the brightest light in his life. He hadn't stopped smiling since they had touched down at the Phoenix Sky Harbor Airport. Xavier didn't know if Grandpa should be grinning so much considering the sad circumstances, but the old man was happy to be reunited with his baby girl. They were now living in the two-story home Xavier's mother had grown up in.

The sound of his mother's muffled sobs caused his stomach to clench as he walked down the hall. She probably thought they had all gone to sleep, but Xavier had stayed up to watch an episode of *That's So Raven* and of *SpongeBob SquarePants*. Sitting on the couch and watching his favorite shows almost made him forget about the last twenty-four hours. He knocked on his mother's bedroom door and slowly turned the knob. The room was softly lit by the small lamp on the bureau. His mother, startled by his appearance, looked over at him with puffy, reddened eyes.

Without saying a word, he rushed to her side and lay down beside her. "Mom, are you all right? Can I get you anything? A cup of tea?" He grabbed a box of tissues from the bedside table and slid them across the bed toward her.

"Don't worry about me, Xavier. I'm fine." She reached out and tousled his head. "We're all going to be just fine once we adjust."

*Adjust?* The word sounded so mechanical. What they'd left behind in Alaska were pieces of their hearts. There was now a hole in the center of his chest that would be impossible to fill. Moose Falls wasn't just any place. It was home. His grandmother had always said there was magic in every snowflake.

"Do you miss Moose Falls?" He swallowed past the huge lump in his throat. He really wanted to ask if she missed his dad, but he worried that doing so might make her even more tearful.

"The real question is how are you doing? I know it's a lot." Her lips trembled. "And I'm sorry, but—"

Xavier shrugged. "I'm doing okay," he said in a low voice, cutting her off. He didn't need to hear her say out loud why they'd left. They all knew it was because of their dad.

"It's important that you get a good night's sleep. You have school in the morning."

Xavier let out a groan. He didn't want to think about his first day at a new school. The other kids would probably think they were just some weirdos from Alaska. I mean, who started a new school in October? Everybody had probably known one another since kindergarten.

"Can't I just stay here with you, Mom? You need me."

She reached out and grazed her fingers across his cheek. "And you need to settle in and meet all the special friends who are going to be part of this new life of ours. I bet you'll come back with a list of names and phone numbers as long as your arm."

He let out a mutinous groan. Nothing would be as perfect as she imagined.

"Being the oldest means setting an example for Landon and Caleb. If you stay home, there's no chance of me getting them to go."

"Just once I want to be the youngest so I don't have to set an example," he grumbled. Xavier folded his arms across his chest and stuck his lip out. He was only ten years old, not a grown-up.

"Oh, Xavier. You're just who you were meant to be. I'm the luckiest mom in the world to have you as my very own." She nestled him against her chest. He wrapped his arms around her. "If you could only see the way Landon and Caleb look at you. In their eyes, you hung the moon. But if it ever gets too much for you, I want to know. Okay?"

He nodded. It *was* kind of cool being the oldest and having two brothers who looked up to him. But sometimes, he wished it didn't feel like such a huge responsibility. What if one day he simply cracked under the pressure? He'd heard his grandmother talking about how his dad couldn't handle pressure. Xavier didn't want to be anything like him. Never in a million years.

"All right," he agreed, wanting to soothe his mother. "I'm going to get ready for bed so I can be up bright and early for school." He made his voice sound cheerful even though he felt lower than an ant's belly.

"That's my boy," she said, a smile tugging at the sides of

her mouth. "I already tucked your brothers in a while ago, but I can tuck you in if you like."

At ten years old, he was getting too old for tuck-ins, although it sounded so comforting. He needed to focus on helping his family adjust to life away from Moose Falls. He needed to be a big boy.

"It's okay. Just get some rest." He winked at her. "You're going to need all your strength to make me chocolate chip pancakes in the morning."

Xavier padded down the hall toward his bedroom after brushing his teeth and splashing his face with water. Getting used to a new house was hard. Everything was different here. He kind of missed sharing a room with his brothers, while at the same time he was looking forward to more privacy.

As he walked past his brothers' room, the soft glow of the moon-shaped night-light drew his attention. Landon had trouble sleeping without one, and he was fascinated by space. The sound of sniffling reached Xavier's ears, and he gently pushed the door open. He knew immediately it was Landon. Xavier quickly looked over at Caleb's twin bed. He was lightly snoring with his sheets all tangled, his legs sprawled.

"Hey, buddy. What's wrong?" Xavier asked as he sank down on the bed beside Landon.

Landon rolled over so they were face-to-face. "I'm scared."

"Of what? You've got your night-light. You're safe and sound," Xavier said, trying to reassure him. He ran his hand across his brother's short-cropped hair in a gesture meant to provide comfort.

"This house makes creaking sounds," Landon whispered. "Like there's a ghost or something. I was watching this documentary about houses with paranormal activity. How do we know this isn't a hot spot?"

Xavier stifled a chuckle. Landon was only seven, but he was the smartest kid on the planet. He loved documentaries, the solar system, and anything science related. "There aren't any ghosts here," he said, trying to sound reassuring. "Mom grew up in this house. She woulda told us."

"Xavier, will you sleep with me? Please! Just tonight." Landon crossed his hands in front of him and pleaded.

Normally Xavier would just say no and leave it at that, but his mother's words were fresh in his memory. *In their eyes, you hung the moon.*

"Okay, just this once," he said, pulling back the covers and sliding beneath them.

"You make everything better," Landon said as he snuggled against Xavier's side.

He was thankful for the room being mostly dark. Xavier wouldn't want Landon to see the tears pooling in his eyes. He had a tough image to uphold, after all. His brother's heartfelt words cut straight to his heart.

Before he knew it, Caleb was standing by the side of the bed. "Scooch over and make room for me." Landon moved over so that he was sandwiched between his two younger brothers. Even though the bed felt way too crowded for a comfortable sleep, Xavier wouldn't have it any other way. In this moment he was exactly where he was meant to be.

# CHAPTER ONE

*Twenty Years Later*

The moment tall, dark, and handsome walked into Northern Exposure, True Everett's stomach lurched as if she'd taken a ride on the Tilt-A-Whirl at the carnival. The last time she had gone on that particular thrill ride, True had been twelve years old and eager for excitement. At twenty-eight years old, she knew better than to look for adventure in a good-looking man. Been there, done that. Having her heart smashed into little pieces had taught her a huge life lesson. She was never going down that road again.

Of course, she knew who the man was on sight. Xavier Stone, a ridiculously handsome ex–football player for the Arizona Cardinals. The Storm was what the fans called him, according to her little brother. There weren't many men in the universe who checked off all the boxes at first glance. This guy packed a solid punch visually.

*Easy there, girl,* she reminded herself. He had "handle with caution" written all over him.

True inhaled a deep, steadying breath as he walked straight toward the bar where she was taking orders. Her insides were now nothing but mush. Even meeting her ex, Garrett, for the first time hadn't yielded this type of visceral reaction. Although Garrett was easy on the eyes, he wasn't a showstopper. Not like this fine work of art handcrafted and dipped in the finest chocolate.

He had to be at least six feet tall. Skin as smooth as a Hershey bar. Full, wide lips. A strong jaw. When he shrugged out of his jacket, True could see his amazing physique. Even while wearing a sweater and jeans, his body popped—strong legs, a powerful chest, and muscled arms.

Body for days! It was enough to make a girl's eyes pop out of her head.

*Good grief!* This man was going to create a feeding frenzy in Moose Falls. Sheer pandemonium would ensue at the mere sight of him. It was almost the setup for a joke—a hot football player walks into an Alaskan tavern. Not a single person can stop staring at him, including the tavern's manager. *Ba dum tss.*

True cast a quick look in his direction. He'd almost made his way over to her. Every step he took was full of swagger. She began the countdown in her head as Xavier advanced, her body tensing with every step he took. *Why am I such a nervous wreck? This is ridiculous.*

"Hi there. Can I put in an order over here? The dining area is pretty packed."

Dang! Even his voice was spectacular. Deep and velvety, like maybe he sang R & B ballads in his spare time.

*Don't look him directly in the eyes!*
*Don't look him directly in the eyes!*
*DON'T LOOK HIM—*

Before she could stop herself, True locked gazes with him. *BAM!* Eyes the color of cognac stared back at her. They were framed by the most striking black lashes. A nice smile showcased perfect white teeth. His pictures hadn't done him justice. A sigh slipped past her lips. She'd just made a huge mistake by looking straight into his soulful brown eyes. True had immediately been swept away into this vortex of warmth and dreaminess and knock-your-socks-off charm.

"Of course. What can I get you?" True asked. *Stay calm*, she reminded herself. Xavier Stone was the last person on earth she wanted to fangirl over. From what she'd read about him, he already had an ego the size of the Chugach Mountains. That's what happened when you were an NFL football player with thousands of fans and buckets of money.

"Great. I'll do a salmon burger with coleslaw and rosemary fries," he said. "And let me have two Yukon Ciders. Apple crisp and wild berry. Please."

"Sure thing. The food will be ready in fifteen minutes or so." She pointed at a spot in the distance. "There's a spot that just freed up over by the pool table. We'll bring your drinks right over."

Instead of walking away to grab the open spot, Xavier couldn't seem to look away from something behind her. "What's with the contest?" he asked, jutting his chin in the direction of the sign hanging on the wall.

"We're having a hot wings promotion. If you can eat a whole platter of wings in five minutes, you win a prize," she explained.

"What's the prize?" Xavier flashed her a wide grin that caused butterflies to flutter around in her stomach. The feeling took her by surprise. Not even her ex-boyfriend, Garrett, had made her feel this way.

"A Northern Exposure T-shirt. And bragging rights." Judging by his expression, he wasn't impressed. "Want to take a whirl?" she asked.

Xavier smirked. "No thanks."

She gave him her best bless-your-heart smile. "I don't blame you. It's not for the faint of heart. Most people can't hack the heat."

Xavier chuckled and shook his head. "Trust and believe, I can eat hot wings with the best of 'em. Matter of fact," he said, puffing out his chest, "I've won my fair share of contests."

"You don't say," True drawled, resisting the urge to roll her eyes.

"No, seriously. I've got a really high tolerance for heat."

"These are pretty hot," she cautioned. "I've known a few grown men who've been on their knees after eating these."

"I can handle it," he said. Xavier sounded cocky to True's ears. Humph. He wasn't even trying to listen to her words of wisdom. A true know-it-all.

"So you're in?" she asked. When he nodded, she said, "It'll be on the house, sort of a welcome to Moose Falls gift." It was the least she could do, considering he was about to be in a world of hurt.

Xavier slapped his palm down on the counter. "You've made me an offer I can't refuse." Once again he smiled at her, causing her knees to buckle a little bit.

True bit her lip. Maybe she *should* try to stop him. He was acting way too eager to devour a platter of hot wings. Just thinking about it caused an acidic taste to rise in her throat. She didn't have a tolerance for anything spicy, never mind an entire platter of fiery chicken baked in the third circle of hell.

"They'll be out in a few minutes," she said in her chirpiest voice. *Keep it light. Be nice.*

"Thanks. By the way, I'm Xavier Stone," he said, sounding way too friendly for her liking.

"I know who you are," she admitted. "One of Hattie's

grandsons, right? The football player. My little brother has had a poster of you in his bedroom for as long as I can remember."

He didn't react at all to hearing about the poster. Instead he knitted his brows together. "Well, I'm at a disadvantage. I don't know your name," he said.

"I'm True Everett, and I run the place." *And I know exactly why you're here in Moose Falls*, she wanted to say. *You're the guy who stands between me and owning Northern Exposure.* But it wasn't her place to call him out. She loved his grandmother too much to risk alienating her. Hattie Stone was a good friend, and it was her most fervent wish to reunite with her grandson. True had the feeling that if Hattie had to pick a side between the two of them, Xavier would win hands down. Although it hurt to admit that fact, True knew the importance of family. Even though she'd tried to create one for her little brother, Jaylen, after the death of their parents, True always felt she was failing miserably.

"Nice to meet you, True."

She slid his ciders across the bar and watched as they landed right in front of him. Her movements were graceful and fast. For some reason it always made her feel accomplished. Even though she was the tavern's manager, True prided herself on being a jack-of-all-trades.

True had a vague recollection of the Stone brothers from childhood. The middle brother, Caleb, had been in her class for a few years. Clearly Xavier didn't remember her, although she couldn't really blame him. He hadn't lived in Moose Falls for decades. Maybe at some later juncture she would remind him.

Xavier jerked his thumb in the direction of the dining area, then picked up his drinks. "I'm going to go grab that table before someone else scoops it up."

True watched him as he walked away from the bar. He looked just as yummy from this angle as he had approaching her. Not many men possessed that skill. *Have mercy!* Miss Hattie's grandson had brought his A game to Moose Falls. He was definitely sending out main-character vibes.

Bonnie Walker, her co-worker and close friend, sidled up to her and said, "Take a picture. It'll last longer." With a peaches-and-cream complexion, freckles, and a mane of dark red hair, Bonnie was adorable.

True playfully swatted her friend. "You have to admit he sure is nice to look at."

Bonnie chuckled. "I'm surprised you're saying it out loud considering the way you've been carrying on about his impending arrival in town." Bonnie looked around. "By the way, where are his brothers?"

True shrugged. "No clue." She'd also wondered about the whereabouts of the Stone brothers, but Xavier hadn't mentioned them. So she hadn't either. "I need to put his food order in. Can you bring him some fresh bread while he waits?"

"My pleasure," Bonnie said with a wink. "Something tells me he'll look even better up close. Maybe I'll take a picture." She wiggled her eyebrows, earning her a chuckle from True.

At least she could laugh about the situation, True realized. That was progress. For months she'd stewed about Hattie's grandsons coming to Moose Falls and the fact they were set to inherit Yukon Cider and all her other holdings, including Northern Exposure. True didn't like feeling helpless, but she wasn't in the driver's seat in this situation. Xavier and his brothers held her fate in their hands. She was at their mercy.

A short while later, Petie, one of her servers, came out of the kitchen with the platter of chicken wings and a small carton of milk in his hands. "I'll take those," True said, reaching for the items. She turned around and walked them over to Xavier. His face lit up as soon as he spotted her.

He rubbed his hands together. "I'm so hungry, my stomach is grumbling. Are you going to be timing me?" he asked.

She reached into her pocket and pulled out her cell phone. "I just need to set my timer. I'll be at the bar, but I'll be watching. As soon as you take your first bite, I'll turn the timer on."

"You can take the milk with you," he said with a wink. "I won't be needing any."

"Are you sure?" she asked. "Hot wings are no joke." She hadn't been expecting this level of bravado.

"Have a little faith in me," Xavier said, subjecting her to another grin. He held up one of the ciders. "I still have some of this to wash it down with."

True walked back to the bar area with the carton of milk in hand.

"Oh no. He's trying to be a hero, isn't he?" Bonnie asked, her eyebrows raised.

True let out a sigh. "Nothing we haven't seen before."

What was it with men and hot wings challenges? They always acted like they were invincible. In her experience, the bigger they were, the harder they fell.

The moment Xavier lifted the first chicken wing to his mouth, True started timing him.

Bonnie grabbed her arm. "Wait. Did you tell him they were ghost pepper wings?"

True slowly shook her head, her eyes never straying from Xavier. He was chowing down on the wings at a record pace. Beads of sweat were now pooling on his forehead. He was fanning himself with his hand. But he continued to eat at a rapid speed.

"I can't say that I did," True admitted, avoiding eye contact with Bonnie.

Her friend let out a shocked gasp. "True! That's terrible."

Bonnie's horrified reaction immediately caused guilt to crash over True.

She turned toward her friend. "What? He was acting so cocky about the challenge, practically calling it lame. Plus, he's an expert at eating hot wings, so who am I to talk him down from the ledge?"

Bonnie shook her head. "You're letting your personal feelings cloud your actions. It's not his fault that he's set to inherit Yukon Cider."

"And Northern Exposure," True muttered. "Don't forget that." A sinking feeling grabbed hold of her. "All of my dreams are going up in smoke."

"That's not true. You're being dramatic." Bonnie covered her hands with her eyes. "I do not want to watch this train wreck."

Unlike Bonnie, True couldn't look away for anything in this world. Xavier picked up another chicken wing and placed it in his mouth, quickly devouring it with finesse. His fingers were long and graceful, like a pianist's. His tongue darted out to lick sauce from the corner of his mouth. Over and over, he picked up a wing and treated it like a precious object. He was making this a spectator sport for the tavern's clientele. A ring of people now surrounded him, shouting words of encouragement. When he devoured the last wing, the group started clapping and cheering. He'd finished with a whole minute to spare.

And even though she'd decided to dislike Xavier on sight, True couldn't help but feel a grudging respect for him. He'd eaten the platter of ghost pepper wings like a boss, even though she suspected he was about to hurl all over her hardwood floors.

🌲

Xavier placed a hand on his throat as a burning sensation threatened to permanently damage his esophagus. *Stay cool.* Surprisingly for this time of the afternoon, the place was packed. People were watching and treating him like a conquering hero. The most beautiful woman in Alaska was gazing at him from a few feet away, and he didn't want to make a fool of himself. Too late, he realized, as hot tears ran down his cheeks. He quickly swiped them away with his sleeve, careful not to get hot wing residue in his eyes. The heat from the wings had invaded his nostrils, his eyes, and the inside of his mouth and throat.

Bring on the fire brigade! He was burning up!

"You did it!" True called out as she made her way over from behind the bar. "And you lived to tell the tale."

"Barely," he croaked.

"Here you go, hotshot. Milk will make it a lot better." True placed a carton of milk and a glass down in front of him. She poured him a healthy serving.

*Hotshot?* The way she tossed the word out made him want to frown. It wasn't exactly a term of endearment. There would be plenty of time later for him to analyze her choice of words, but for now all he wanted was to guzzle down this glass of milk. Xavier had never chugged milk so fast in his life. The only thing he could compare this experience to was when he'd gobbled down a box of fireball candy as a kid. His mouth had been on fire for what felt like hours. But this! *This was worse. Way, way worse.*

"Are you all right?" True asked, concern flaring in her stunning brown eyes.

"I—I think so. Are my lips still here?" he asked. "I can't feel them." He raised his hand to his mouth. Or at least what used to be his mouth. A few minutes ago, it had been tingly, but now he felt nothing. Had he burned his lips off?

Even though it had been a minute since he'd smooched anyone, he still wanted to be able to kiss someone. The thought had crossed his mind that True's lips looked very kissable.

She was quite the looker, Xavier noted. Up close she was even more beautiful than at first glance. A short hairstyle highlighted flawless bone structure and a heart-shaped face. Her tawny skin was complemented by big hazel-brown eyes. Her soulful eyes were hard to look away from. She was no more than five foot four with a curvy figure.

Maybe he wouldn't be bored to death in this little town after all.

Tiny freckles dotted the bridge of her nose, and a small scar rested above her right eye. The slight imperfection did nothing to dim her beauty. How, he wondered, had she gotten that keepsake? Had she broken up a bar fight? Fallen out of a tree as a kid? Been cut by a piece of glass?

Suddenly she was leaning toward him and perusing his face. "I can tell you with absolute certainty that your lips are still attached to your face." The sides of her mouth twitched with mirth.

If she hadn't been standing next to him, he might have let out a howl of pain. But he didn't want True to view him as a wuss, even if he felt like one. Xavier imagined that this was what it felt like to drink gasoline.

*Suck it up, buttercup.* As a professional athlete, he had endured way worse pain than this. That's why he was back here in Moose Falls after a twenty-year absence. A tough hit in a championship game had given him a severe concussion and loss of peripheral vision in his left eye. As a result, his stellar NFL career had crashed and burned in a single instant. He'd lost everything, including his fiancée, Heather Denton, who'd replaced him in her affections with one of Xavier's teammates. A friend, no less. He couldn't be certain when the cheating had begun, but finding out about the affair after his injury had been gut wrenching.

"You're a good sport," True said, patting him on the shoulder.

"W-what was in the sauce? Molten lava?" he asked, panting. He took another swig of milk, then filled his glass up again.

True shifted from one foot to the other, then chewed her lip. "Hot peppers."

"I've had hot peppers before. Do they grow them differently here in Alaska?"

She mumbled something he couldn't quite hear.

"What was that?" he asked.

"Ghost peppers. They're ghost pepper wings."

Xavier's jaw dropped. "And you're just telling me that now?"

"Hey, you were pretty insistent about taking on the challenge." She smiled at him brightly. "Congratulations. You won a Northern Exposure T-shirt."

He scowled at her. "And bragging rights," he said dryly.

"Exactly," True said. "Let me know if you need any more milk. The rest of your food will be out shortly."

Once she'd stepped away, Xavier let out a grunt. As if he could eat anything else after consuming those death-defying wings. He could barely remember what he'd originally ordered. Maybe the wings had fried his brain in addition to every other part of his body.

What a wild day this had been. Due to her terminal illness, his long-lost grandmother, Hattie Stone, had invited Xavier and his younger brothers, Caleb and Landon, to come back to Moose Falls to take over Yukon Cider. Because he had nothing to lose and everything to gain, Xavier had jumped at the opportunity. Basically, he and his brothers had a year to decide whether to run the company or sell it. The decision had to be unanimous, or they would forfeit the company. Although he couldn't imagine relocating permanently to this remote Alaskan town, he'd agreed to keep an open mind.

He felt guilty admitting it even to himself, but despite his curiosity about the lucrative hard cider company, Xavier was simply biding his time in Moose Falls. If the Stone brothers stuck it out in Alaska for three hundred and sixty-five days per their grandmother's request, they could sell Yukon Cider and hit the proverbial jackpot. He didn't want to be mercenary, but Xavier desperately needed the cash. If his career hadn't imploded after his injuries, he wouldn't be in this precarious position. For the last year, bill collectors had been blowing up his phone and sending him threatening demand letters. He had received so much correspondence with *FINAL ATTEMPT* stamped in red ink, he was beginning to sweat every time the postman made a delivery.

After all he'd been through in the last few years, he deserved something good to come his way. He was tired of playing by the rules. All it had ever given him was heartache. No more Mr. Nice Guy.

True let out a snort. The Stone brothers. Frankly she was sick and tired of hearing about them. The grandsons were all Hattie talked about anymore. She was surprised Xavier hadn't floated in on a cloud with a halo over his head. She wished that she could be happy for Hattie being reunited with her family, but the whole situation annoyed her to no end. A feeling of resentment rose inside of her. Where had they been all this time when Hattie had needed them? Xavier had been chasing NFL glory and supermodels, while Caleb had been making a fool of himself on reality television. And Landon had been spending his days in a laboratory trying to be the next Albert Einstein. As if!

She'd done her research! All three of Hattie's grandsons were selfish to the bone, only thinking of themselves. Now that their lives and careers had hit rock bottom, they were running home to Moose Falls with their tails between their legs.

Hattie was like her very own fairy godmother, as well as her boss, so it hurt a little to know that these virtual strangers meant the world to Hattie. They would be her heirs, while True would be nothing more than the tavern's manager. She wasn't jealous or anything. Yukon Cider had never been on her radar very much, but Northern Exposure was her baby, an establishment she'd nurtured for the last seven years. She'd begun working here as soon as she was of legal drinking age, right after the death of her parents. In record time True had worked her way up to the role of manager. She had been hungry to support herself and Jaylen.

True loved this place. Northern Exposure was her pride and joy. *Hers!* Even though she didn't own the tavern, she had shed blood, sweat, and tears to whip it into shape over the years. All her hard work had paid off, and now it was a top-notch venue in this part of Alaska. She had brought on an amazing chef, Laurie Ito, who had brought her culinary skills and creativity to the tavern. Anyone who thought it was just a bar was dead wrong!

Maybe she shouldn't feel a certain type of way toward Xavier and his brothers. She didn't even know them, but it sucked big time that they would be in control of her destiny.

What did they know about Moose Falls or running this unique establishment? Absolutely nothing, she would wager. But because the tavern owner's blood flowed in their veins and due to Hattie feeling nostalgic about "the boys," they were poised to inherit it all. And, if they didn't want the businesses, they could sell the entire lot a year from now.

What would happen to True when the Stone brothers owned Northern Exposure lock, stock, and barrel? Would she still have a job? She'd seen new owners completely turn establishments upside down after acquiring them. She needed this position at Northern Exposure. How else would she continue to support her nine-year-old little brother? In terms of family, they were all each other had in the world since the accident that had ripped their lives apart.

Tears of frustration mixed with fear stung her eyes, and she headed to the back office to gather her composure. She hated being afraid. In many ways Xavier could determine her future. And she couldn't help but hate him for it.

🌲

Xavier swept his gaze around the establishment, marveling at the setup. The interior of Northern Exposure was rustic and full of charm. The flooring was hardwood and slightly scuffed, as if many a patron had trod all over it. Pictures of Alaskan wildlife graced the walls—bears, moose, foxes, caribou—lending the place a rugged vibe. Large flat-screen televisions hung from various vantage points around the bar and dining area. All the counters were gleaming as if they'd been polished just this morning. A cedar smell drifted in the air along with another sweeter aroma.

The waitress who'd introduced herself as Bonnie brought over his salmon burger and fries. The scent of the food was incredible, and his hunger kicked up a little in response. She sent him a sympathetic look. "I took the liberty of bringing you another cider in case you wanted to try another flavor. This one is black cherry, a bestseller in these parts."

"I really appreciate that, Bonnie."

She favored him with a wide grin. "Please let me know if you need anything. Any kin of Hattie's is tops in my book," Bonnie said enthusiastically.

"That's really nice to hear," Xavier said, slightly startled that she also knew his identity. Had Hattie announced to all of Moose Falls that her grandsons were coming to town and inheriting her business? Or had True clued her co-worker in?

As soon as Bonnie walked off toward another customer, he cracked open the tab and took a hearty sip of the drink. The flavors crackled on his tongue as he took a swig, providing a soothing distraction from the lingering effects of the chicken wings. Whereas the apple cider had been like a crisp walk in fall, the black cherry was explosive, packing quite a punch.

"Very nice," he said aloud before taking another sip. So far he was discovering that Yukon Cider's products were amazing. He now knew why his grandmother's company was thriving. So far, each cider had a different personality and distinct flavor. Hattie produced a fantastic product. Yukon Cider. From what he'd found out, the hard cider company was an extremely lucrative enterprise. According to his research, Yukon Cider was a household name in Alaska and the Pacific Northwest. The company was valued at several million dollars.

Thoughts of his grandmother flitted through his mind. Xavier dug into his pocket and retrieved the letter he'd received from her roughly six weeks ago. He smoothed out the wrinkles and began to read it to himself, even though he practically knew it by heart. The delicate cursive scrawl tugged at his heart.

*Dear Xavier,*

*Oh precious one. It's been too many years since I've looked into those deep brown eyes of yours and held you in my arms. My sweet little X. Before I get down to business, it's important that you know I've never stopped loving you for a single second. I've thought of you each and every day since you and your brothers left Moose Falls. I want you to remember that the things that separated us won't ever be as important as the ones binding us together.*

*My doctor tells me my time on earth is coming to an end. I'm in late-stage renal failure after many years of treatment. As a result, I think it's pertinent to get my affairs in order. So, here goes. After one year of residing in Moose Falls, you and your brothers are to receive one hundred percent ownership of Yukon Cider. At the end of one year, you may decide to keep or sell the company. The decision is yours. It has always been my intention to make the three of you my heirs. I've built up Yukon Cider so that you three could carry on its legacy and learn the craft of making cider. I truly believe love is always the answer, no matter what the question is.*

*Love always,*
*Granny*

His throat tightened with emotion as the words washed over him. He must have reread the letter a dozen times in the last few weeks. It was still hard to believe he, along with Caleb and Landon, was set to inherit a hard cider company from a grandmother none of them had seen in two decades. And now here he was in the wilds of Alaska, on the brink of reconnecting with his long-lost granny and their roots.

His mother, Daisy Stone, hadn't been too thrilled about the fact that her three sons were returning to Moose Falls. For her it was a complicated issue. He had always been in awe of the way she'd packed up and left an unhealthy marriage with her three sons in tow. She'd raised them as a single mother with zero help from their dad. Surely his mother wouldn't hold it against her sons that they were reaching out for the brass ring once she recovered from the shocking news. It wasn't as if they were going to have anything to do with their father. He let out a snort. Calling him *father* was an act of generosity since Paul Stone hadn't done a single thing to earn the title.

Xavier let out a shout as soon as he spotted Landon and Caleb walking into the tavern. His brothers were supposed to have beaten him to Moose Falls by an hour or so, but due to mechanical issues with their plane, they had missed their connecting flight.

Caleb's personality was always on full display with his wide smile, matching set of dimples, russet-colored skin, and the movie-star good looks that had earned him the nickname "Hollywood" back in high school. Landon was also a good-looking guy with a lean, athletic physique, fine features, and warm-brown skin. He tended to put himself under the radar and didn't usually engage in social situations. Spending most of his time locked away in a laboratory hadn't done him any favors in the getting-himself-out-there department. He was definitely an introvert.

His brothers rushed over to his table, and Xavier wasted no time sweeping them up in a tight bear hug. Words couldn't express how good it was to be a threesome once again. Due to his living in a different state than both of them, he hadn't seen them in person for at least three months.

"It's great to see you guys," Xavier said as he finally let go of them. He felt his shoulders relax. Now he wouldn't have to go it alone in a town he wasn't familiar with. Things would be so much better with his brothers by his side. Although they were nothing alike, the three of them couldn't be closer. As strange as this situation was regarding their return to Moose Falls, Xavier knew he could handle any potential challenges with these two by his side. The Three Musketeers had nothing on them!

"It's been a day of travel headaches, so we're really glad to be here," Caleb said, sounding exhausted. He sank into a seat, mirrored by Landon, who appeared just as weary. All three of them needed to get a good night's sleep as soon as they met Hattie and settled in.

Within minutes they'd put in an order with Bonnie for nachos and queso to share between them since they'd grabbed something to eat earlier. Xavier put in an order for more ciders so his brothers could sample Hattie's amazing product.

"Who's that?" Caleb asked, his gaze focused on True. Leave it to Caleb to notice the gorgeous woman behind the bar. Of the three of them, Caleb was the one most likely to find female companionship in Moose Falls even though he'd sworn off women. Xavier didn't buy it for one second. Caleb and women went together like a Super Bowl party and nachos.

Xavier's gaze lingered on True. "That's True Everett. She runs the place." He splayed his hand on the table. "I'm pretty sure she knows all about us and why we're in Moose Falls."

Landon pushed his glasses up to the bridge of his nose. "Seriously? I guess word gets out fast in small towns."

Xavier bit down on the inside of his cheeks. His mouth was still fiery. "Don't let her sweet façade fool you. She set me up to eat some ghost pepper chicken wings that practically obliterated my esophagus. I can't put my finger on it, but she's sending out some strange vibes...like maybe we're not wanted here. At least by her."

Caleb let out a throaty chuckle. "And here I thought this town was going to be a snooze fest." He rubbed his hands together. "Sounds like the drama is just getting started."

Landon bristled. "Why would she have any negative feelings about us being here? She doesn't even know us."

Xavier shrugged. "Maybe she's close to Hattie and wants to shield her from the big bad wolves."

Landon's expression radiated confusion. Caleb leaned over and gripped his shoulder. "He means the three of us," Caleb informed him. "*We're* the big bad wolves."

"That's ridiculous! Personally speaking, I've never hurt a woman in my life." Landon quirked his mouth. "Most women consider me a gentleman. I open car doors. I call or text after a first date. I never ask a woman to split the check at a restaurant." Landon seemed mighty pleased with himself, Xavier noticed. To listen to him talk, one might think he had a prolific dating history. In reality, Xavier couldn't remember Landon ever having a girlfriend.

Caleb leaned in and peered closely at Landon's chest as if examining the fabric.

Landon frowned. "What are you looking for?" he asked, swatting him away.

Caleb's lips twitched. "Your Boy Scout badge. From the sound of it, you're still a proud card-carrying member," Caleb drawled.

"Very funny," Landon said, jabbing him in the side. "Laugh all you want, but I'm proud to have learned so much from the Scouts. It made me into the man I am today."

Xavier stifled a laugh. Caleb was right on the money about their younger brother. Landon meant well, but he tended to act a bit superior at times. He had a case of the Goody Two-Shoes. Perhaps it had something to do with him being a brainiac and a member of Mensa with an IQ of 150. He needed to let loose a little bit, in Xavier's opinion. Maybe even take a walk on the wild side. Just the thought of Landon doing so caused Xavier to burst into a chuckle.

Both Caleb and Landon glanced over at him with curious gazes. Before they could even ask, Xavier held up his hand and said, "Inside joke. I was just remembering something."

Caleb smirked at him but said nothing further. Xavier felt bad for a moment. Their younger brother was often the butt of their jokes. Although he had always chalked it up to the fact that Landon was the youngest, Xavier also suspected he and Caleb poked fun at Landon due to his being a scientist and very different from the two of them. Xavier was beginning to sense the ribbing was getting old for Landon, especially with everything going on. He'd had such a tough time of it after being fired from his coveted lab position and being accused of falsifying lab results. Nothing could be further from the truth. Xavier would stake his life on it.

"So, do you think we'll see . . . Dad?" Landon asked, mentioning the one topic they tended to avoid like the plague. Paul Stone, otherwise known as Red, names none of them ever brought up due to their long-term estrangement. On occasion they referred to him as the invisible man based on his absence in their lives. Hattie had given him the nickname Red due to the light coloring of his hair as a child.

Landon tripped over the D word, clearly uncomfortable

with it. As they all knew, Red had never been a father to them. Once they had left Alaska, he'd made only a few feeble attempts to contact them. Just thinking about the man caused Xavier to feel uncomfortable, as if a heavy weight had landed on his shoulders. They'd all learned to navigate life without a father.

A hissing sound escaped Caleb's lips. "Let's hope not," he muttered. "Mom said he hasn't lived in Moose Falls for years," he added with a shrug.

Xavier twisted his mouth. "Well, Papa *was* a rolling stone."

All three of them laughed at the pun, although Xavier knew deep down that the joke wasn't all that funny. They had lost out on a lot of moments through the years due to their father's inability to be present in their lives. It was hard to really find humor in being left by your father. Although it wasn't something they had openly delved into among themselves, their bottled-up feelings had risen to the surface on a few occasions. As the oldest, Xavier hated to see his brothers in pain. So, over time they'd all learned to stuff down any memories of their father and pretend that not having him around hadn't gutted them. Xavier had grown up watching all the other kids have their fathers at every single football game while his own dad hadn't seen a single one of his. That had left a huge, gaping hole in his heart.

*There's nothing you can do to change the past, but the future is yours!* he reminded himself. Xavier had the power to shape his own destiny. Wallowing in past hurts wouldn't do him any good. All it ever accomplished was to make him doubt himself. He couldn't afford to wallow at the moment. Being in Moose Falls signified a huge reversal in all their fortunes.

Xavier clapped his hands together. "All right, bros. It's

time to rock and roll. Let's go meet our long-lost granny."
He took out some cash from his wallet and plopped it down
next to the bill Bonnie had left on their table. He left a little
extra than his normal tip amount, which might not have been
the smartest move considering his current financial woes.
Living beyond his means and trying to keep Heather happy
with lavish gifts had backfired. Xavier hadn't listened to
his financial advisor until the situation was dire. He wasn't
going to dwell on his dwindling bank balance at the moment.
Bonnie was a sweetheart, and she'd shown him nothing but
kindness. He was currently living a more frugal life, and
by living here in Moose Falls he was saving money. He had
even taken the drastic move of listing his house in Arizona
for sale.

He and his brothers stood from the table and began moving toward the exit.

"Hey! Stone!" A raised voice called out after them.
Xavier, Landon, and Caleb all turned around at the sound
of their last name. True was standing a few feet away with a
wad of cash in her hand.

"Your money's no good here," True said, her gaze locking with Xavier's own as she held out the money. Raw emotion flickered in her pretty brown eyes. He had no idea what
she was talking about. What was wrong with his cash?

"What do you mean?" he asked, sputtering with confusion. Had he done something to make her angry? He took a
step closer, closing the distance between them. There was no
way he was taking his money back. "What's the problem?"
Maybe this was some sort of prank for outsiders? Xavier
folded his arms across his chest. "Am I being blackballed? Is
this because of the hot wings challenge?"

Xavier swore the corners of her mouth twitched a little
before straightening back into a straight line. She blew out a

huff of air. "I can't take your money because Hattie wouldn't like it," she said. Her lush, full lips pursed, distracting him for a moment from the matter at hand. If things were different, he would really enjoy kissing those perfect ruby lips. He wasn't sure True was into him like that. But he was curious to find out.

Xavier frowned. "What do you mean? What does my grandmother have to do with this?"

Now she was definitely smirking. "She owns the place, Stone. So, you see, your money is literally no good here." She advanced toward him and stuffed the cash in his jacket pocket. "I kept the tip portion for Bonnie. She deserves it."

"She sure does. And by the way, feel free to call me Xavier," he said. Try as he might, he couldn't stop himself from grinning at her.

"Got it," she said. "See ya around, Xavier."

*I sure hope so.* The thought popped into his mind as she turned away from him. True was growing on him by the minute. She was stunning and hardworking with a sly sense of humor. Once he'd fully recovered from the ghost pepper wings, he might even view it as slightly humorous.

When he turned around to face his brothers, Xavier was greeted with near-identical grins. They had clearly been enjoying the show. Neither of them had the sense to try to pretend that they weren't all in his business.

"I think you were wrong about the manager. She's *truly* into you," Caleb said with a snicker. He jabbed Landon in the side as if he'd just cracked the funniest joke ever.

"Ain't that the *truth*," Landon added, chuckling along with Caleb. "The two of you were setting off more smoke than those hot wings you ate."

His brothers were laughing so hard, they had to hold on to each other for support. Clearly they had both forgotten that he had sworn off women courtesy of his ex-fiancée.

"Very funny," Xavier said. "Let's get outta here before she hears you. We've got things to do, places to go, and a long-lost grandmother to meet."

Jacques Chaplin, their grandmother's driver, was waiting for them outside Northern Exposure. The older man jumped out of the cream-colored Cadillac El Dorado at the sight of them, opening the back door with a flourish. With his cap of gray hair, wire-rimmed glasses, and handlebar mustache, Jacques resembled someone who had time traveled from the late 1800s. With a complexion the color of sand, he resembled the actor Sam Elliott. So far, he was proving himself to be a cool dude as far as Xavier was concerned. Jacques had picked Xavier up earlier from the marina and transported him to the tavern so he could get something to eat while he waited for his brothers to arrive.

Xavier took a quick glance behind him before sliding into the vehicle. Through the window he could just make out the sight of True. She was different from most women in his orbit, leaving him with a desire to know more about her.

The woman had given him mixed vibes, but he couldn't ignore the sparks flying between them. At first she'd seemed a bit wary of him. If he didn't know any better, he might think she was one of the many women he'd hooked up with during his early days in the league. Xavier had been a bit of a player back then, emboldened by his NFL status and feeling like a man on a mission to pursue every attractive woman in his path. Then he'd met Heather, and everything had changed. He had been so smitten with the stunning model that he'd never looked elsewhere. What a cliché. The football player and the model. Yet he'd never felt a false note about their relationship until she'd blindsided him and trampled over his heart.

So much for his killer instincts!

True was the very first woman who'd given him butterflies since his ex-fiancée walked out of his life and left him
for dead. This feeling fluttering around inside of him wasn't
one he'd expected to experience on his first day in town, but
he couldn't deny that it gave him a little spring in his step. At
the moment he felt more alive than he had in a very long time.

# CHAPTER THREE

For a moment there True had forgotten all about her dislike for Xavier Stone. That's what she found scary about men like him. They possessed so much charm that you ended up sucked in until you couldn't see straight. Smiling. Grinning. Flirting. She let out a sigh. Xavier probably thought he had her wrapped around his little finger.

"Xavier seems really nice, plus he's a good tipper," Bonnie said to True as she tucked her hefty tip into her apron pocket. A satisfied smile lit up her face. "And he's easy on the eyes. Hubba-hubba. I wish we had more customers like Hattie's grandsons."

True let out an indelicate snort and rolled her eyes. "*Seems* being the operative word. It's really easy to put on a nice grin and say all the right things, isn't it? Especially when you're being handed a literal fortune for no reason at all other than you share the same bloodline."

Bonnie reached out and patted True on the arm. "Maybe it's time you let this go. Some things are not in your control." She held her fingers up in the air and said, "Just breathe."

"Maybe you shouldn't always accept people at face value," True said in a chirpy voice. "That's when you get blindsided." *And I'm not going down that road. Never again!*

Bonnie made a tutting sound. "Oh, True. Not everyone is like Garrett. You can't take your anger out on every man you come across."

True felt her cheeks getting flushed. "This has nothing to do with *him*," she huffed. "I don't want Hattie to get bamboozled by her grandsons, that's all. I see nothing but red flags with this entire situation. She hasn't seen or heard from these dudes in almost twenty years."

Bonnie pursed her lips. "Honestly, it's not for us to judge," she said, folding her arms across her chest. "Didn't you hear Hattie when she said that her wildest dreams were coming true with the return of her grandsons? She wants this reunion more than anything else in the world."

True chewed her lip. "That's what worries me. Her expectations are sky-high. She's wearing her heart on her sleeve, which means it can easily be broken. I want the last moments of Hattie's life to be filled with joy, not sorrow." She teared up at the thought of Hattie's terminal illness. The notion of losing her dear friend caused a twisting sensation in her stomach.

Bonnie threw her hands in the air. "And hopefully they will be. Stop being such a pessimist. I've known Hattie Stone my entire life, and if there's one thing I know for sure, it's that she's as savvy as they come. She's not going to fall for any schemes."

True nodded. Bonnie was right. Hattie was highly intelligent, but she was also steeped in nostalgia about the past. How many times had Hattie spoken about what might have been if her grandsons had stayed in Moose Falls? Sometimes emotions got in the way of pragmatic thinking. And if

Xavier, Caleb, and Landon were hustlers, they might know how to manipulate their grandmother. The very idea of her sweet friend being played for a fool gutted True.

"And if I were you, I'd be extra nice to the Stone brothers," Bonnie said in a warning tone. "They're going to own Northern Exposure...and become our bosses." Bonnie widened her eyes and arched her brows for emphasis.

"Or sell it to the highest bidder," True drawled. Just saying the words out loud hurt like stepping on cut glass. If only she had the money to buy the place. Owning Northern Exposure was her dream, but she wasn't even close to saving up the funds for such a monumental purchase. Maybe Bonnie was right. Her mother used to always tell her that a person could catch more flies with honey than with vinegar. Perhaps it was time for her to turn on the charm with Xavier rather than shower him with saltiness. Getting on his good side would be a smart move on her part, she realized. Down the road it might work in her favor.

The thought of schmoozing with the attractive former football player caused heat to flow through her. Xavier was the hottest man she'd ever laid eyes on in her life. He was a little bit out of her league if she was being honest. Her research on him before his arrival in town revealed a dating history full of models, video vixens, and socialites. *How typical*, she thought. Not a cashier or teacher or librarian in the bunch. Somewhere in the mix was a former fiancée who was a dead ringer for Beyoncé.

His brothers were attractive as well, but Xavier stood out from the pack. He looked as if he'd been sculpted by Michelangelo himself. Xavier was the sort of man people would break their necks trying to look at as he passed them by on the street. And if he happened to return the stare, it would feel like you had been struck by lightning.

*Stop it!* she chided herself. Yes, Hattie's grandson was certified eye candy, but that didn't mean True had to drool over him or lose her head. There would be plenty of that type of pandemonium in the weeks and months to come from the residents of Moose Falls. She had a feeling that they were going to be celebrating the arrival of the Stone brothers as if it were Christmas morning, Easter, and the Fourth of July all wrapped up in a single moment.

A hushed silence enveloped the Cadillac as Jacques drove the Stone brothers to Hattie's house for their reunion. *Granny? Hattie?* Xavier still wasn't sure what he should call the woman he barely remembered. Perhaps he would leave that in her court to decide. He looked out the window during the ride and absorbed the lush Alaskan scenery. Everything was pristine, like a picture-perfect postcard. He couldn't help but gasp as the mountains rose right before his eyes. They seemed so close, almost as if he could reach out with his hand and touch the jagged rocks. Snow blanketed the ground, and the fluffy white stuff covered what looked like pine and Sitka trees. He'd done a little research over the past few weeks to familiarize himself with Alaska, and those types of trees were abundant in Moose Falls. Even though he wasn't exactly stoked about relocating here for an entire year, he had to admit that this town—and Alaska in general—was visually spectacular.

The picturesque surroundings served as a great distraction from the upcoming meeting. He was battling an onslaught of nerves. He didn't know why his palms were suddenly moist and his heart was beating at a rapid pace. *This*, he thought, *is a first step toward a better future.* There was absolutely nothing to feel stressed about. As always, he needed to set the tone for his younger brothers and stay strong. Of the three of them, Xavier had been the one pushing the most for them to accept Hattie's offer. He intended to see this thing through until they could figure out whether to stick around or sell Yukon Cider.

Approximately ten minutes after leaving Northern Exposure, Jacques pulled up in front of a large sky-blue Victorian home. The house was magnificent, an architectural masterpiece in Xavier's opinion. The impressive structure reminded him of grand homes he'd seen over the years in California and Martha's Vineyard.

Once he stepped outside the vehicle, Xavier craned his neck so he could capture the full scope of the structure. It was three stories high with a pitched roof and cylindrical turrets. A wraparound porch with lattice work and tomato-red Adirondack chairs lent the home an inviting air. A niggling feeling of déjà vu washed over him. He couldn't shake off the feeling that this place had been important to him.

Caleb let out a low whistle. "I'm guessing the Victorian style is pretty unique for Alaska."

"Very unusual," Jacques said. "Hattie's father—your great-grandfather—came to Moose Falls from Oregon. He had his mind set on a sweet Victorian the color of a robin's egg." Jacques let out a chuckle. "I'll let Hattie tell you the rest. You hail from a very interesting family."

All of a sudden, a memory sparked in Xavier's brain of him sitting at a grand table drinking tea while being surrounded by an array of teacups, saucers, and a light-brown teddy bear he'd named Kodiak. He had a strong feeling the afternoon tea had taken place inside this very house.

How could he have stuffed those memories down for such a long period of time? He knew this place. Xavier had believed that a lot of his memories of Moose Falls had evaporated way back when. Gone in a puff of smoke. Over the years he'd struggled to recall details about his hometown and the years he'd spent here. Sadly, many of his memories revolved around the fighting and tension between his parents that precipitated their departure from Alaska. That ugliness had been seared into his soul. But there had been joyful times. He wondered if the trauma of leaving Moose Falls and having to build a new life in Arizona had short-circuited his recollections. Now that he was back, the warm and fuzzy memories were creeping back to him.

"We played hide-and-seek here. The dumbwaiter was my favorite hiding spot," Caleb said as he gazed at the house. His expression was shuttered so that Xavier couldn't read his emotions, but he sensed he was also dealing with childhood remembrances.

"I remember making gingerbread cookies," Landon added, grinning. "With lots of icing."

Both of them appeared as surprised as he was at the memories that were flooding back to them. Not once had the three of them ever discussed this house, Hattie, or their life in Moose Falls. It was only as he stood a mere fifty feet from the entrance that Xavier realized there had been a code of silence among him and his brothers throughout the years. Not the healthiest way to deal with the past, he realized. No wonder their lives were a hot mess.

Once they stepped inside the house, they smelled the fragrance of lemons wafting in the air. Another memory kicked in. Lemons sitting in big glass bowls. He and his brothers had gotten in trouble one time for using the lemons as footballs inside the house. Even as a small kid, Xavier had dreamed of football glory. He tried to shake off all the cobwebs and focus on the present.

Jacques led them to a room with large bay windows, gleaming hardwood floors, and shelves upon shelves of books.

"Sweetness," Landon said, looking around the room with wide eyes. Landon had never met a library he hadn't fallen in love with on first sight. Xavier knew his brother was geeking out about the fact that their grandmother had an in-house library stocked with hundreds of books. After all Landon had been through as of late, it made Xavier happy to see Landon so excited about something. For months Xavier's youngest brother had barely been able to get out of bed after getting the boot from Abbott Laboratories. He never wanted to see him so down in the dumps again.

"Would you boys...I mean gentlemen...like a beverage?" Jacques asked.

"I think we're good on drinks," Xavier responded. "If it's easier for us to go to Hattie, we can do that." If she was bedridden, he didn't want their grandmother to exert herself coming downstairs to welcome them. That wouldn't feel right at all.

A smile tugged at the corners of Jacques's lips. "That's not possible at the moment. She hasn't gotten back yet."

The brothers exchanged a glance. "She's not here?" Landon asked. A tinge of outrage laced his tone. Xavier knew all three of them were thinking the same thing. They had traveled all this way at Hattie's request, yet she wasn't at the house to greet them.

"No worries. Her plane just landed," Jacques explained. "It won't be long now."

"Where was she?" Caleb asked, blurting out the question Xavier himself wanted to ask.

"She was attending a blackjack tournament," Jacques said, wiggling his eyebrows. "In Vegas."

A shocked gasp slipped past Landon's lips. Caleb tried to hide a chuckle behind his palm. Xavier didn't know what to think. If Hattie was so sick, what was she doing gambling at casinos? He wasn't judging her at all, but the plot was thickening right before his eyes. In all his communications with Hattie, she'd made it sound as if she was waiting on pins and needles for their arrival in Moose Falls. Maybe that wasn't the case after all. Doubt began to creep in. Were they being punked?

His mother's words rang in his ears. *Be careful. Don't take everything at face value. Everyone has an agenda.*

Jacques excused himself, leaving Xavier, Landon, and Caleb in the cavernous library by themselves.

"Vegas?" Xavier asked as soon as they were alone, looking back and forth between his brothers. "I didn't have that on my Alaska bingo card."

"I kind of love it," Caleb said, walking over to the sofa and sinking down onto it. "She's clearly a woman who seeks out adventure."

"Unless of course she has a gambling problem," Landon said, quirking his mouth.

"You always go from zero to a hundred in a split second," Caleb said, shaking his head reproachfully at Landon.

Landon shrugged. "Don't be a hater. It's a proven fact that smarter people think faster." He began to scan the books on the shelves, making a whistling sound as he ran his fingers along the spines.

Caleb let out a groan and slapped his hand to his forehead. "Ugh. Here we go again. You always have to point out that you're the smartest one in the room. Big deal. You're a nerd."

Landon turned around and scowled at Caleb. "It *is* a big deal!"

Caleb scoffed. "To *you*. Not for the rest of us. We don't care."

"Will the two of you knock it off? The bickering is getting really old," Xavier spat out. "You're giving me a headache." He took a deep breath. "This is a really stressful situation, so we have to keep our eyes on the prize and try to dial back the infighting. It's been a really long day, and we're all a bit on edge."

"Sorry," Landon mumbled, his expression sheepish.

"Sorry," Caleb added, nodding in Landon's direction.

For a second, Xavier flashed back to childhood when the fights had been fast and furious, usually over something mundane.

"Come on, guys. Hug it out like Mom always used to make us do," Xavier said with a deep chuckle as he motioned with his hands for them to come together. Caleb and Landon let out groans but followed Xavier's suggestion and hugged.

Just then the clicking sound of the door opening drew their attention to the doorway.

"Sorry to keep you boys waiting," an older woman said in a husky voice as she crossed the threshold and entered the library. Dressed in a floor-length caftan, Ugg-style boots, and dark leggings, Hattie Stone sure knew how to make an impressive entrance, Xavier thought. As many times as he'd imagined coming face-to-face with his grandmother, he hadn't been fully prepared for the full effect of the imposing woman. The lady standing before them did not look as if she was in ill health. Nor did she resemble the little old woman he'd imagined. At a commanding height of at least five foot ten, she entered the room like a runway model. She was striking in every way possible, from her pecan-colored skin to the blue mane of hair she was sporting.

"She's got blue hair," Landon hissed in a loud stage whisper.

Xavier resisted the urge to slap his youngest brother in the back of his head for being so rude, but he was trying to be kinder and gentler toward him. Instead he sent Landon a pointed look that spoke volumes. As usual, his glare worked. Landon stopped talking.

Hattie let out a deep-throated cackle. "I do, indeed. My hairdresser calls it royal blue." She ran her hand over her hair. "It makes me feel like a queen. At my age I deserve it. YOLO."

"Indeed," Caleb drawled, sending her a nod of approval.

Xavier couldn't take his eyes off her. The only word that came to mind was *badass*. For some reason he hadn't been able to find any current pictures of her online, and he hadn't wanted to ask his mother for any, so his imagination had run wild. He couldn't have been more wrong. She was no little old lady. Instead she was vibrant and lively. A firecracker.

"I know we haven't seen each other in a very long time, but I'd love a hug or two." For a moment none of them moved. A hug seemed so intimate as far as Xavier was concerned. Other than some DNA, there wasn't anything tying them together.

Nope. He was wrong. There was something else. Yukon Cider and their inheritance. His path to a better future. A way to start fresh.

Caleb was the first one to step forward and wrap his arms around Hattie in a tight bear hug. When he was done, Landon tentatively walked over and awkwardly embraced their grandmother. Before Xavier could decide on how to approach the situation, Hattie rushed toward him, reaching him in a few strides. She threw herself against his chest and said, "If it isn't my little X-man all grown up." When she finally let go of him, Hattie brushed tears away from her cheeks. "Forgive my emotion, but I wasn't sure I'd ever see the three of you again."

"It's been a long time," Xavier said, patting her arm. He didn't know what had prompted him to comfort her, but in the moment, it felt right. At the same time, Xavier felt bad that he wasn't feeling the same emotional response to seeing her again. She still seemed like a stranger to him. Had they once been close?

"I can't tell you how tickled I am that you've come to Moose Falls," their grandmother said, her face lit up as if she had just won the lottery. "I'm sure it was a difficult decision, but I think you're going to love it here as much as you used to." She clapped her hands together. "I can't wait to show you my cider company, among other things."

"We're looking forward to it," Caleb said, flashing his signature Hollywood grin. "And for the record, we're all really sorry about your illness."

"Thank you for saying so," Hattie said, returning the grin. "I am dying," she said. "But I'm also living."

Hattie's comment was pretty profound, and it said a lot about the way she lived her life, Xavier realized. He wasn't sure he would handle a death sentence quite as well as his grandmother.

"Is that why you went to Vegas?" Landon asked. "To kick up your heels?"

"One hundred percent, Landon. I'm going to be sick wherever I am, so why not hop on a plane and give the black-jack tables a whirl?" Hattie asked.

"Makes sense," Xavier said, "especially if you won."

Hattie, Landon, and Caleb all chuckled, which eased the tension in the room. He couldn't put into words how surreal this whole situation felt for him. He imagined his brothers were experiencing similar emotions. Throw in travel fatigue, and they were all operating on nothing but fumes. He could barely keep his eyes open.

"I can see you're all bone tired from the journey. Why don't you retire to your rooms until dinnertime?" Hattie riffled through her desk drawer and pulled out three folders. Hattie beckoned them toward her. "These are for you. It's a contract that I'd like you boys to look over. Signing will mean that you agree to stay in Moose Falls for a full year to work at Yukon Cider, at which time you get to decide whether to stay on and run the company or sell. There's a lot of legalese in there, but it's pretty straightforward. I'm here to answer any questions and walk you through the agreement if necessary."

Within minutes they were all settled in their individual rooms. Their luggage, courtesy of Jacques, had been placed in the hall outside their doors.

Xavier's bedroom was a large suite with a bathroom and walk-in closet attached. The walls were a soothing eggshell color. A red velvet sofa sat at the base of the mahogany-colored sleigh bed. An antique mahogany desk sat by the window.

Although he was exhausted and wanted nothing more than to lie down on the comfy-looking king-size bed, Xavier couldn't resist a look at the contract. As a former professional football player, he knew a lot about contracts. Good ones. Bad ones. And those in between. He sat down at the desk and began thumbing through the paperwork, feeling pleasantly surprised at the transparency of the agreement. He and his brothers would be getting a salary for their work at the company over the course of the next year. As the contract stipulated, if they couldn't reach a consensus about remaining in Moose Falls and running Yukon Cider, they would forfeit rights to the company. They were being asked to keep the contents of the contract confidential so as to avoid town gossip about the arrangement. It wasn't until he reached the last page of the document that he froze in his tracks. He couldn't believe what he was reading.

"There's no way in hell," Xavier murmured.

He read the sentence once. Twice. Three times.

Of course there was a catch. In life, as he'd always experienced it, there was always a catch. Anger rose inside him at the thought that he and his brothers had been bamboozled. Tricked. They'd come all this way and uprooted their lives for a setup. They were being treated like puppets on a string.

No matter how many times he read the sentence, it continued to send chills down his spine. He could feel the beginnings of one of his headaches coming on, a lingering side effect from his traumatic brain injury (TBI). He read the words once again. These headaches caused extreme tension and blurred vision.

*It is stipulated that Caleb, Landon, and Xavier Stone must work with Paul Stone during their year at Yukon Cider. Failure to do so will render this agreement null and void.*

Paul Stone, aka their deadbeat dad. Their grandmother was trying to force them to have a working relationship with a man who'd left his sons in the lurch for decades. A sorry excuse for a dad. Absentee father. There was no way this was going to fly with him or his brothers.

What in the world was Hattie thinking?

# CHAPTER FOUR

"So did you get the Storm's autograph for me?"

True let out a sigh. She'd been answering questions about Xavier Stone for the last twenty minutes. Ever since she had crossed the threshold of their cozy three-bedroom home, her little brother had been relentless. He was obsessed with the new resident of Moose Falls. Honestly, it didn't surprise her, since Jaylen considered himself to be a mega fan of the Storm.

"Jaylen, finish your dinner, please. I've already told you a dozen times," True said. "I didn't ask him for an autograph. The timing wasn't right." True continued to eat her taco casserole. She had made the meal a few days ago and put it in the fridge for an easy dinner to heat and serve. Maybe Jaylen would follow her lead and clean his plate so she could check his homework and get him ready for bed. Lately, True felt that going over Jaylen's work was futile. More times than not, he didn't get a single question wrong.

Instead of polishing off his meal, Jaylen placed his elbows on the table and leaned forward. "Okay, last question.

Was he nice? Do you think he'll give me an autograph if I ask him?" As usual, he made True's heart thump like the Energizer bunny's drum. With his warm-brown skin and gap-toothed smile, he was irresistible to his big sister and absolutely adorable. At moments like this one, True wished her parents were here to see their sweet boy.

"He was nice," True answered. So nice that she felt a little bad about the ghost pepper wings she had served him. Xavier had handled the situation with grace. And humor. "I'm sure he would love to give you an autograph if you ever meet him."

Jaylen's brown eyes widened. "Do you think I'll ever get the chance to meet him?"

"So much for last question," True said. It was all there in his eyes—the hope, the expectation, the adoration. Her insides clenched. Jaylen held Xavier in such high esteem. She'd rip his heart out if he hurt Jaylen. He had already been through enough heartaches for a lifetime.

"Last one. I promise," Jaylen said. He picked up his fork and began taking a few bites of his meal.

"Well, with Xavier staying here in town, you'll definitely cross paths with him. Moose Falls is teeny tiny," she said, wrinkling her nose. "Smaller than a postage stamp." It was something their mom used to say about Moose Falls, and it always made Jaylen grin.

"I'd skip school to meet him," Jaylen said in a wistful voice.

"That's not happening," True said with a shake of her head.

"Why not? He's a legend. And I'm his biggest fan." His tone was full of outrage. "Life experiences matter."

"Because I'm not down with playing hooky. Fourth grade matters too, especially for a great student like yourself.

You'll just have to meet him outside school hours." When had she become such a grown-up? Her words rang in her ears, sounding so much like True's own parents.

Jaylen rubbed his hands together and let out a squeal. "I can't believe he's here. We have someone famous living right here in Moose Falls." If she could bottle up a nine-year-old's enthusiasm and sell it to the highest bidder, True wouldn't have a single financial worry.

"For now," True muttered. She couldn't wrap her head around the infamous Stone brothers permanently relocating to small-town Alaska. It simply didn't compute. She didn't know all the details of their arrangement with their grandmother, but she figured they could simply sell Yukon Cider after Hattie's death and get out of Dodge. Northern Exposure could be a casualty of the Stone brothers' whims. She was kicking herself for not being in a position to have made Hattie an offer outright.

"Before I forget to tell you, Miss Hattie invited me to a reception. It's tomorrow night. She wants everyone to roll out the red carpet for her grandsons."

Jaylen let out a groan. "You are so lucky. Can I be your plus-one?"

True sputtered. "What do you know about plus-ones?"

He puffed out his chest, seemingly proud of himself. "I remember Garrett saying it once." Suddenly, Jaylen's face fell, and he began stumbling with his words. "I—I'm sorry, True, for mentioning him."

"No biggie," she said. "That was a long time ago."

Two years, three months, and some odd days. Who was she kidding? It really wasn't that long ago as far as her heart was concerned. Garrett was like the gum stuck on the bottom of her shoes. No matter how hard she'd tried to disentangle him from her heart, he was still stuck there like a permanent tattoo. He served as a reminder of her foolishness. Her feelings for him had been over-the-top and epic. He'd made her believe in happily-ever-afters, unicorns, and white picket fences. She had felt like the luckiest girl in all of Alaska to be *his* woman. And then he'd vanished into thin air, ghosting her in the cruelest manner. At first she had been frantic about his safety until he'd popped up on Instagram at a ski resort with a very sexy plus-one.

Months later they had run into each other at a local market, and Garrett hadn't batted an eyelash. He'd made a point to tell her how great she looked and remarked on how long it had been since they'd gotten together. Garrett had waltzed away before True could recover enough to tell him off. To this day it astounded her how he'd acted as if nothing had ever happened. She was in a better place emotionally now, but he'd left her a bit jaded about romance in general. It would be a challenge to put herself out there again.

"I don't have a plus-one," she explained, "so Bonnie's going to watch you. You can order Thai food. Your favorite." She reached over and tousled the top of his head.

He pumped his fist in the air. "Yes! I love hanging out with Bonnie. We can play *Animal Crossing* and *Mario Brothers*." Jaylen began shoveling taco casserole into his mouth. "She's almost as good as I am," he said with a mouth full of food.

"Don't talk with your mouth full, kiddo," True cautioned.

"Excusez-moi, mademoiselle," Jaylen said in a thick impersonation of a French accent. A smile tugged at her lips. Even though it was her job to correct her brother's manners and raise him up into a well-rounded man, at moments like this one all she could focus on was the joy he brought into her world. He was the living, breathing embodiment of a sugar rush.

Jaylen was an incredibly cool kid and full of so much exuberance for one who'd lost his entire world at such an early age. He didn't carry any loss around with him. Becoming a stand-in parent for a two-year-old hadn't been easy, but Jaylen had made it more meaningful than she ever could have imagined. Losing their parents in a small plane crash had devastated True, but she'd picked herself up, staggered through her grief, and immersed herself in Jaylen. From potty training to nursery school to birthday parties, she'd done it all. And loved him fiercely every step of the way. And if, as she suspected, there would be no marriage or kids in her future, this would all be enough. Making taco casserole for Jaylen, baking cupcakes for his school's bake sale, and tucking him at night would always be more than enough.

🌲

After reading through the contract, Xavier didn't waste any time gathering Caleb and Landon to his room. There was no way they could let Hattie's contract stand with this insane stipulation. Xavier's thoughts raced all over the place. Raw emotion welled up inside him. He was a grown man now, and even though there had been countless moments when he'd ached for a dad, he no longer needed one. That ship had sailed.

Was this his grandmother's hidden agenda for getting them back to Alaska after all these years? If so, she was about to get a reality check. This wasn't one of those cutesy movies like *The Parent Trap* where decades-long divides could be made up for over the course of a few weeks. His father's absence in their formative years had negatively impacted all three of them. There was no coming back from that type of betrayal. Hattie might as well try to part the Bering Sea.

Once he was behind closed doors with his brothers, Xavier let loose.

"Did you look over the contract?" Xavier asked, waving the paperwork in the air.

Landon nodded. His mouth was set in a grim line. "I did. Plot twist."

A sheepish expression passed over Caleb's face. "I kind of skimmed it if I'm being honest," he admitted.

Xavier rolled his eyes. "Seriously? This is important stuff, Caleb. We didn't come all this way for the scenery. We need to be on the same page."

Caleb held up his hands. "Sorry. My bad. I nodded off." He looked back and forth between his brothers. "What? Did I miss something important?"

Landon arched an eyebrow. "I'm guessing you didn't read the stipulation stating that we're required to work with—" At this point Landon swallowed before continuing. "With Dad." His voice came out in a raspy whisper as if he was afraid to say it out loud.

"What? You've got to be kidding me!" Caleb said. He ran a shaky hand over his face.

"He's dead serious," Xavier said. "It's right here in black-and-white on page three."

"What is she thinking?" Caleb asked as he reached for the document and scanned the passage. Seconds later he slammed his palm against his forehead and let out a groan.

Xavier couldn't come up with a single reasonable explanation. Coming home to Moose Falls had been hard enough, but the notion of working with Paul Stone was mind-boggling.

"Perhaps it's her dying wish," Landon said with a shrug. "It's not uncommon for folks to try to sort out their affairs before they pass." He twisted his lips. "I mean, that's the main reason why we're here, isn't it? So she can go to the great beyond with her business all tied up with a neat red bow."

"We came here for Yukon Cider, not for the invisible man," Xavier muttered. "I don't have a desire to make nice with him after all these years. That's not happening!" Xavier didn't even know what to call him other than *sperm donor*. Anything paternal like *dad* or *pop* was far too generous. And he wasn't in the mood to play nice. He was tired and hungry and in need of some relaxation. True's face flashed before his eyes. He should have gotten her number so they could hang out. She was definitely a silver lining in this tiny Alaskan village.

"I agree," Caleb said, folding his arms across his chest. "It's not like he's ever tried to be a part of our lives."

"Other than the random visits when we were kids," Landon pointed out. "Remember that time he took us to the circus? Caleb ate so much popcorn, he threw up on the way home." Landon chuckled at the memory.

Both Xavier and Caleb turned their heads to frown at him.

"What?" Landon asked, adjusting the bridge of his glasses. "I'm just stating the facts. Let's not lose all objectivity here. I feel the same way as the two of you about him, but I'm not going to pretend as if there wasn't a time when he seemed to care about us. It wasn't all bad."

"I don't remember it that way," Xavier said. It pained him to go down this road, but it was too late to reverse course now. Some things a person never forgot. "I remember how Mom cried for days before he came and how frightened she was that he wasn't going to bring us back home. I remember how he checked his watch the whole time we were at the circus and screamed at Caleb when he got sick." He could see all those moments in his mind's eye so clearly, almost as if it weren't nearly two decades ago. Considering how long he'd stuffed these memories down, it was a miracle they had resurfaced. After all this time, they still made his stomach hurt.

A tense silence descended over them. This wasn't a topic they had ever been comfortable discussing. There was so much wrapped up in it—pain, embarrassment, loss, and anger. Most kids took having a father for granted. For the Stone brothers, there had always been a huge hole sitting smack-dab in the center of their lives. No Pops sitting in the stands at his football games. No Pops cheering Caleb on at the school play or attending Landon's science fairs. Although their mom had always been there for them, she shouldn't have had to do the heavy lifting by herself. Even if they were no longer married, he could have offered his support.

And now Hattie expected them to put all those things aside? It just wasn't possible.

"Let's not fight," Landon said in a soft voice. He folded his arms across his chest. Xavier knew it was Landon's tell. He was trying to protect himself. That was exactly what Xavier was trying to do—protect the three of them.

"This isn't fighting," Caleb said. "We're just talking it out."

Seeing Landon's crushed expression gave Xavier pause. He hadn't meant to sound so fierce, but old wounds were being reopened.

Xavier reached out and placed his arm around Landon and pulled him close. "We're not on opposite sides. It's always team Stone brothers. No matter what. You all right?"

Landon's shoulders sagged, and he let out a breath. "Okay. I'm good. It's just been a stressful day."

Of the three of them, Landon was the most sensitive.

In the heat of the moment, Xavier tended to forget that his youngest brother had always taken things to heart. When they'd left Moose Falls as kids, Landon had cried nonstop for days. Xavier and Caleb had been stoic about leaving the only home they'd ever known and their father. To this day Xavier wondered if he would've been better off if he hadn't stuffed down his emotions. Maybe he should've cried his eyes out, but he'd wanted to be strong for their mom. Over the years that had become his pattern—to push away his feelings when faced with heartbreak.

"So, what now?" Caleb asked, sinking down on the plush bed.

"Let's get downstairs and let Hattie know where we stand on this," Xavier suggested. "She needs to understand that we're not just going to roll over and agree to something unreasonable."

"Right. It's nonnegotiable," Landon said, nodding in agreement. "And we need to get this squared away."

They made their way downstairs, pausing along the way to check out their surroundings. Ornate gold-and-green wallpaper lined the walls. There was something about this hallway that tugged at Xavier's brain. A rush of memory washed over him: Xavier and his brothers chasing one another up and down this hallway and then sliding down the banister to the first floor. He let out a chuckle at the thought of it. They had experienced happy times in this house!

Xavier stopped short when he spotted a framed photo hanging by the spiral staircase. He reached out and ran his finger across the picture of him, Caleb, and Landon. From what he could tell, the photo had been taken right before they'd left Moose Falls. They were all wearing matching blue jackets and hats, set against a backdrop of snow and Sitka trees. He sucked in a steadying breath. He hadn't quite prepared himself for the fact that the past would be infused in every nook and cranny of their grandmother's grand home.

When they reached the library, Xavier gently knocked on the door. After hearing Hattie's voice inviting them in, Caleb pushed open the door so they could step inside. Xavier's brothers ushered him inside first. A sigh slipped past his lips. *Here we go again*, he thought. Caleb and Landon expected him to be the mouthpiece for all of them. Just once he wished that they would take the lead.

"Hello, boys." Hattie's voice was full of enthusiasm as she greeted them. "I hope you had a chance to rest up before dinner."

Xavier nodded. "We actually read through the contract so we could get the formalities out of the way."

"Makes sense. I hope you found everything to your satisfaction. I'd love to show you the factory and have you hit the ground running." Hattie rubbed her hands together and grinned.

Xavier shifted from one foot to the other. "We're a bit confused about one of the stipulations."

Hattie peered at him from over the rim of her spectacles. "Is that right? Take a seat, boys. If you would be so kind as to point me toward the section you're concerned about, I'd be grateful."

"It's the section about working with…Paul," Caleb blurted out. His voice didn't sound normal. He was looking at Hattie as if she were a tiger ready to bite him. Xavier almost wanted to laugh out loud. Finally, Caleb had come across someone who intimidated him.

She wrinkled her nose. "It's pretty straightforward. I can't cut my only child out of the company, so I figured it should be in the contract, so there's no confusion. Red will be working at Yukon Cider, although he won't be part of the ownership."

Frustration got the better of Xavier. "So we're supposed to work alongside our deadbeat dad?" *Whoosh.* He'd used the D word, one he normally didn't say out loud.

He watched his grandmother's face tighten as her cheeks became flushed and a vein bulged on her forehead. Hattie waved a finger at him. "I prefer the term *absentee father*, Xavier." There was a sharpness to her tone that let them know she wasn't playing around. She was ticked off, which only seemed fair, since he was as well.

Xavier felt the back of his neck getting heated. Of course she was defending her son! Suddenly all the old wounds were opening, triggered by the mention of their father.

"With all due respect, you shouldn't have sprung this on us." He kept his tone cordial, even though he wasn't feeling warm and fuzzy at all. All his defenses were up. And he was kicking himself for believing things would be straightfor-ward. After all, it was a bit unusual to inherit a company from a woman they hadn't seen in decades.

"You're angry. I understand, Xavier. Believe me, I do. But you're going to have to trust me on this one." She reached out and clasped his hand in hers. "I would never do a single thing to harm any of you. That's one of the reasons I stayed away for so long. I know it's confusing, but I don't intend to go meet my maker with any unfinished business. And your relationship with Red isn't finished," she said, shifting her body in the chair. "Not by a long shot."

Xavier looked over at his brothers. Both had bewildered, annoyed expressions etched on their faces. But they all knew Hattie had them over a barrel. At this point they either had to sign the agreement or leave Alaska before they had even gotten a chance to settle in. And all three of them had sublet their condos, which meant they literally had no place to go other than their mom's house.

As the oldest brother, Xavier considered it his role to be the outspoken one. The decision maker. He and his brothers had come to Moose Falls for an inheritance from their grandmother and to enrich their lives. It had been a rookie mistake not to request the paperwork ahead of time. But if Granny Hattie thought she could force them to have a relationship with Paul "Red" Stone, she had another think coming!

He cleared his throat. "With all due respect, there are some things in life you can't force. You can stipulate that we work with him, but that's as far as it'll go." He gritted his teeth. "I'll email my attorney the documents so she can look them over for us."

Hattie nodded her head. "Now that we've hashed things out, let's eat. I'm famished. I hope the three of you like venison stew and salmon." Hattie stood from her chair, and Xavier quickly made his way to her side, offering his arm to her for support. For a moment there she'd seemed unsteady on her feet. She tightly grabbed hold of him. Caleb went to her other side and looped his arm through hers.

Her eyes grew moist right before their eyes. Xavier could feel her arm trembling.

"I might just be the luckiest woman in all Alaska to have three handsome grandsons as my dining companions," she gushed.

Xavier had the feeling Hattie was laying it on a little thick. Truth was, she had them right where she wanted them. He would email the papers to his attorney to look over, but Xavier knew the three of them would sign on the dotted line. At this point, after traveling all this way, what choice did they really have?

# CHAPTER FIVE

True studied herself in the full-length mirror. She tugged at the hem of her navy-blue dress, biting her lip as she gazed at her reflection. She wasn't used to getting decked out in fancy clothes, and this outfit did nothing to hide her curves. It wasn't as if she was ashamed of her body, but she never wore clothes that accentuated her physical attributes. For most of her life, she had rocked the tomboy image and worn unisex clothing. That had shifted a little bit due to her role as tavern manager. She'd tried to mix up her wardrobe a bit with a combination of trendy and business casual for meetings.

The few pounds she'd gained over the last year had settled around her hips, making her body shapelier. That wasn't something she had a problem with, since it suited her, but wearing formfitting clothing made her feel slightly out of her comfort zone. It wasn't something she often did.

Bonnie let out a loud whistle. "Woo-hoo. You're smokin' hot in that number."

True bit her lip. "I don't know, Bonnie. I feel a bit exposed in this dress."

Bonnie waved her off. "What are you talking about? It just hugs your body a little bit. You're barely showing any skin."

"I just feel...naked," True admitted. Or maybe she just felt exposed. Her regular work attire wasn't anything fancy, just sweaters and jeans. Slacks and a jacket on the rare occasion when she met with Hattie. She'd always considered it a perk of working at Northern Exposure that she got to wear comfortable clothes. Her lifestyle didn't afford her many opportunities to get decked out. She might put on a nice silk shirt for teacher-parent conferences, but for the most part, True lived in comfy clothing.

"Honestly, if I had a body like yours, I wouldn't even bother with clothes. I'd throw them all away or donate them to a worthy cause." Bonnie put her hands on her hips and looked True up and down, her eyes full of approval. "You're a total smoke show. You'll have everyone in town drooling, including the Stone brothers."

True shook her head as Bonnie let out a boisterous laugh. Bonnie was the best hype woman in the game, always boosting True up to the stratosphere. A true bestie.

"Thanks for the vote of confidence," she drawled as an image of one particular Stone brother flashed before her eyes. She wouldn't complain if Xavier Stone treated her like eye candy. He was hot enough to melt the snow in Alaska.

"Seriously, True. I know you never work out, so I think it's safe to assume you hit the genetic lottery." Bonnie let out a sound of disgust. "Which once again proves that life isn't fair. I owe my physique to potato farmers in Ireland."

True chuckled. "Both of my parents were total knockouts. Extremely easy on the eyes." Her mom had been a plus-size queen with flawless mocha skin and a close-cropped Afro, while her dad had resembled a male model with hair flowing to his shoulders, a mahogany complexion, and muscles for days.

"Lou and Jessie *were* both smoking hot. I used to have the biggest crush on your dad," Bonnie said, her voice sounding wistful. "I remember this one time he walked into the bowling alley wearing these tight Levi's jeans. I swear he stayed in my dreams for weeks."

True clapped her hands over her ears. "La la la la. TMI. I don't want to hear another word about those jeans. Or any of your scandalous dreams. I'm serious."

Bonnie smirked and wiggled her eyebrows. "Sorry, but I speak the truth. He was my first crush. But more than anything, I liked seeing them together. Watching him open doors for her or hold her hand made me believe I could have what they had someday."

Tears pricked True's eyes. She'd had no idea how impactful her folks had been. "Thanks, Bonnie."

"For what?" Bonnie asked, sending her a quizzical look.

"Well, for starters, thanks for watching Jaylen tonight. And for talking to me about my parents." She wiped a stray tear away from her cheek. "No one here in town ever does. It's like everyone is so wrapped up in how they died, it's impossible for them to remember how they lived." A malfunction in a seaplane's engine had taken them in the prime of their lives. Their deaths had rocked their small town, highlighting the fragility of life and showcasing the reality that tomorrows weren't promised to anyone. Her parents had been beloved in Moose Falls, making the tragedy even more poignant.

Bonnie reached out and clasped True's hand in hers. "Are you kidding me? Spending time with him is always a blast. As you know, he's an amazing kid," Bonnie said. "And that's in large part due to you, True. You've been big sis, Mom and Dad, plus a soft place to fall all wrapped up in one."

"You're going to make me cry, which means you'll have to do my makeup all over again." Bonnie was masterful at blending eye shadow, creating a cat eye with eyeliner, and picking the perfect lipstick. She claimed to have learned her skills on TikTok and YouTube. If she started charging folks, Bonnie could have a nice side hustle.

Bonnie reached out and hugged her. "I'll do your makeup one hundred times if you ask me to. I want you to shine tonight." Her lips twitched. "It isn't every day you get invited to the mayor's mansion."

"I wish you were attending too," True said. The event would be a lot more fun with her BFF by her side. Although Bonnie was a good eleven years older than True, they had bonded at Northern Exposure over the past six years and become besties. Her friend had come to Moose Falls to evade a boyfriend who liked to use his fists on her when he got mad. Words couldn't describe what Bonnie meant to True. She was the most loyal and generous person True had ever known. She hoped that one of these days Bonnie would get everything she deserved in this world.

"Honestly, I think that I got the better end of the deal, staying inside where it's nice and cozy with the coolest kiddo in Alaska and ordering Thai food." Bonnie made a shooing motion with her hands. "Go on and get outta here so you're not late. And remember, I want all the details." Bonnie winked at her. "I wouldn't complain if you snagged a few snaps of the Stone brothers while you're at it."

True laughed out loud at Bonnie's outrageous request. She wasn't going to embarrass herself by getting caught taking photos of Hattie's smoking-hot grandsons. She could just see Xavier now looking at her with raised eyebrows.

True heeded Bonnie's advice and hustled out of the house after quizzing Jaylen about his homework and kissing him on the forehead. She tried not to feel bad when Jaylen cuddled up to Bonnie on the sofa, appearing as happy as a kid on Christmas morning. He had barely seemed to notice her exit. *He's growing up*, she reminded herself. *And pretty soon I'm going to have to share him with the world. Sports. Dates. College.* It was all coming at her with the force of a rushing river. Sometimes True just wanted everything to slow down. Or maybe she was afraid of being alone. Jaylen had filled a huge void in her life after the death of her parents. Raising him had been a distraction from grief.

As she drove up to the mayor's mansion, True let out a contented sigh. The driveway leading to the mansion was lit up with sparkling lights strewn across Sitka trees and mounds of snow. The building itself was an architectural dream. Marble columns stood on either side of the entrance. Two brass knockers in the shape of bald eagles decorated the door. The Alaskan flag flew proudly from a spot above the balcony.

After parking her truck in the designated area, True made her way over to the mansion. Thankfully, she'd decided to wear her XTRATUF boots until she got inside. Otherwise she'd be slipping and sliding all over the place in snow and slush.

True let out a gasp as soon as the attendant opened the doors and ushered her inside. She caught sight of the magnificent spiral staircase and the gleaming black-and-white marble floors. She had only been here once before for a business workshop, and the place had lived rent-free in her head ever since. Although she would never admit it to a single soul, True had fantasized about getting married here in a simple yet romantic ceremony filled with loved ones, close friends, and lots of forget-me-nots, the official Alaska state flower. She wasn't a very sentimental person, so this particular dream always managed to take her by surprise.

*Shoot.* In her rush to leave the house, she'd left her bag with the heels. They were sitting on her entryway table. Now she would have to walk around the reception in her sturdy winter boots. Either that or simply go with stockinged feet. The hell with it. She was going to rock her winter boots. Maybe everyone would think it was a deliberate fashion choice instead of a faux pas.

*A confident woman can pull off anything.*

Pearls of wisdom from her mentor and the woman who had invited her to the mayor's mansion this evening. Hattie Stone. True didn't think her friend had ever lacked bravado a day in her life. Hattie was the fiercest woman she had ever known. Businesswoman. Creator. True wanted to be just like her when she grew up. With the exception of her complex familial relationships. True didn't know the truth behind Hattie's estrangement from her grandsons, but twenty years was a long time for them to be MIA.

True checked her jacket with the coatroom attendant, then stashed the ticket in the small evening bag that by some miracle matched her dress to perfection. In keeping with Hattie's motto, True glided into the room as if she were the special guest of the evening. Two steps into the room, and True clapped eyes on one of the guests of honor. Xavier!

She hadn't been wrong in her initial assessment of him. Not one little bit. He looked even more handsome than she'd originally thought, decked out in a dark suit and a crisp white shirt. And he was heading straight toward her. Suddenly her palms moistened, and she lost her train of thought. Not even Garrett had made her feel this type of nervousness mixed with anticipation. A gut rush.

He stopped in front of her, greeting her with a wide smile that showcased perfect teeth. "Hey there, True. Nice to see you again."

He remembered her name. Why did that make her feel giddy? And her pulse was racing.

"Hey, hotshot. Fancy meeting you here."

Xavier frowned at her. "If it's all the same, I prefer my given name. Xavier." He winced. "*Hotshot* reminds me of my old football coach. That's what he called me. And it wasn't a good nickname. He thought I was a showboat."

She quirked her mouth. "And were you?"

He grinned at her, momentarily knocking her off-kilter. Maybe it was a good thing she wasn't wearing heels. She was feeling a little wobbly.

He shrugged. "Perhaps just a little bit. I was thirteen years old and really feeling myself. It was the first time in my life I was good at something, and having those skills made me feel like I was wearing a Superman cape." The chuckle that came out of his mouth was rich and throaty. "It's funny how certain memories stay sharp in our minds. I don't think I'll ever forget it."

She could imagine him in her mind's eye as a cocky teenager ready to take the football world by storm. The pint-sized version of him must have been adorable. "Okay, Xavier it is," she said with a nod.

"You clean up well," he said, his eyes full of masculine appreciation. She liked the way he was looking at her. He wasn't leering, but he was letting her know that he liked what he saw. It had been ages since a man had looked at her like this. His eyes were the deepest brown, the type a person could get lost in. *If* a person were open to that sort of romantic entanglement.

"So you think I needed cleaning up, huh?" she asked, frowning at him.

"No, not at all. I—I didn't mean it like that. I just meant that you look like you spruced yourself up." He ran a shaky hand over his face and let out a groan. "That didn't come out right. I really must be out of practice flirting with a beautiful woman."

True threw her head back with laughter at the dumbfounded expression on his face while inwardly basking in the compliment. "I'm messing with you, Xavier. I knew what you meant." She wrinkled her nose. "It's a bit rare to get decked out for a night on the town here. Moose Falls is more low-key casual than fancy."

He heaved a relieved sigh. "Phew. It's only my second day in Moose Falls. I don't want to burn any bridges that fast."

A server holding a tray of hors d'oeuvres stopped beside them. "Crab cake?" he asked.

She wasn't about to turn down Alaskan crab! Not in this lifetime or any other.

True reached for a mini crab cake and a napkin while Xavier did the same. "No worries," she told him. "I don't get offended easily. Talk trash about my tavern or my little brother, and then you're going to be on my bad side. Anything else, I'm flexible."

"Noted," Xavier said, popping the rest of his appetizer in his mouth.

Just as she was about to let him know that Jaylen was a super fan of his and try to finagle an autograph, True's gaze landed on a surprising face in the crowd.

"Hey! Isn't that your dad over there?" She jutted her chin in the direction of Paul "Red" Stone standing by the bar. His features were sharp and attention grabbing. He was almost as handsome as Xavier. "I haven't seen him in years, but it looks like he's back in town."

The moment the words left her mouth, Xavier's expression shifted. His jaw tightened. He shifted from one foot to the other, leaving no doubt that he was uncomfortable. One would have thought she'd told him that a werewolf had sauntered into the ballroom.

*Way to go, True. You've just opened your mouth and inserted your big ole booted foot inside it.*

🌲

Xavier's entire body froze the moment he locked eyes with his father from across the room. Although he had been expecting to cross paths with him at some point, it still served as a shock to the system to see the invisible man calmly drinking champagne and nodding in his direction. Xavier had to give it to him. The years had been kind to Red. Salt-and-pepper hair only made him look more distinguished. The athletic frame he'd passed on to Xavier was still on point.

Xavier looked back at True. Her eyes were full of questions he didn't really want to answer. "Yeah...umm, in a manner of speaking, yes." His voice sounded awkward to his own ears. He couldn't even manage to string a coherent sentence together at the moment. *Stay cool*, he reminded himself. *Don't let him get under your skin.*

"It's complicated, huh?" she asked softly. *Nope. Nope.* He instantly rejected the sympathy emanating from her soulful brown eyes. Been there, done that. He wasn't going down that road again.

"Yes," he said in a clipped tone. He didn't intend to air his family's laundry at a social event. And he didn't really know True. He had been burned enough in the past by friends and acquaintances who had sold him out to the tabloids.

Xavier was a bit surprised that True didn't seem to know about his messed-up relationship with Red. The blank expression etched on her face spoke volumes. And she'd said Red had been away from Moose Falls for a few years. Had he come back due to Hattie's illness?

Xavier glanced quickly around the room in an effort to locate Landon and Caleb. He didn't want them to be blind-sided. Caleb was deep in conversation with a good-looking redhead, while Landon stood a few feet away with their grandmother. Xavier should have checked in on Landon by now. He was an introvert who hated social engagements. Landon was the polar opposite of Caleb, who thrived on moments like this one.

The moment Hattie had told them about the reception during dinner last night, Caleb had stood up a little straighter, and his eyes sparkled. With his dark good looks and bright Colgate smile, he really fit the part of an aspiring actor. Becoming a famous Hollywood star had been his life's ambition. Starring on a reality show had been a stepping stone for Caleb. Or so they'd all thought.

"A reception?" he'd asked. "For the three of us?"

"Yes, at the mayor's mansion," Hattie had answered. "I want the entire town to roll out the red carpet for my grandsons."

Caleb lived for meet-and-greets. He came alive in the presence of others. That was why he'd made such a splash on the reality show. At first. Rather than fame, Caleb's stint on *Love Him or Leave Him* led to ridicule and heartache and ruin. Somehow, he still was holding on to his dream of becoming the next Michael B. Jordan.

Xavier tried to get Caleb's attention from across the room, but his brother was in his element, flirting and schmoozing. Xavier liked seeing him shine. Ever since the reality show debacle, Caleb hadn't been his true self. Caleb had been sincere in his desire to find love on the show, but everything had gone wrong when he'd fallen madly in love with the leading lady's sister. Turns out it was all a setup for ratings, and Caleb had been labeled a scheming cheater as well as had his heart broken by the woman he loved. In the end, everyone had come out smelling like a rose except Caleb.

Now, instead of walking around with that special glow of his, he had a dark cloud hanging over him. Maybe being far away from the glare of the tabloids was exactly what Caleb needed to get out of his funk and get back in the game.

All of a sudden, his grandmother was speaking into a microphone and calling Xavier, Caleb, and Landon to her side. When Xavier hesitated, True gave him a little shove and a nod of encouragement. "Don't leave her hanging," True urged in a low voice. Once all three of them joined Hattie onstage, she began her speech.

"I'd like to welcome everyone to the mayor's mansion," Hattie said, smoothing back her hair. In her glittery dress and elaborate jewelry, his grandmother resembled a flapper from days gone by. Hattie turned toward the town's mayor, Fred Sparks, giving him a thumbs-up sign. The mayor was balding with a fair complexion and a portly frame. "Thanks, Fred, for hosting us at your gorgeous home. It's the perfect setting for welcoming my three gorgeous grandsons back to Moose Falls. Please, everyone, give a nice round of applause for the next generation of Stones. Xavier, Landon, and Caleb. The future is yours."

Thunderous applause greeted Hattie's announcement. Xavier's gaze went straight to where True stood in the crowd. He couldn't help himself—the woman attracted him like a magnet. True held up a champagne glass and nodded in his direction. Caleb must have noticed the interaction, since he jabbed him in the side and smirked. "So you've forgiven her for the ghost wings?" Caleb asked with a raised eyebrow.

"She's pretty incredible," Xavier murmured. "It would take more than ghost wings to scare me away."

"I never thought I'd hear you say that again," Caleb said,

surprise registering in his voice. "Not too long ago, you swore off all women, so it's nice that you've had a change of heart."

"I'm not looking for anything serious." He didn't want Caleb to get the wrong impression. This would just be a little flirtation to get him back in the groove again. For so long now, he'd been acting like a wounded bird, afraid to make any connections out of fear of getting burned again. His attraction to True was making him reconsider his stance. Connecting with her was already making Moose Falls a more interesting place.

As soon as Hattie finished up, Xavier made a beeline right back to True. He didn't get the impression she was with anyone tonight, but he also wasn't sure if she was single. Yeah, she wasn't giving out any vibes that she was taken, although perhaps that was just wishful thinking on his part. A woman like True would have a lot of options.

"It's great seeing Hattie so full of joy," True said as soon as he reached her side. "She's glowing. I can't remember the last time I've seen her so happy."

"That's good to know, especially since she's so sick." Ever since they had landed in Moose Falls, he'd almost forgotten that Hattie was suffering from a terminal illness. So far all they had seen was her strong will and might.

True shot him a look filled with meaning. "I think having her family back in Moose Falls gives her strength."

He remembered a strong woman from his childhood, a matriarch. Hattie's presence had loomed large in their lives. Even though some of the details were fuzzy, there were memories that still stuck with him. Her vibrant clothing. The big parties she used to host. Her over-the-top laugh. The no-nonsense attitude that kept everyone in line. A true boss.

"I wasn't expecting to be front and center up there. My

grandmother is full of surprises." He reached for a glass of champagne as one of the servers walked past him.

"No? Aren't you used to it, though? Being a big football star and all." True's voice was light and teasing. For a moment he wondered if she was making fun of his current status, but one look at her face dispelled that notion. She was simply being playful while he was being paranoid. For so long he had felt like a joke in the media and the ranks of the NFL. It was hard for him not to automatically go there.

"I'm not sure I ever got used to that aspect of being an NFL player. I loved playing football, not the glare of the spotlight." He shrugged. Most people didn't understand what it was like to be hounded by the press until it felt like you couldn't breathe. With his on-the-field injury, losing his career, and being dumped by Heather, he had been fodder for the tabloids.

"Well, it must have had its advantages, such as being adored by millions of people. My little brother is your biggest fan."

"Don't you mean *was*?" he asked. It was hard to believe people still looked up to him. Fans tended to move on when you were sidelined. There was always a bigger and better player ready to take your place.

She frowned at him. "Is," she repeated. "I'm supposed to be getting your autograph for him. He's going to torture me if I don't deliver the goods."

Xavier felt a smile tugging at his lips. "That can be arranged." Giving out autographs was one of the most rewarding parts of being in the NFL. He was good with kids. They were genuine and had no filters. He'd always known where he stood with them. Almost 100 percent of the time they didn't hesitate to speak their minds.

True tapped the side of her champagne flute. "I'm still

stuck on the fact that you don't enjoy being famous." True was eyeing him with skepticism.

"The limelight wasn't all it was cracked up to be. Trust me, it comes with a downside. My brother Caleb eats that stuff up even though he got burned by the media," he said with a shake of his head. Even now Caleb was posing for photos and glad-handing the townsfolk.

"I noticed," she said. "Wasn't he on that reality show with the twins?"

Xavier winced. "Yeah, although we're not allowed to talk about that. Not sure if you followed the show, but things didn't end well for Caleb."

True made a tutting sound. "I didn't watch, but I heard what happened. What a mess."

And that was putting it mildly. Caleb's image had been completely and utterly trashed. He'd been dragged online by thousands of women who'd called him everything in the book. Cheat. Liar. Scam artist. He'd earned the nickname Love Rat. As a result, no casting people would take him seriously. The only offers he received now were from male revue shows in Vegas. And there was no way Caleb was going to strut around onstage showing off his goodies. He wasn't that desperate.

"Incoming," True said, her eyes wide as she focused on a spot in the distance.

Xavier followed her gaze. Red was walking straight toward him. Xavier opened his mouth to say something to True, but the words were stuck in his throat. His chest tightened. All of a sudden, his breathing felt shallow. The walls started closing in on him.

"I've got to get out of here," he said. Before he knew it, his legs were taking him away from True and out of the ballroom.

# CHAPTER SIX

The rush of cold air greeted Xavier as he pushed past the ornate front doors and into the biting chill of an Alaskan night. He took a deep breath and sucked in the pristine air. Snowflakes fell gracefully from the inky sky, and he lifted his face upward, enjoying the feather-light sensation. He couldn't think of the last time he'd seen this much snow falling. It had probably been around four years ago when the Cardinals had played the Broncos in Denver. A random snowstorm had taken everyone by surprise. The game had been a career high for him. He'd completed twenty of twenty-seven passes. If he closed his eyes, Xavier could picture the actual moment they'd won the game in overtime. He'd never experienced such a rush, not before or since.

Right now all he could feel was a dull ache in the center of his chest.

"Xavier. Are you all right?" True's honeyed voice dragged him from his thoughts. She was standing next to him on the steps, shivering despite her thick parka. He was glad she'd had the sense to grab a coat. He, on the other hand, had beaten a fast path out of the mansion before considering the elements. Fight or flight.

Red-hot embarrassment washed over him. He'd made himself look like an idiot, and there was no telling what True thought of him. For so long now he'd obsessed about the opinions of others. Ever since his life had imploded, he'd felt like a massive failure. Being a grown man who had run away from the sight of his father was pitiful.

"I'm good. Other than making a fool of myself by walking out of there, I'm okay." He couldn't even look her in the eye. Instead he focused on a sign posted by the entrance. *Moose Falls. Established in 1868.*

He felt a tugging sensation on the sleeve of his suit jacket. "Hey! You're overthinking things," True said. "Nobody noticed other than me…and I'm guessing Red." She twisted her lips. "And considering I'm wearing boots because I left my cute little heels at home, I win the making-a-fool-of-oneself contest."

Xavier's eyes trailed down to her feet, then back up to her little blue dress. "I hadn't even noticed the boots. And I guarantee you that most of the folks in that room only saw you wearing that dress." He felt a grin breaking out on his face. "And you *are* wearing it, Miss Everett."

"Aww, thanks," she said, smiling at him. "Hattie gave me the moxie to go out of my comfort zone and wear it," True admitted. "That lady is truly exceptional."

"I wish we knew her better, to be honest," he said with a shrug. "According to my mother, Hattie's health was a big reason why her visits to Arizona stopped."

"I'm sorry," True said. "That must have been hard."

"Not having Red in our lives was even harder. That type of absence leaves a gaping hole," he admitted. "I admire my grandmother for trying to bridge the gap by inviting us back."

"They don't make 'em like Hattie anymore." Her eyes misted over. "And they never will," she added.

"Are *you* okay?" he asked, noticing the swift change in her.

"I'm fine." She drew in a breath. "Just thinking about her not being around anymore makes me emotional. She's very special, not just to me but for everyone here in Moose Falls."

Their eyes held and locked. Xavier felt a little hum pulsing in the air between them. He hadn't experienced anything like it in years. After Heather's betrayal he had sworn off women. What was the point when your heart had been trampled on by someone you'd wanted to be with forever? A person you'd given your all to?

"Something tells me you're pretty special yourself. I like you, True." The words slipped out of his mouth. Maybe it was the champagne or the frostbite he was currently experiencing. Perhaps it was being so far away from his failures back in Arizona, but he felt lighter. He had been in the same room with his father, and it hadn't killed him. He was still breathing. His heart had been broken into a million jagged pieces. Yet he was still breathing.

And he did like True. Not only was she a knockout, but he liked a woman with a wry wit and a sense of humor. She had a self-deprecating air about her, as if she had no clue that she was sexy as all get-out. He wasn't used to a woman not knowing her appeal. The women he had dated ever since college had been well aware of their charms. In some cases, their egos had been completely out of control.

True's lips opened—wide, full kissable lips—and he couldn't take his eyes off them.

Just then the doors were flung open. Landon was standing on the threshold, panic etched on his face. "Xavier. You need to get inside. It's Granny Hattie. She just collapsed."

Seeing Hattie in such a vulnerable position was agonizing for True. The sweet older woman was lying on the ballroom's marble floor, her head propped up on her son's lap. Caleb was fanning her with his hand. Xavier was on his knees by her side, murmuring words of comfort and squeezing her hand. Landon was frantically pacing back and forth, wringing his hands and muttering. People were crowded around her.

True motioned toward the crowd. "Please take a few steps back so she can breathe," she commanded in a raised voice. Having a no-nonsense reputation helped in situations like this one. Everyone immediately complied and moved several feet away.

"Where am I? What happened?" Hattie asked, appearing confused.

"You fainted, Mama. We're at the mayor's mansion. You're hosting a reception for the boys," Red said, his features creased with worry. The resemblance between Xavier and his dad was uncanny. True hadn't noticed it before, but now she couldn't ignore it as they were mere inches away from each other.

Hattie beckoned Xavier closer, then whispered something in his ear. In one swooping motion, he lifted her off the floor and carried her out of the ballroom. Immediately the room began buzzing. Xavier looked like a freakin' superhero coming to the rescue. It certainly wasn't the time or the place to gawk at the man, but Xavier was quite a sight to behold. His buff arms strained against the fabric of his jacket while his strong legs powered him out of the room.

True trailed behind the family as they hustled out of the ballroom. Even though she wasn't related by blood to

Hattie, she was family in every way that mattered to True. If this was something catastrophic, True wanted to be by her friend's side as a source of comfort.

Xavier headed straight down the hall toward the mayor's office. Red stepped in front of him and opened the door. Xavier gently placed his grandmother down on a velvet couch and propped a pillow behind her neck. "How's that?" he asked, sounding tender.

"It's just perfect." Hattie patted his hand. "You've always been such a sweet boy. I'm glad to see that hasn't changed despite all your challenges." Although she hadn't gotten all her color back, True thought Hattie seemed a bit better. She was speaking clearly and seemed to know her surroundings, since she'd led Xavier to this office.

"Let me get you some water," True suggested, heading over toward the watercooler in the corner of the room and filling a plastic cup. When she turned around, Xavier was standing there looking frazzled.

"What just happened?" he asked, running a shaky hand across his face.

"She fainted. Maybe she's dehydrated," True suggested. When a person was terminally ill, it could be any number of things.

Xavier folded his arms across his chest. "But she seemed fine earlier."

This wasn't good. Had Hattie glossed over her illness? Xavier didn't seem to have a clue about the fact that Hattie had been dealing with kidney failure for a long time. With renal failure the side effects were vast. Nausea. Loss of appetite. Fatigue and weakness. The list went on and on. Surely the Stone brothers weren't of the belief that everything in Moose Falls would be kicks and giggles. Hattie was dying. There would be agonizing moments on the road ahead.

"She's sick, Xavier. No matter how good she looks or how she manages to hold things together, Hattie's living on borrowed time."

The expression on his face gutted her. She hadn't imagined that he truly cared about Hattie, but she instantly realized her mistake. Who was she to judge why he and his brothers had stayed away for so long? Obviously Hattie didn't hold it against them. There could be a hundred reasons that had caused a divide. Although it was none of her business, she had a hunch that Red Stone had everything to do with it. The look on Xavier's face when he had first seen Paul was even more tortured than the expression on his face right now.

"I know she's terminally ill," Xavier said. "But she just seems so...full of life."

"You're not wrong about that," True said, "but she puts on a brave front. I've been to a few dialysis treatments with her, and it's a lot for someone to endure at her age. She's made of tough stuff, but she's not invincible."

"Dialysis?" Xavier stammered. "I had no idea. She told us about being terminally ill with renal failure, but nothing more." He let out a frustrated sound. "I should have asked more questions, but I didn't want to push."

"Don't beat yourself up about it," True said. "She's actually doing the treatments at home now while she's sleeping. I'll let her tell you."

She didn't want to disclose too much of Hattie's medical information. Although she didn't think her friend would mind, True didn't want to overstep. Clearly Hattie's grandsons weren't privy to her complete medical history. She knew that the treatments were a big reason her visits to Arizona had stopped, but it wasn't her story to tell.

"I need to bring Hattie this water," True said curtly.

Although Xavier seemed to care about Hattie, True was still concerned about her friend's welfare and the inheritance issue. Maybe it wasn't any of her business, but someone had to put Hattie's well-being first, considering her precarious health. Ownership of Yukon Cider and her own aspirations regarding Northern Exposure weren't nearly as important.

Hattie slowly raised herself to a sitting position and reached for the cup of water True held out to her. Red attempted to assist her, but she waved him away.

"Stop. I'm not an invalid yet," she barked.

"Take it easy," Red said. "You're pushing yourself too much."

"Hush, Red. I'm fine." Her tone matched his, and for a moment the resemblance was uncanny. True almost felt sorry for him—a baby cub going up against a lioness.

Red raised an eyebrow. "You just collapsed. That's not fine in my book. Your doctor is on the way over here. Hopefully he can talk some sense into you."

"I don't need a doctor!" Hattie protested. "Now don't get on my back, but I forgot to eat lunch earlier...and maybe breakfast too, if I'm being honest."

"Mama!" Red said in a shocked voice. "Now you know that's foolish for someone in your condition."

"I don't need a lecture," she snapped, rolling her eyes.

"You need something," Red said, frowning sternly.

Hattie reached out and patted her son's cheek. "We're all on borrowed time, son. I'm not going to obsess over it. It's important for me to live my life. YOLO."

If it weren't so serious, True would have cackled. Lately, Hattie loved using the term YOLO. She said using the acronym made her feel young.

Hattie's grandsons were watching the back-and-forth like they were viewing a tennis match between Venus and

Serena. Anyone watching could sense the battle of wills between mother and son. Perhaps this was why Red had been so scarce these past few years. Or maybe they were at odds because he hadn't been present as much as Hattie would have liked.

"Hattie, are you feeling any better?" True asked. She needed to hear it from her friend's lips and break up the tension-filled dynamic between her and Red.

"I am. I'm so sorry that I ruined the reception," Hattie said, darting a glance at her grandsons. Her expression was so pitiful, it caused a little hitch in the region of True's heart.

"Are you kidding me?" Caleb asked, winking at her. "You spiced it up. Everyone will be talking about this event for weeks."

Hattie let out a groan and placed her head in her hands. Her shoulders shook as she chuckled, immediately lifting the tension. Laughter broke out in the room. It was a relief to see Hattie so lighthearted after her episode.

Perhaps having her grandsons back in Moose Falls was medicine for Hattie's soul.

Just being in the Stone brothers' orbit allowed True to home in on their personalities. Caleb was the life of the party, always smiling and performing. Landon was the sensitive one, the worrywart. Xavier was the protector. She'd known it the moment he had scooped Hattie up in his arms and taken her to a quiet spot. True had noticed him holding his grandmother's hand and the way he'd taken the lead in the situation. Even though she found herself going back and forth in her mind about Xavier's intentions, she sensed that he was a protector at his core. And even though it frustrated her to be so uncertain about Xavier, she vowed to keep an open mind about him.

So, if Xavier was the caretaker, who watched over him?

she wondered. When the world became too much to bear,
who did Xavier turn to?

🌲

By the time Dr. Benjy Akash arrived at the venue, Hattie was back to her normal self. Or at least she seemed to
be. She wasn't complaining of a headache, but the doctor
wanted to make sure Hattie hadn't hit her head when she'd
fallen. Everyone except Red and True left the room when
he examined her. Xavier and his brothers headed back to
the ballroom, where they circulated around the room and
mingled with guests in Hattie's absence.

Xavier met a lot of interesting people. The mayor, Fred
Sparks. Restauranteurs. Fishermen. A local glassworks artist. One woman named Claudine told him that she'd been in
a funk band with his mother. It made him wonder when the
music had stopped for Daisy Stone. Other than crooning in
the shower, his mother wasn't much of a musician. He made
a mental note to ask her about it. Like most things related to
their past in Moose Falls, she'd kept it under wraps. Sometimes Xavier felt as if he barely knew the woman who'd
raised him.

The respect everyone held for Hattie was awe-inspiring.
Left and right he was answering questions about her condition and reassuring folks that his grandmother had recovered from her fainting spell. She was embedded in the fabric
of Moose Falls, and an entire room full of people cared
about her well-being. Although fans had been invested in his
recovery after his TBI, Xavier knew it had been more about
his viability as a quarterback than about him as a person.

*Out of sight, out of mind.* The league, his fans, and his
former fiancée had all moved on once the pundits declared

that his career was finished. Xavier Stone was nothing more than a footnote in NFL history.

For the second time this evening, Xavier realized that his father was heading straight toward him. He couldn't very well dip out of the ballroom a second time. Xavier took a steadying breath. Throughout his NFL career, he'd always done the same thing before hitting the field as a way of mentally preparing himself for battle. Sadly, this was another form of combat.

Now that they were standing face-to-face, Xavier could see the signs of wear and tear that the years had wrought. Fine lines surrounded Red's eyes, and his hairline was now slightly receded. He was still in incredible physical shape. It was the one thing his father had given him—the body of an athlete. "It's good to see you, son," Red said, his gaze intense.

*Son.* That word coming out of Red's mouth was like nails on a chalkboard. It was hard to fathom that he thought of Xavier that way.

Red was a few inches shorter than him, which took Xavier by surprise. When Xavier was a kid, his father had always seemed like a larger-than-life figure.

"Red," he said with a nod, acknowledging his presence.

Red drew his brows together. "Can we talk, Xavier? I think it's best we clear the air."

"Okay, that's fine, but this might not be the time or the place." Xavier looked around him. Too many people were milling around. It already was awkward. No need for an audience.

"We're going to be working together, so I don't want there to be any tension," Red announced, his arms folded across his chest.

Xavier almost laughed out loud. Their relationship had

always been tense until it became nonexistent. Red had bailed on Xavier, Caleb, and Landon in every way imaginable as they'd made their way through adolescence into adulthood. Xavier couldn't even remember the last time he'd seen the man. In all likelihood, he didn't want to hold on to that memory.

"Of course not. No one wants that," Xavier said. He didn't *want* to go down this road with his father. This conversation seemed as if it should have happened decades ago. Maybe then he would have cared to listen. But having a heart-to-heart now felt too little, too late. Did his father think that their talking would result in a Hallmark television moment where everything was forgiven?

Red studied him for a moment. Xavier could see he was deep in thought about something. "Just so you know, I didn't ask Hattie to put that stipulation in the contract. It's important that you understand that. I'm not trying to manipulate anything." He eased his shoulders back, creating tension in the seams of his jacket. "I wouldn't do that to you."

Xavier shrugged. "We signed on the dotted line, so it's a nonissue. My brothers and I want to learn everything there is to know about running Yukon Cider. That's our priority ... and Hattie's as well."

"She loves the three of you. Always has. You're the future of Yukon Cider. You might not understand her reasoning, but she wants her company to be a symbol."

"Of what?" Xavier asked, his curiosity piqued.

"Family. Unity. The things that matter most."

Okay, Xavier was calling BS. Since when had those things meant anything to Red? Suddenly, all Xavier's defenses were up. His mother had warned him about falling for Red's charms. He couldn't allow himself to fall into the trap so easily.

Xavier needed an exit plan from this conversation. Fast. Otherwise, he might just lose his cool.

"If you don't mind, I need to track someone down," he said, sounding clunky. He needed to focus on something else.

Someone else. True. Where was she?

"Sure thing. We have plenty of time to talk later." Red placed his hand on Xavier's shoulder and lightly squeezed it.

Xavier walked away, his head spinning with a million different thoughts. For so long now, he had viewed Red in a monstrous light, and those negative feelings were still churning around inside of him, threatening to spill over. There were so many questions he'd wanted to hurl at him. Why did you abandon your sons? It really was time to concentrate on something other than Red, especially since Xavier's head was pounding from all the stress.

Where had True gone? Xavier hadn't seen her since they were all gathered with Hattie in the mayor's office. Both Red and Hattie had resurfaced in the ballroom, but there hadn't been any sign of True. Xavier looked out across the room, searching for a stunning brunette in a little blue dress. He couldn't find her anywhere!

She was gone. Vanished. Poof. He had scoured the ballroom, walked down the hall, and even ventured upstairs. No sign of True.

When it sank in that True had left the reception, Xavier felt a little bummed about her not saying goodbye. They had bonded tonight. Or at least he'd thought they had. He'd been out of the game for so long now, maybe he had misinterpreted things. Maybe she was simply being friendly to Hattie's grandson. That was possible, but his gut instinct didn't usually lie to him. She had given him all the feels. The push and pull of attraction. Subtle flirting and a hunger to spend more time with her. To explore the possibilities. To kiss those beautiful lips.

Once all the guests began to head out for the evening, Jacques drove them back to Hattie's house. On the drive, his grandmother fell asleep on Xavier's shoulder. He didn't have the heart to wake her up after the night she'd had. A few more minutes of resting her head on his shoulder wouldn't do any harm, he figured.

"Jacques, could you loop around the lake one more time?" Xavier asked, giving in to a sentimental urge.

Jacques nodded. He turned his head and smiled at Xavier. "I think that's a great idea."

As Jacques drove around the lake area, Xavier's thoughts turned to True. She had made the night enjoyable even in the midst of his grandmother's fainting spell and Red's unexpected presence. She had been incredibly sensitive about his lack of knowledge regarding Hattie's illness. True hadn't judged him. She had stayed by Hattie's side, supporting her with friendship and words of assurance. He wanted . . . no, he needed to see True again.

# CHAPTER SEVEN

"So, tell me all about the reception. I didn't want to pester you last night for the juicy details." Bonnie leaned over the bar, waiting with bated breath for True to deliver the piping-hot tea. Bonnie would deny it if pressed, but she lived for town gossip.

"It was a lot of fun," True answered. Her thoughts immediately went to Xavier. She felt bad about not saying goodbye to him last night, but she hadn't wanted to pull him away from an intense conversation with Red. From what she'd gleaned, their relationship needed a lot of TLC. Hattie would be ecstatic if they managed to mend their issues with each other.

"Did you snag a photo of the genetically blessed brothers?" Bonnie asked. She crossed her hands prayerfully in front of her and gazed at True with puppy-dog eyes.

True chuckled. "Yes, I did, although I almost got caught by Xavier snapping the pic." She'd managed to snag a photo without anyone being the wiser. She dug into her back pocket and pulled out her cell phone. A few seconds later, she was sharing the photo with Bonnie.

"Good golly, Miss Molly. Make sure to text that to me." Bonnie fanned herself with a menu. "How did you keep your equilibrium with all that testosterone in one room?"

"I managed just fine," True said, shaking her head. Bonnie was a trip. She wasn't letting up on this. In many ways her friend was all talk. At thirty-nine Bonnie had experienced a lot of failed relationships and disappointments. But for the past two years, she'd been dating Tucker Jennings, a local who worked at Yukon Cider. Although Bonnie always tried to downplay the relationship, True sensed things were getting serious between them.

"I heard about Hattie collapsing. How's she doing?" Bonnie asked, her brows knitted together with worry.

"I haven't heard anything today, but she was able to recuperate at home instead of having to go to the hospital. Turns out she'd skipped meals and didn't properly hydrate," True explained. "I need to give her a call later to check in."

Hattie's collapse had been terrifying. At her age, and considering her illness, no one should have been surprised. Considering all the hours she'd been working, it was almost inevitable that Hattie would crash. It served as a reminder that Hattie's health was precarious. True knew all too well that tomorrow wasn't promised.

A few minutes later, True headed to her office in the back of the establishment. She had decorated the space in bright, cheery colors to offset the occasionally gloomy Alaskan weather. Her walls were robin's-egg blue with accents of cream. A faux Tiffany lamp with colorful stained glass sat on her desk. She had splurged on the sepia leather chair, but it had proven to be well worth the cost. Once she sank into it, True felt as if she were floating on air.

Northern Exposure had been slow all day, which was a cause for worry, True realized. Lately, business hadn't been as bustling as usual. As manager, it was True's job to figure out why there had been a decline in business and what she could do to turn things around. Hattie hadn't said anything to True about the downturn in revenue, but as a sharp businesswoman, Hattie must have noticed.

Not the best impression to make if one aspired to own the business. And even though she knew it might not be a practical goal considering the state of her finances, her heart wouldn't allow her to let go of the dream. True still aspired to own the tavern.

A sudden knock on the door drew her attention. "Come in," she called out.

Nico, one of her servers, stood in the doorway. With his black mohawk and variety of tattoos displayed across his neck, he was her youngest employee at twenty years old. Sweet and reliable, Nico was an incredible asset at the tavern.

"Hey, True. Someone's here asking for you. Last name Stone."

Her heart began to thunder wildly in her chest. "Okay. You can send him back here. Thanks." Once Nico was gone, True smoothed her hair back and rummaged in her desk for a lip moisturizer. Why hadn't she worn a better outfit today? The last time Xavier had seen her, she'd looked like the absolute best version of herself.

*It's what's inside that counts.* Her mother's words roared in her ears. *Yeah, right*, True thought. She let out an undignified snort. That might be true, but she still wanted to look presentable.

Seconds later there was another knock on the door. Once again Nico opened it and ushered her visitor inside. Her stomach fluttered in anticipation while her palms moistened. She was dying to know what had brought Xavier over to Northern Exposure.

Disappointment seized her by the throat when she laid eyes on Red Stone as he entered her office. She put her game face on and tried not to let her feelings show.

"True, it's good to see you again," Red said, nodding as he entered her office.

"Hey, Red. Likewise. What brings you by Northern Exposure?" she asked. Her curiosity was piqued by him showing up at her place of business. Red had been away from Moose Falls for years, and to her recollection, he'd never shown any interest in the tavern. This visit was a bit unusual.

"For starters, I want to thank you for being such a great friend to my mother. As you know, life hasn't been easy for her as of late." Red's tone was far from upbeat. He seemed a bit subdued and more than a little stressed. True attributed his demeanor to Hattie's fading health. She imagined he might be feeling guilty about being away from home for so long.

True splayed her hands on the desk. "There's no need to thank me. Hattie's done more for me than I could ever pay back over several lifetimes. I love her dearly."

When he grinned at her, Red looked exactly like Xavier. Same perfectly shaped lips. The deep-set brown eyes. Even their expressions were similar.

"So, I'm here today to talk about the tavern."

Suddenly, True felt uneasy. The tavern was her baby, and she felt very protective of the place. What did Red want to know about Northern Exposure?

"Take a seat and make yourself comfortable," she said, gesturing toward one of her plush velvet seats. She wasn't feeling very cordial all of a sudden, but she couldn't very well snub the boss's son. What was it with these Stone men taking over?

Red pulled off his coat and draped it over the back of

his chair. Once he was done, Red leaned across the desk. "Hattie is pulling me into the family business," he explained as he sat down, "and she wants me to brainstorm some ideas with you to ratchet up business."

She knitted her brows together. Why hadn't Hattie come to True herself with this? It stung a little that she'd sent her son to have this conversation rather than broach it with True directly. They had always been so close. This visit from Hattie's son only served to magnify her feelings of being on the outside looking in, especially now that Hattie's beloved grandsons were back in town.

"I know sales have been down recently, but I've been trying to research the reasons for it." She was on the defensive now after being blindsided by Red's unexpected visit.

"Did you come up with anything?" Red asked. "This isn't an interrogation, by the way. You're not on the hot seat."

"I brainstormed some ideas to get more customers in." She reached into her desk drawer for her notebook. "More dining specials, special events, tie-ins with the Yukon Cider merchandise, wine and food tastings."

"Those sound really promising. Why don't we get together next week and go over this?" He made a face. "I know you weren't expecting me, so I apologize for just popping up. I was actually picking up a pumpkin bagel for my mother. After last night we're all going to make sure she's not skipping meals."

"That's a brilliant idea. How is she today?" True asked. She felt guilty for not checking in on her friend earlier.

Red shook his head. "I thought she should take the day off, but she's eager to show her grandsons Yukon Cider. According to Hattie, she's fine, but last night made everything all too real for me." He let out a huge sigh. "She's mortal like the rest of us."

Compassion flared inside her. Clearly, Red loved his mother, yet he was helpless to protect her against the ravages of illness. She knew exactly what he meant. Hattie Stone was a larger-than-life figure who seemed invincible. Accepting the fact that she was terminally ill was something True struggled with. Obviously she wasn't alone.

"I know I'm not a blood relation, but Hattie's always been like family to me. Believe me, I've always viewed her as my she-ro. Superwoman's got nothing on her." She let out a chuckle that quickly transformed into a sob. The more she tried to choke the tears back, the harder she cried. Red reached across the desk to pat her hand.

"I'm so sorry. I don't know where that came from," she apologized. Embarrassment threatened to swallow her up. Usually she was able to easily keep her emotions in check, but lately she had been struggling to hold it all in.

"No need to apologize. As to where it came from, you're human. And you love Hattie. That means you're grappling with the idea of losing her. Trust me, we all are." Sorrow emanated from his dark brown eyes. Suddenly, True wanted to know more about this man. Why was he estranged from his sons? What had taken him away from his hometown for so many years?

"Thanks for understanding," True said with a nod. Loss had been such a huge part of her life. In many ways losing both of her parents had shaped her adulthood. She had been trying to recover ever since. With the anniversary of her parents' death rapidly approaching, True knew all her emotions were resting on the surface.

"I'll be in touch, True," Red said as he stood. "I appreciate you hearing me out."

"Of course," she said, standing to see him to the door. "I'd love for you to come to our karaoke night on Wednesday.

It'll give you a feel for the place and what we're doing for events."

He smiled at her, giving the impression he was considering it. "I might just pop in, True. Thanks for the invite."

Red immediately gestured for her to sit back down. Before she knew it, he'd sailed out the door.

Another knock on her door caused her to let out a huge groan. What was it now? Unless it was actually Xavier Stone standing in her doorway, she didn't want to be bothered. Seconds later Bonnie appeared, her eyes brimming with curiosity.

"Wasn't that Hattie's son I just saw walking past me?" Bonnie asked. She was smacking her gum so loudly, it resembled the sound of popcorn popping on the stove.

"Yes, that was Paul Stone, otherwise known as Red."

"I haven't seen him in years. Hubba-hubba. He's aging like a fine wine." Bonnie's excitement was palpable. "I almost bowed when I saw him. He's fifty percent responsible for those hunky Stone brothers." She winked at True. "He should get a medal."

"Please tell me you didn't say that to him." Sometimes Bonnie went rogue. True fervently hoped this wasn't one of those times. She had to handle this business situation as a consummate professional. She would have to cross all her *t*'s if she meant to follow through with her plan to buy Hattie out. Now that the Stone brothers were in town and poised to inherit Hattie's empire, she felt a sense of urgency. More than ever True realized how much she wanted to own Northern Exposure. She had put in a lot of blood, sweat, and tears to make the establishment a success. Maybe it was a long shot, but she needed to pursue this dream.

"C'mon, True. I'm not that out there. That would be inappropriate." Bonnie made a prim face and shot True a sweet smile. At the moment she looked as if butter wouldn't melt in her mouth. True knew better. She loved Bonnie to death, but she was a wild card.

"It would be," True murmured, "considering this is a place of business that his family owns." She could feel the corners of her lips twitching, but True didn't want to encourage Bonnie.

"Honestly, he's mighty fine himself. I'm open to dating a zaddy."

True had held in her laughter as long as she could. Bonnie's last comment sent her over the edge. True put her face in her hands, and with quivering shoulders, she began to howl with laughter. She really needed this moment of levity. Thoughts of Hattie's impending death, combined with the upcoming anniversary of her parents' tragic plane crash, had been weighing heavily on her. This was the perfect outlet.

"Bonnie, what would I do without you?" she asked, wiping away tears of laughter.

"Girlfriend, we're not ever going to find out." She approached True's desk and held up her hand for a high five. After they'd slapped palms, Bonnie quickly turned to leave. "Gotta get back to the grind. It's almost time for Amos's lunch."

Amos Duggan had been a regular customer since the tavern opened its doors fifty years earlier. Every single day—even during snowstorms and major holidays—Amos showed up for lunch. And he ordered the same meal each time—a cup of Alaskan clam chowder, a barbecue burger, and rosemary fries. He was the sweetest man in the world with his pure white beard, twinkling blue eyes, and slight potbelly. He flirted madly with Bonnie every single day she was on the schedule and pitched a small fit when she had a day off. If a human being could be a mascot, then Amos was it for the tavern.

After Bonnie's departure, True's thoughts veered back to her unexpected encounter with Red Stone. True barely knew him at all. Over the years she'd only seen him a handful of times. He had been in and out of Moose Falls for the past twenty years, always having one foot in and the other foot out. To her knowledge he hadn't ever worked for Yukon Cider. But now, with Hattie's terminal illness, everything had shifted. If only True had been in a position years ago to make a bid for ownership of Northern Exposure, things wouldn't feel so precarious right now.

And now, it seemed as if the opportunity was rapidly slipping through her fingers without there being a single thing she could do about it.

🌲

"Isn't Moose Falls beautiful?" Hattie asked from the front passenger seat. Bundled up in her long purple puffer jacket and knit hat, she appeared to be in fine shape. She'd made a nice recovery from last night's fainting spell. Dr. Akash had warned her strenuously about the hazards of skipping meals. As much as he could, Xavier intended to make sure his grandmother ate heartily.

"It really is scenic," Xavier said. No one could dispute that simple fact. He had to focus on the road, but he could still soak in his magnificent surroundings. Rugged mountains rose in the distance. They loomed so large, it almost seemed as if he could reach out and touch them. Snow-dotted trees—Sitka spruce, mountain hemlock, quaking aspen—were in abundance.

He had a vague memory of this view, which was fairly shocking to him. Xavier was learning more and more each day that he'd retained way more about his hometown than he had ever imagined. Just being here in Moose Falls was bringing it all back like ocean waves crashing against the shore.

Today Xavier was driving one of his grandmother's cars. If he was going to be living in Alaska for a solid year, he needed to become proficient at driving in snowy conditions. Back in Arizona snow tires and chains were nonexistent. He was being careful and driving slowly until he became acclimated to the roads and weather conditions. So far, he was doing a pretty good job.

Like Hattie said, *It's not the speed of the train, it's the destination.* He was going to have to start writing down her Hattie-isms.

Moose Falls was located on Kachemak Bay in the southern tip of the Kenai Peninsula. Due to its proximity to the water, fishing had always been a major industry in town. But, due to Hattie's ingenuity, the small town was now known for Yukon Cider. It was a major draw for tourists, allowing visitors to enjoy an authentic Alaskan experience with a stay at the Moose Falls Inn and a tour and taste at Yukon Cider.

"So, how did Yukon Cider originate?" Xavier asked. "Was it a family business?" Although he had done a little research into the company prior to coming to Alaska, he still didn't know much about the founding of the business.

Hattie let out a throaty laugh. "My father was a preacher who didn't believe in drinking. He would have frowned upon Yukon Cider. The business came to pass when I was widowed after Jack's death. I had very little money and a small boy to raise, so I had to think fast to find a way for us to survive." She looked out the window and ran her finger along the pane of glass. "I've always loved apples, and I hated the taste of beer, so I decided to do some experimenting one day. I fooled around with fermented apples, and one thing led to another. Voilà. Yukon Cider was born."

"That's quite a story," Caleb said, letting out a low whistle. "You really did the thing, didn't you?" He reached over into the front seat and squeezed her shoulder.

"I did indeed," Hattie said, her voice bursting with pride.

"You were a bit of a scientist," Landon said. "I must've inherited that from you."

"I bet you did," Hattie said. Xavier darted a glance at his grandmother. She was grinning from ear to ear. He was noticing that it didn't take much to make her happy: a sweet compliment on her blouse or a tidbit they shared with her about their lives.

"Did you know that Alaska has more coastline than the rest of the United States combined?" Landon asked as he peered out the window.

"Is that a serious question?" Caleb asked. He was busy snapping photos on his cell phone, ones that no doubt would end up on his Instagram page within minutes. Caleb was all about rehabbing his image in the hope of jump-starting an acting career. So far it really wasn't working all that well. Caleb couldn't manage to shake the public's perception that he was a lying, cheating snake. Every time he went on an audition, casting directors brought up his unfortunate stint on the most popular reality show on television.

"That's fascinating, Landon," Hattie remarked. "I appreciate how you're being a man of facts. You could probably rake in the dough on *Jeopardy!*" she said with a chuckle.

From the rearview mirror, Xavier could see Landon grinning. "Thank you, Granny. I consider that a huge compliment. I appreciate someone who's always seeking knowledge."

As they continued to travel along the road, Xavier slowed down when they came across a "Moose Crossing" sign. He'd been warned by both Hattie and Jacques about driving in Moose Falls in remote areas. Hitting a thousand-pound moose was the last thing he wanted to do on their first day at the factory.

"We're coming up on it now," Hattie announced. "Make this right turn and pull into the lot."

A large, oval, red-and-white sign announced that they had arrived at Yukon Cider. Although Xavier had never imagined he would get so excited at the sight of Hattie's cider company, goose bumps rose on the back of his neck. What his grandmother had achieved was monumental. It was even more impressive that she had built her company up from nothing after being widowed and raising Red as a single mother. He wondered why their mother hadn't ever told them about all their grandmother had achieved. Xavier knew there had been bad blood after the divorce, but they had really taken their beef to new levels.

Once they exited the car and walked into the building, there were employees waiting to greet them. They stood by the entrance with a sign that read "Welcome back to Moose Falls." Each of their names was written at the top in bold red letters. Everyone was smiling and jovial. Hattie seemed to know every single one of them by name.

"Laying it on a bit thick, aren't they," Caleb said in a low voice. His lips were twitching. Despite everything he'd been through, Xavier appreciated the fact that Caleb's sense of humor was still intact. Caleb never lost his sense of self, despite being portrayed in the media as someone he wasn't.

"I think it's nice," Landon said. "They're rolling out the welcome wagon."

Even though he wouldn't admit it out loud, Xavier thought it was nice too. Because they were important to Hattie, he and his brothers were being welcomed with open arms. It reminded him of the days when a new player arrived in the Cardinals' locker room. There had always been a little bit of razzing, but mostly they'd showered the newcomer with love.

"They like us," Xavier said. "They really like us."

Xavier knew better than to look at his brothers. It would only result in a fit of inappropriate laughter, which wouldn't go over well with Hattie. Yukon Cider was her pride and joy. The way she talked about the company, Xavier didn't know where she began and Yukon Cider ended. Maybe in time, all would be revealed. He had so many questions to ask her, things his mother hadn't ever wanted to discuss.

Why had she been absent from their lives for the most part? There had been visits in their early years, but those had faded out. Sure, she had sent plenty of gifts and checks for birthdays and graduations, but her physical presence had been lacking. Why? Clearly she loved them and always had. What had gone down between his parents that had been so terrible that the entire family had splintered?

One way or the other, Xavier was determined to uncover the truth. After all, he'd only been waiting for twenty years to find out.

# CHAPTER EIGHT

The next few days were a whirlwind of activity, with Xavier and his brothers getting a crash course in all things related to Yukon Cider. So much so that his dreams were filled with a laundry list of all the things he needed to learn over the next year. Even though he was skeptical about the idea of living in Moose Falls and running Hattie's company, he knew that keeping an open mind was only fair. After all, it was his grandmother's life's work, and the fate of Yukon Cider would affect lots of people here in town. From what he had gleaned from a few employees, the company fueled the economy in Moose Falls.

They met lots of Hattie's employees over the next few days—wonderful, hardworking Alaskans who were devoted to the cider company. Either way—stay or sell—the fate of the company was of vital importance to the townsfolk. Which meant there was a lot resting on his shoulders—and Caleb's and Landon's. Had Xavier really thought this out before he had packed up his life in Arizona and headed back to Alaska?

And now, he'd decided to spend some time at Northern Exposure in an effort to decompress a little bit. According to Jacques, they held a karaoke night every Wednesday. Xavier wasn't planning to get onstage and perform, but Caleb was determined to belt out a few songs.

"This is a little out of my element," Landon announced as they walked through the doors of Northern Exposure. Xavier had had to coax Landon to join them tonight. His view of a night out was a visit to the planetarium. Because Landon was his little brother, Xavier found it endearing, but he also thought it was high time he mixed it up a little bit. His romantic life had always been a snooze fest. Even though it seemed as if his brother wanted to make a connection with someone, so far nothing had clicked. Maybe coming to Alaska would get him out of the safety zone.

"It's a tavern, Landon," Xavier said, clapping his brother on the back. "Not a strip club."

Landon's eyes widened. "I should hope not." He adjusted his glasses and cleared his throat. Xavier's baby brother was looking around the place with wide eyes.

"Haven't you ever done karaoke?" Caleb asked, frowning. "Back in L.A. I do it a few times a month."

"I guess I've never had the opportunity," Landon answered with a shrug.

Caleb threw his arm around him. "That's okay," he said with a wink. "Just follow my lead. You'll be great."

Landon sputtered. "Oh, no. Thank you very much, but I'll be watching you from the cheap seats. I'm not a performer."

"I need a wing man or two, so you're definitely joining me," Caleb insisted. "I'm not taking no for an answer."

As the two went back and forth, Xavier found himself looking for a True sighting. So far he hadn't gotten a glimpse of her. Even though she was petite, she was definitely a woman who would stand out in a crowd. Her friend Bonnie was behind the bar serving customers while a few servers were on the floor taking orders.

Just as he was beginning to wonder if True was even working tonight, she appeared. He watched as she strode out of the kitchen with a platter in her hands. She stopped at a large table of guests to deliver the food, then paused to chat with them. Her attitude was relaxed, as if she knew the patrons and was at ease with them. He liked watching her in action. She was comfortable in her own skin. So far there wasn't anything he didn't like about this woman.

When she was within a few feet of Xavier, True spotted him and walked over. Tonight she was dressed more casually in skinny jeans and a pink-and-gray flannel button-down. She was wearing pink Timberland boots on her feet, which, in his opinion, upped her adorable quotient into the stratosphere. There wasn't a single flaw in this woman as far as he could see.

"Hey there, Xavier. Welcome to karaoke night." True greeted him with a wide smile. His belly was doing wild somersaults. He was getting that feeling again, the one that transformed him into a goofy teenage boy.

*Easy, hotshot. She's just a girl.*

"Thanks. The place looks great," he said, looking around at the colorful decorations and the makeshift stage set up with microphones, speakers, and a mixer. He'd done a few karaoke nights back home, and although it had never been his thing, he was excited to spend more time in True's orbit.

"This is the fun part of my job," she said. "I like watching everyone cutting loose and singing their hearts out. Are you a big karaoke fan?" Her expressive face was lit up with excitement.

"Not really. I was getting a little stir-crazy at the house," he explained. "So far we've really only been going from Hattie's place and Yukon Cider. That's getting a bit boring if I'm being honest. It's nice to get out and check out the nightlife."

True snorted with laughter. "Nightlife? I sure hope you're not disappointed. Karaoke night is the ultimate night out on the town in Moose Falls. You're not going to experience what you're used to back in Arizona, I'm sure, but it's a fun time."

"Okay, well, judging by the way this place is filling up, it's a crowd favorite." People were entering the tavern left and right, with the tables by the stage already occupied. This event might be standing room only.

"As I said, karaoke night is sacred in Moose Falls. Folks in these parts take it very seriously."

"Will you be taking the stage?" Xavier asked. He liked the idea of her doing her thing and letting loose onstage. If he had to guess, he'd peg her as a Beyoncé fan. Maybe Lady Gaga.

"Not a chance," True said, making a face. She pointed toward the bar. "I'll be too busy making sure everyone has food and drinks. I also oversee the bartenders to make sure no one is overserved."

"Smart," Xavier said. He had frequented a lot of bars during his time in the NFL, and he knew all too well how many people ended up leaving totally wasted with car keys in their hands.

"It's one of the first things that I learned from Hattie," True told him. "She's one wise woman."

He was getting the distinct impression that True had a little hero worship going on toward his grandmother. It made sense. Hattie was her boss and a woman who had carved out her own empire in Moose Falls. She was a town legend.

"She is indeed," he agreed. "I'm pretty much a sponge

at this point at Yukon Cider, soaking up all of Granny's knowledge."

True bobbed her head. "Keep soaking it up. Hattie is masterful at her job."

"I'm beginning to discover that."

"I better check on my patrons before the karaoke starts."

"Well, I'll be sitting over there with my brothers," Xavier said, jutting his chin in the direction of Landon and Caleb. "Swing by if you have time. I'll save you a seat."

"Okay," she said, smiling. "I'll try my best." And then she was off, heading back toward the kitchen, where he imagined True was overseeing her employees. When it came to the tavern, she seemed to be a perfectionist, much like Hattie.

He'd thrown the offer out there to join him at his table in the hope that True would get the message. He was interested in her. By the end of the night, he intended to get True's number and make plans for them to go out. He had no idea what date nights looked like in Moose Falls other than kara-oke nights at the tavern, but he sure intended to find out.

🌲

Was Xavier coming on to her or simply being friendly? Seri-ously? Was she this out of practice with men that she wasn't even sure if the hottest guy in town was interested in her? Maybe a part of her couldn't wrap her head around the pos-sibility that a famous athlete would find her appealing. True knew that Xavier had been engaged to a glamorous semi-famous model. Clearly, that's what he was used to. Why on earth would she appeal to him?

All the old insecurities rose inside her. Her relationship with Garrett had taught her to watch out for red flags. Xavier was hot and famous. Those weren't bad things on their own, but the combination could be trouble. She imagined he was used to women falling at his feet. Maybe he was the type of guy who expected it. If that was the case, she would have to set him straight. She was not one to go gaga over a man. Never again.

*Put your game face on. Don't melt over the man.* Sure, he had a smokin' body and a face straight from the pages of *GQ*, but he also had warning signs all over him. He had been involved in a highly publicized breakup not too long ago, so he might be on the rebound. He was also her boss's grandson.

She would have to be an idiot to fall for an athlete's charms. They were known for playing the field. But that didn't mean she couldn't go out with him, did it? What would be the harm in hanging out with the new guy in town? It wasn't as if she was going to marry him or anything. She certainly had no intention of giving her heart away. True let out a groan. She was already caving and coming up with reasons she should go out with Xavier. Not that he had asked her out yet, but she was getting interested vibes from him.

True stayed in the kitchen for as long as she possibly could. She knew it was avoidance, but just thinking about Xavier Stone made her way too giddy. And she wasn't a giddy person at all. Just before the MC was about to take the stage, True headed back to the dining area.

"Where have you been?" Bonnie asked as soon as she arrived on the floor. With her shoulder-length hair in two high ponytails, she looked like a teenager. "They're about to start the festivities. AJ's in rare form tonight."

"Well, we couldn't ask for a better hype man," True said.

AJ was True's cousin. The best word to describe him was *eclectic*. His personality was high energy and vibrant. He was beloved by everyone in town. He dabbled in all types of music; there wasn't a genre AJ didn't like. He was determined to be the next Lenny Kravitz, but until that day came, he was content to host karaoke night at Northern Exposure and perform gigs in the Kenai Peninsula.

AJ was on the makeshift stage getting the crowd revved up by doing a sing-along of "YMCA." If ever there was a song to pump up the audience, this was the one. Patrons were even jumping out of their seats and dancing around, forming the YMCA letters with their arms.

She casually scanned the crowd for a glimpse of Xavier. There were so many people here tonight, it was tricky finding him.

"He's sitting at a table over by the beam. And he's looking straight this way," Bonnie said, practically shouting over the din. "Something tells me it's not me he's looking at."

True locked eyes with Xavier, and he beckoned her over to him. He was sitting with his brothers, and as promised, there was an empty seat next to him. He patted the seat of the chair, making his invitation clear.

"What are you waiting for? YOLO," Bonnie shouted before turning back to serve thirsty customers.

"YOLO," True said to herself as encouragement as she walked toward Xavier.

"Hey," he said, shouting over the din as she reached his table.

"Hey," she answered, also trying to be heard over the loud singing.

"Take a load off," Xavier said, pulling the chair back from the table. True sat down, her knees brushing against him as she did so. Even though there were dozens of people in the space, she was acutely aware of Xavier. A woodsy, cedar smell rose to her nostrils. When he rolled up the sleeves of his button-down shirt, she couldn't help but notice his muscled, toned arms.

AJ began calling up performers after announcing that the winner, as determined by the crowd, would receive a cash prize and a winner's trophy. AJ's enthusiasm got the crowd riled up, and for a moment True wished that Red had shown up to witness the lively atmosphere. Maybe then he would understand that great things were happening at Northern Exposure and pass it on to Hattie. She wondered if Red was lying low due to the tension between him and his sons. Sooner or later, they needed to hash out their differences.

It was nice sitting with Xavier and his brothers. Their reactions to the performers were a beautiful sight to behold. Their interactions with one another showcased the tight bonds that flowed between them. They were all charming in different ways, with Caleb being a huge extrovert and Landon being the complete opposite. She loved how Xavier seemed comfortable in his own skin without flexing his athlete status.

Suddenly, Caleb jumped onstage and positioned himself at the microphone. "We did this one for my mom's birthday, so I'd like to perform it again tonight. *If* I can get my brothers up here." Caleb motioned for them to join him onstage. "What do you say, boys?" he asked.

"I'm going to strangle you," Xavier muttered while Landon covered his face with his hands.

"Come on. Don't make me beg," Caleb said into the microphone. For emphasis he put his hands in a prayer-like pose. Every single woman except True let out an "aaah" sound. True wondered if undies would soon be flying toward the stage.

Xavier and Landon let out simultaneous groans. "Oh, we should have seen this coming," Landon said, shuddering. "Is it too late for me to slink out the back entrance?"

"It's way too late, bro," Xavier said. "This crowd isn't going to let us off that easy."

"You're right about that. You can't leave him hanging," True said, jabbing Xavier in the side.

"Oh, yes, I can. I did not come here tonight to do karaoke." He twisted his perfectly shaped lips. Then he rolled his eyes. Hard.

True laughed out loud. It was funny seeing him so upset. He was really bent out of shape about the prospect of performing. "You know what they say, Xavier. The best-laid plans often go astray." She covered her mouth with her hand so Xavier didn't see her grin.

"Can everyone help me get them up here? I promise it'll be worth it," Caleb pleaded with the crowd. He began to clap. "Get onstage!" he chanted. The audience eagerly cooperated, yelling "Get onstage! Get onstage!"

True turned to look at Xavier. He was glaring at Caleb, who was grinning back at him while still chanting along with the audience. He had them firmly in the palm of his hand, and he knew it. True got a mental image of what the dynamic must have been like between them as kids.

"Let's just get this over with," Xavier said, standing and motioning for Landon to do the same. Landon let out a deep breath before standing up and following Xavier toward the stage. Caleb raised his hands in a gesture of triumph. The brothers huddled up and began having an animated conversation. After a few minutes, they stood side by side facing the audience.

Caleb looked over at AJ and gave him a signal. The strains of Whitney Houston began to ring out. Within seconds the Brothers Stone began to belt out the lyrics to "I Wanna Dance with Somebody." With Caleb in the middle as lead singer, Xavier and Landon had positioned themselves on either side of him. They began to bust out the moves, their steps synchronized as they entertained the crowd. Landon was shy at first, but after a few minutes he got into the groove along with his brothers. They dipped and turned and snapped their fingers, all in perfect sync with the music and each other.

True couldn't take her eyes off Xavier as he moved his hips to the beat and sang his little heart out. He was hysterically funny and hot at the same time. A potent combination!

As the song came to a climax, the room erupted into applause as they rewarded the Stone brothers with a standing ovation. True got to her feet and put her fingers to her mouth, letting out a loud whistle. This performance had definitely made True's night and won over the crowd.

Xavier had been reluctant to take the stage, but he'd performed like a pro. She liked that he was a team player. And he sure knew how to move those hips, she thought as she fanned herself with her hand.

"A round of drinks is on Caleb," Xavier informed Bonnie, who quickly let the crowd know the good news. An immediate roar ripped through the patrons.

"Hey!" Caleb protested. "I never said that!"

"And I never said I would do karaoke tonight," Xavier said, shooting him a pointed look. "Why don't you settle up our tab as well," Xavier suggested. Caleb shook his head and headed off toward the bar with Landon. Xavier could hear him grumbling as he walked away.

"Bravo!" True told Xavier as he sat back down.

"Thanks. So, what do you do on a night off?" Xavier asked, his eyes like laser beams as he stared at her.

"A night off? What's that?" she asked in a teasing tone. She needed to do something to defuse the electric tension between them. It was so combustible, she thought flames might erupt.

"Well, I'm hoping we can hang out sometime. Maybe you can show me around Moose Falls. Or you can teach me how to bowl." His smile was flirtatious, and there was no doubt now that he was interested in her. It was written all over his beautiful face.

"I don't want to be anyone's winter bae," she blurted out.

There. She'd said it. Gotten it off her chest. Only now Xavier was gaping at her as if she were an alien from outer space.

"Come again?" he asked, a look of confusion etched on his face.

"A winter bae. You know, someone to keep you warm during the winter. I'm not looking for anything serious right now, but I also don't want to have a fling with my boss's grandson."

Xavier's jaw dropped. He began to sputter. "True, no offense, but your mind is a terrifying place. I have no idea what you're talking about with this winter bae thing." Xavier held up his hands. "And to be honest, I'm not sure I want to know."

True folded her arms across her chest. "I'm just a realist. Imagine you're me for a second. I run a tavern in the wilds of Alaska." She jerked her chin at him. "You are a famous athlete. I'm sure you're used to getting any woman you want."

He made a face. "Not true."

She felt a little bad about making that statement since she knew his ex-fiancée had broken up with him. True couldn't conceive of a woman ending a relationship with this delicious man. But maybe he had a ton of flaws she hadn't yet seen. After all, she barely knew the man.

"Don't get me wrong. I like myself. I'm reasonably attractive, hardworking, and trustworthy. But I'm not used to dating... football players. And I'm guessing you haven't gone out with many tavern managers."

"Reasonably attractive?" Xavier asked, raising an eyebrow.

"Don't sell yourself short. Have you looked in the mirror lately? You're gorgeous. And that's not why I want to spend time with you. You fascinate me, True. And if I'm being completely honest, it's been a long time since I've wanted to hang out with a woman. I'm not saying we should get married or anything," he said with a chuckle, "but keeping each other company might be fun."

"So, why me?" she asked. She was genuinely intrigued. It sounded like they were both very casual in their outlooks on dating.

"Why not you? You're interesting and funny as hell. You make me laugh even when you're plotting against me with ghost pepper wings. And trust me, I haven't laughed a lot over the past few years. That's a huge plus for me."

True nibbled on her lip. "Did I apologize for the wings? It wasn't the best way to welcome you to town."

He cocked his head to the side. "I have the feeling that you had your reasons. Am I right?"

"Maybe a little bit," she admitted. She didn't want to tell him that his arrival in Moose Falls had felt a bit threatening to her. If she did, Xavier would probably think she was petty. And he wouldn't be wrong. Serving him the ghost pepper wings had been a ridiculous reaction to his arrival in town. Now that she was getting to know him better, True was ashamed to have gone down that road. He was proving to be quite different than she'd imagined.

For lack of a better word, he was dreamy.

"I'll let you tell me all about it when we go out." He locked eyes with her, pinning her with his intense gaze. He exuded confidence.

Suddenly, she was tongue-tied. He had this magnetic effect on her. True couldn't come up with a single plausible reason not to hang out with him.

"Can I see your phone?" he asked, holding out his palm.

True took her cell phone out of her back pocket and handed it over.

"I'm going to put my name and number in your contacts." His fingers began moving across her phone. "The ball is in your court," he said, handing her phone back over to her. "No pressure."

"Okay," she said, still feeling flustered. This so wasn't her! She was feisty and independent. True didn't fold in the presence of a gorgeous man. She had learned her lesson with Garrett. Or had she? Xavier Stone had her all twisted up in knots.

*Just breathe*, she told herself.

"My brothers are waiting for me outside, so I'm going to call it a night, unless you need help closing up the place."

"I appreciate the offer, but I'm good. I'll be heading out right behind you," True said. His offer to help her out was sweet. The truth was, it was hard for her to accept help, especially when it came to Northern Exposure. But with everything shifting with the arrival of Red and the Stone brothers, she might just have to bend a little. Change was coming whether she liked it or not.

"Night," Xavier said, pulling on his coat. She didn't mean to stare, but he made the act of putting on his jacket a spectator sport. He was definitely the finest man ever to step foot in Moose Falls. Maybe in all of Alaska, if she was being honest.

"Good night," True said, battling the urge to ask him to stick around a bit longer. It was a foreign feeling considering she was always eager to get home to Jaylen and relieve her sitter. Her brother would be asleep by now, but just being at home with him was always satisfying.

"Just a sec. I forgot something," Xavier murmured,

moving toward her and not stopping until their bodies were mere inches away from each other. He looked down at her and cupped her chin in his hand. She noticed little caramel flecks in his eyes as he dipped his head down. "I've been wanting to do this since the day we met." True had a few seconds to step away from the incoming kiss, but there wasn't a single question in her mind that she wanted this to happen.

The moment his lips landed on hers, True leaned against him and sank into the kiss. His lips were tender and inviting, shifting from warmth to blazing like a roaring fire. They tasted like peaches. She kissed him back, her hands reaching out to grab ahold of his jacket for leverage. Xavier's lips moved over hers with a mixture of tenderness and urgency. She parted her lips, inviting him in. They explored each other for a few moments as the kiss deepened. True felt as if she were soaring, flying to a destination she'd never been to before. All of her nerve endings were tingling. She felt achingly, wonderfully alive.

Way too soon for True's liking, the kiss ended.

"I'll be seeing you, True," he said with a glint in his eyes.

The way he spoke his parting words had her convinced that he meant them.

"Mm-hmm," she murmured, her brain still foggy from the best kiss she'd ever experienced in her twenty-eight years of life. As she watched Xavier exit Northern Exposure, all she could think about was how fast things were moving. A few days ago, the name Xavier Stone had been tied up with Jaylen's hero worship and Hattie's desire to reunite with her beloved grandsons. The very mention of his name had annoyed True. But now, after just a few days of him being in Moose Falls, she was acting like a smitten kitten.

And she didn't like it one bit.

# CHAPTER NINE

"Xavier, I'd like you to attend a meeting with me this morning." Xavier had barely crossed the threshold of the dining room before Hattie barked at him. He was discovering that her demeanor tended to be gruff at times, particularly in the morning.

"Good morning to you too, Hattie," Xavier said as he sat down at the mahogany-colored dining room table.

Hattie paused before responding. "Good morning, beautiful boy. I hope you slept well last night." She daintily lifted her teacup and brought it to her lips. "I'm sorry for being so abrupt with you. It feels like there's never enough time in the day to get everything done. Now, it's more important than ever."

Xavier heard the stress laced in Hattie's voice. Although his grandmother put up a brave front, Xavier could now see the cracks in her façade. Her hand shook slightly as she poured more hot water into her cup. He couldn't help but wonder if the pressure of her terminal diagnosis was weighing on her. If so, who could blame her? He couldn't imagine what it would be like to discover you were living on borrowed time.

"Are you feeling okay?" Xavier asked. He knew Hattie was a proud woman who hated showing any weakness, but he had to ask. Even though they weren't close, he felt a responsibility toward her. In some ways she reminded him of his mother in the way she spoke effusively about her love for him and his brothers. He felt bad that he couldn't return the favor, but after so many years apart, their relationship was starting from scratch. Xavier didn't use the L word indiscriminately.

"I'm right as rain," she said. "Never felt better."

Xavier sensed she wasn't being totally honest with him, but he wasn't going to call her on it. He was quickly learning that Hattie Stone marched to the beat of her own drum.

Xavier reached for a cheese Danish followed by scrambled eggs and sausage. Before he knew it, his plate was full. He felt a pair of eyes trained on him. When he looked up from his plate, Hattie was staring at him, a sweet smile plastered on her face.

"You have no idea how much I've missed you." Hattie threw the comment out, and he had no idea how to respond. He'd gotten used to life without a grandmother, and over the years, he'd pushed memories of her and his childhood in Moose Falls below the surface. Anything he said about missing her would sound phony. Best to change the subject and talk about something else.

"Your hair," Xavier said, noticing that the hue was now a vivid orange color. The fiery shade suited Hattie better than the blue. She was a chameleon, always shifting gears.

Hattie patted her curls. "I've always wanted to be a redhead. Shades of *I Love Lucy*. That Lucille Ball was something else."

Just then his brothers walked in and sat down at the table.

Caleb, not being a morning person, grunted a good morning while Landon stopped by Hattie's chair and leaned down to press a kiss on her cheek. The gesture made her grin so hard, Xavier worried her face might crack. Landon was way more sentimental than his brothers. Sometimes Xavier wished that he could be more like Landon, but he knew all too well that his role as the oldest brother in the family had shaped him into the man he'd become.

All he knew right now was that Landon made Hattie beam with happiness, and it made Xavier proud of him.

As they headed out the front door after breakfast concluded, Xavier walked in lock step with Hattie. "Tell me more about the meeting." Xavier was such a newbie at Yukon Cider that he was still learning how the company operated. He didn't want to embarrass himself. Why hadn't his grandmother prepped him earlier? Xavier prided himself on his work ethic and doing well in all aspects of his life. He wouldn't allow himself to fall on his face. He wanted to excel in every endeavor he tried.

"The meeting is with True Everett, who manages Northern Exposure. I've asked Red to brainstorm with her about the tavern, so he'll be there as well." She wrinkled her nose. "It's been hemorrhaging money lately, so something's gotta give. We need to examine the problem and try to come up with some solutions."

Xavier stood up a bit straighter at the mention of True's name. He hadn't been able to get their kiss out of his mind. There was nothing he wanted more than to share more alone time with True. And more kisses. Unfortunately, she hadn't reached out to him, and almost a week had gone by since karaoke night. She didn't seem the type to play games the way some people did with phone numbers and waiting a week or more to play it cool.

He had never played games like that. If he liked someone, he hadn't hesitated to let them know. Even now, after
being jerked around by Heather, he still held that belief deep
at his core. Games were for little children.

By the time he entered the conference room an hour later,
Hattie was already seated at the table, talking animatedly with
True. He sucked in a deep breath at the sight of her, taking a
moment to remind himself that this was a business meeting.
As always, she looked beautiful. A light floral scent hung in
the air, one he associated with True. Xavier couldn't allow
himself to be distracted by True's presence despite her close
physical proximity. Moments after he sat down next to Hattie, Red walked into the room and took the seat beside True.

He sat through the meeting, listening as the tavern was
discussed. True was the star of the show. Today she'd dressed
in a pair of cream-colored slacks, a matching blazer, and
black flats. She knew the establishment backward, forward,
and upside down. Her love for what she did for a living was
apparent every time she opened her mouth. She was a bit
nervous, though, which didn't mesh with her usual confident
vibe. Maybe she perceived this meeting as a critique of her
managerial skills. He sure hoped not. Hattie was lucky to
have her at the helm.

Thankfully, Hattie took a moment to praise her managerial efforts. "True, you've done a fantastic job with the tavern. This isn't personal at all." She looked at her from over
the top of her glasses. "Moreover, I think we need to update
the model. Perhaps tweak a few things to get business rolling
again. With the launch of our new line of ciders, I'm hoping
we can come up with a profitable tie-in."

"That's a great idea," True said. "Patrons always get
excited about new flavors."

"I've heard a lot of great things about the chef," Red

remarked. "It would be interesting to do some pairings with her meals and the new ciders."

"I really like that idea," True said, typing notes on her iPad.

"Me too," Hattie said, rubbing her hands together. "Let's do this!" She turned toward Xavier. "You've been awfully quiet. Got anything to add?"

"Not really, but having frequented the tavern on a few occasions, I can attest to the great ambiance and food selections." He glanced over at True. "And the karaoke is a lot of fun. The place was packed with patrons."

"Thanks for your vote of confidence," True said, meeting his gaze. Xavier didn't want to look at her too long, in case Hattie picked up on any vibes. The last thing they needed was for her to be involved in whatever was brewing between them.

*If* there was anything. At the moment he wasn't so sure.

Once the meeting concluded, Xavier wasted no time catching up to True in the corridor.

"Hey, True! Wait up!" he called out.

When she stopped in her tracks and turned back toward him, he tapped his wristwatch. "Still waiting for that call." He placed his other hand on his chest and made a painful, wounded sound.

True looked away from him, casting her gaze downward. He waited for her to say something. If she sent out any signals that she wasn't interested, he wouldn't make any further attempts to pursue her. The last thing he wanted to do was become a pest.

"It's not that I didn't want to reach out to you, but time kind of got away from me," she explained, shifting from one foot to the other.

"Mm-hmm," Xavier said. It was a pretty lame excuse.

Maybe she really wasn't feeling him, which caused disappointment to nearly swallow him whole. He was so out of practice, he had probably read the whole situation wrong between them. That would leave him no choice but to walk away from the situation.

*No way!* He hadn't imagined their blazing chemistry. He'd kissed enough women to know if there was heat or not. And there had definitely been fireworks. A five-alarm fire, if he was being honest.

"And now, I'm thinking...are we working together?" True frowned. "Because that might get awkward. I don't date co-workers."

Xavier quirked his mouth. "I think that would only be a problem if I were your superior or you were mine. That's not the case at all. We don't have any power over each other, and I'm not working at Northern Exposure."

She raised a brow. "Well, you are Hattie's grandson."

"Meaning?"

She let out a sigh. "Are you serious? That holds a lot of weight in Moose Falls. It's like you're a Kennedy or something."

Xavier burst out laughing. Never in his life had he been compared to a member of the illustrious Kennedy family. But True wasn't laughing along with him. She was gazing at him with a concerned expression stamped on her face.

He didn't want to be in the position of twisting her arm to get her to go out on a date. At this point his ego was a bit wounded. Maybe he should just quit while he was ahead.

"I have a theory," he said, scratching his jaw.

True groaned. "Oh, no. Do I want to hear this?"

"People make time for what they want to. So, if you're not interested, that's cool. But if you're just finding reasons not to call me, maybe you should ask yourself why." He leaned in and whispered, "I promise that I don't bite."

True clutched her purse to her chest. "Okay, here's the thing. I'm raising my little brother. The one who happens to be your biggest fan. He thinks you walk on water, by the way." True made a face, letting him know she didn't agree with her brother's assessment. "I spend most of my free time with Jaylen. Cooking for him, helping him with homework, driving him to his events. But I do have a window this Saturday if you want to meet up."

Relief swept through him. "Yes. I do. That would be great."

He mentally patted himself on the back. He hadn't lost his mojo. Even if True seemed hesitant, she'd said yes.

"Okay, I can show you a little bit of Moose Falls." She grinned at him. "It's changed a bit over the last twenty years."

"I'm looking forward to it already," he said. And he was. True was not what he had expected to find in his little Alaskan hometown. Matter of fact, Xavier hadn't anticipated that he would feel any romantic stirrings at all while he was in Alaska. Life had taught him that the best things happened when a person wasn't looking for them. Serendipity. His mother's favorite word. Perhaps he needed to embrace more serendipitous moments in life. Perhaps this was the big lesson he needed to learn in Moose Falls.

If so, he was excited that True Everett would be his teacher.

🌲

True left the Yukon Cider offices feeling upbeat. When Hattie had called True in for this impromptu meeting, she had been full of trepidation. After Red's unexpected appearance at Northern Exposure, she'd been questioning her role as the establishment's manager. With so much up in the air with Hattie's illness and the future of her holdings, True's confidence had been shaky.

But things had gone smoothly. Red did not give her the vibe of someone who was planning to usurp her authority or try to take over her position at the tavern. Honestly, he'd given her the impression that he just wanted a seat at the table after being away for so long. His position was understandable, considering there were so many things at play—Hattie's illness and his sons returning after such a long absence from Moose Falls.

Seeing Xavier earlier had been a shock to her system. For the past week, she had thought of nothing else but the blazing kiss they had shared. She had relived that moment countless times, relishing their chemistry and the way he'd made her feel. She wasn't used to being desired. Wanted. Pursued. Growing up she had chased salamanders, worked on cars with her dad, and built forts in the woods. None of the boys had lined up to ask her out on dates. She hadn't gone to prom. Her first kiss had been at eighteen. Being a stand-in parent in her early twenties had made romance out of the question. And then, when she had been ready for a partner, True discovered that her taste in men was pitiful. Selfish, narcissistic, gaslighting men who were less mature than her baby brother.

Until now. Xavier didn't present as any of those things, which worried her. Was he too good to be true? No pun intended. Hadn't that been one of the reasons that she hadn't contacted him? On some level she didn't feel good enough to be with a man like Xavier. Although she talked a good game, the men in her past had done a number on her self-esteem.

Why had all her relationships crashed and burned? Was she the common denominator?

True checked the time on her dashboard. She had a

meeting at Jaylen's school with the principal. Her thoughts whirled as she parked in front of Moose Falls Elementary. She didn't want to let her imagination go wild, but over the phone, Principal Dandridge had sounded somber. Jaylen was a great student who had perfect attendance, so she couldn't imagine he was in any trouble. *He better not be!* Raising him right meant a lot to True. She had tried her best to be nurturing and loving, all the while teaching him to respect others and himself. Her pulse quickened at the thought that maybe he was being bullied by a fellow student.

When she entered the school, True was ushered into the principal's office with her heart beating wildly in her chest. *Why was this so nerve-racking?*

"Good afternoon, Principal Dandridge," True said upon entering her office. With high cheekbones, a dramatic widow's peak, and onyx-colored eyes, Priscilla Dandridge had striking looks. She was a member of the Yupik tribe, who were among the first Alaskan inhabitants.

"True, we've known each other a long time. Call me Priscilla."

She was right. Priscilla had been Jaylen's principal ever since he'd started school.

"Okay, Priscilla. Thanks for making time for me today," True said, smiling despite her nervousness. True had always known Priscilla to be a kind and wise woman, which lessened her anxiety.

Priscilla gestured toward one of the chairs in front of her desk. "Please take a seat."

True sat down and placed her purse in the chair next to her. Although she tried to read Priscilla's face, she wasn't giving off any cues.

"So, the reason I asked you to come is because Jaylen is exhibiting signs of being academically gifted."

True gulped, then leaned forward in her seat. "Excuse me. What did you say?" *Gifted?*

"Although he goes to great pains to conceal the fact that's he's advanced, Jaylen is testing way past his grade level. He's not just bright, True. He's exceptional."

"B-but I've never heard this before from any of his teachers. How could I have missed something like this? I help him with his homework all the time." True slapped her palm to her forehead. "But of course he doesn't really need my help." Guilt crept in like a thief, immediately causing her to question herself rather than celebrate this amazing news. How could she not have wondered about the fast rate at which Jaylen finished his work, breezed through books, and learned the scientific element tables? She had been so thrilled that he had been well-adjusted and content that she hadn't seen the obvious. She'd been complicit in holding him back. And it gutted her.

"Don't beat yourself up, True," Priscilla said. "We all knew he was smart, but it's my belief that Jaylen hasn't wanted to stand out. Instead, he's done well, but not too well."

"And why would he do that?" True asked, knitting her brows together.

"So he can fit in," Priscilla explained. "That's my guess."

"But he's always fit in. Hasn't he?" True asked. Jaylen had loads of friends, was always invited to birthdays and sleepovers, and had been tight with his bestie, Tai, since nursery school. For a nine-year-old, what else was there?

"Jaylen has always been very popular." Priscilla laid her hands on the desk. "I don't want to overanalyze the situation, since I'm not a therapist, but as a child who's suffered major losses in his life, he probably feels different than other kids. Why would he want to make himself stand out even more by being super smart?"

True sucked in a deep breath. She felt as if this information was a sucker punch. All this time she'd been of the belief that her brother was well-adjusted. She had even given herself pats on the back for doing a great job as a stand-in parent. But the truth was, Jaylen was hiding his light under a bushel. That was the last thing she wanted for him.

"True, I can tell you're internalizing this. And that's the last thing any of us wants. We want to make sure we do everything possible to support and guide Jaylen and meet all his educational needs."

"What does that mean?" True asked. She had never felt so completely in over her head in a situation before. She wasn't used to feeling like a complete and utter failure.

Priscilla stood and went over to her mini fridge, taking out two bottled waters. She slid one across the desk toward True. "It may or may not appeal to you, but promoting him to a higher grade is a viable option. There's also an academy in Homer that teaches gifted students. They offer scholarships, and I think Jaylen would be a great candidate."

"Homer?" True asked, her voice radiating her shock. "That's so far from home."

"Students board there, so he would be living in Homer," Priscilla explained. "Eagle River Academy teaches the best and brightest students from all over Alaska."

All True could do was sputter. She jumped to her feet.

"Absolutely not!" She grabbed her purse. "I'm not farming Jaylen out to some school hundreds of miles away from home."

"Even if it's what's best for him?" Priscilla asked.

All True could see was a red haze. Ever since the death of her parents, people had been trying to tell her that she couldn't raise her brother on her own as a twenty-something. Members of her extended family had even tried to adopt

Jaylen out from under her. And now, after seven years of raising Jaylen, she was supposed to hand him over to a school in Homer? Nope, it wasn't happening. She may not have given birth to Jaylen, but she was still a fierce mama bear.

"Please don't ever suggest that you know what's best for him. I know the type of life my parents wanted for their child. And it involved him having me present in his life." She let out a ragged sigh. "This meeting is over. Thank you for the information."

"True, please don't leave like this."

True turned toward the door and wrenched it open, ignoring Priscilla's calls for her to come back and talk to her. Through a mist of tears, True made her way outside to where her truck was parked. Once she was inside, she burst into sobs. If someone had asked her why she was crying, True wouldn't have been able to explain it. She was experiencing so many emotions all at once. Anger. Sadness. Pride. Fear. Guilt. It was all mixed together like a bouillabaisse. Trying to analyze the situation felt impossible. She had always done her best by Jaylen, but now, in this moment, she wasn't sure about next steps. Where did he go from here?

Education had always been important to her parents, and in True's dreams she envisioned Jaylen graduating from college and pursuing graduate studies. She wanted him to go beyond her wildest dreams and soar.

So what now? First, she would sit down with her brother and have a serious conversation about his schoolwork. He needed to know that he should never dim his own light. Jaylen was her entire world. Everything revolved around him. True would continue to make him her number one priority, which meant finding a way to tap into his intellect without sending him away from Moose Falls.

# CHAPTER TEN

"So, I saw you talking earlier to True. What's up with you two?" Caleb was in Xavier's office perched on the edge of his desk, chowing down on a snack and eyeing him with curiosity. Hattie had divided one large office into three units so each brother could have their own private work space.

"None of your business. What were you doing? Lurking in the hallway?" Xavier asked. For someone who had been the victim of the celebrity gossip world, Caleb sure enjoyed digging into other people's business.

"I never lurk. That's creepy. I was heading toward the break room for a snack," he said through a mouthful of food. "Did you guys know that there's a snack table there completely free of charge?" He held up a stick of beef jerky. "Remember this from when we were kids? Jack's Jerky?"

"Wow. I remember those," Xavier said. "Give me a bite." Jack's Jerky had been their choice of snack back in the day, with all three Stone brothers loving the product.

Caleb pulled it behind his back. "Get your own."

Landon came up behind him and snatched the jerky

before quickly tossing it to Xavier, who held it over his head out of Caleb's reach.

"Hey! Give it back!" he protested, trying to grab it from Xavier, who stood two inches taller than him.

"Take it from me," Xavier said, using the same line as when they were kids and Caleb was trying to get the football out of his possession. Old habits died hard. It never took them very long to revert to their childhood selves.

All of a sudden, the door opened, and Red was standing in the doorway. "Hey, I knocked, but I don't think you guys heard me. Seems not a lot has changed between you boys since the old days," Red said, chuckling.

"Except we're not boys anymore," Xavier said. The words slipped past his lips before he could rein them in. Landon looked at him with big eyes. Caleb's expression didn't change.

Red let out a sigh. "No, you're not, which is why I'm here. I want to get reacquainted with the three of you. I know that I can't get a do-over, but I sincerely want to spend time with you, maybe get a chance to know you."

"Why now?" Caleb asked, sounding genuinely confused.

Red quirked his mouth. "I like to think I'm wiser now and more in tune with my deficits. I'm also back in Moose Falls after years of rolling around the world. We're in the same place at the same time for the first time in decades. I'm taking advantage of our proximity and the fact that Hattie has us all working together." He looked around at them. "What do you say?"

Xavier wanted to say no and let his father know it wasn't happening. At the same time, he sensed Red wasn't going to give up. They might as well deal with him head-on and get it over with. As usual, Caleb and Landon looked in his direction to determine which way he was leaning. "Okay, what did you have in mind?"

"Why don't we start with dinner at my place?" Red suggested. "Tonight?"

"We like dinner," Landon said, causing all of them to laugh. Red slapped him lightly on the back. Xavier noticed how Landon lit up at the contact from Red. More than Caleb and Xavier, Landon had always voiced his desire to reconnect with their father. He had never been able to shake off the need for a father figure, and he hadn't been shy about saying so.

"Sounds good," Xavier said, reminding himself that this was simply checking off something on his to-do list. This didn't matter to him, not like the prospect of going out with True. The pint-size version of himself would have been excited, but after dozens of no-shows and disappointments, he'd stopped wishing for miracles. Daisy Stone had been a kick-ass single mother, the best the world had to offer. For a long time, Xavier had learned to lean on her as his sole parent. No dinner with Red could ever fix what their father had torn down.

The rest of the day passed swiftly, and before Xavier knew it, they were headed to Red's house with Caleb in the driver's seat. As soon as they pulled up, Xavier drew in a sharp breath.

The ranch-style structure was unmistakable. It was their childhood home. From what he remembered, not much had changed since they were kids. No add-ons or major reconstruction. It almost felt like he was in a time warp.

"Is this—" Caleb said before Xavier cut him off.

"Yeah, it is," Xavier said, turning to look out the window from the passenger seat.

"What? What am I missing?" Landon asked, leaning into the front seat.

"Our childhood home," Caleb answered. "You were too young to remember, I guess."

"Oh, wow," Landon said. "It's amazing how much I can't recall from our time here in Moose Falls. Honestly, it sucks. Makes me feel as if I wasn't even there."

"That's not true! You remembered us making gingerbread." Xavier tousled his head. "You were there, bro. The best baby brother we could have asked for."

"Truth," Caleb said as he parked the car in the driveway. "You were never a snitch, and you looked up to us the way baby brothers should."

Landon let out a snort. "Aww. You're all heart, Caleb."

"Let's get this over with," Xavier muttered, wrenching open the car door.

As they walked toward the house, Xavier studied the exterior. Not a single thing had changed. It was kind of eerie how it seemed as if it had been bubble-wrapped for the last twenty years.

"Be nice," Landon said, looping his arm around Xavier. "Don't start any trouble."

Xavier let out a low grunt in response. He wasn't the bad guy here. Not by a long shot. Frankly, he was being pretty magnanimous to even accept this dinner invite.

Red opened the door as soon as they knocked. The smell of amazing cooking wafted under their noses. Spaghetti Bolognese with sourdough bread. Xavier was discovering that sensory memories were just as powerful as visual ones. The aromas took him straight back to Friday night dinners at their kitchen table. As a kid he'd loved the fact that sourdough bread was traced all the way back to the Yukon Gold Rush. As a child who loved adventure, that fun fact had impressed him.

After Red ushered them inside, they each took off their boots and placed them on the mat right beside the door. Xavier breathed a sigh of relief after taking a quick look around him. The place had been completely renovated. All new furniture. Gleaming appliances. Colorful paintings on the walls. Brand-spanking-new paint. Now the interior looked modern and bright. He stopped short when he spotted a framed black-and-white photo of himself, Landon, and Caleb. In the photo they were all wearing party hats, and a big birthday cake with candles sat in front of them.

Red, seeing Xavier staring at the photo, came up beside him. He tapped the glass and said, "I remember this day like it was yesterday. It was your ninth birthday, and all you wanted was a football, even though there weren't any youth teams back then in Moose Falls."

A lot had changed in that regard over the years. Now, with the arrival of nine-man team football, things had really opened up. His former teammate, Richie Akuna, had lived in Alaska for many years and frequently talked about the evolution of youth football in the state.

"I remember that birthday," Xavier said. That football had changed his life, even though he hadn't played once in Alaska. How could he have forgotten that life-altering gift from his father? It hadn't been all bad.

"You slept with that football every night," Caleb said. "It was your first girlfriend." He cracked up at his own joke.

Xavier fake-laughed, then leaned in. "Don't forget I'm still bigger than you." The unsettled look on Caleb's face caused Xavier to let out a genuine laugh.

"If you guys are hungry, we don't need to stand on ceremony," Red said. "We can head into the kitchen and eat."

"You don't need to tell me twice. I'm starving," Landon said, beating a fast path down the hall.

When they had all assembled in the kitchen, Red motioned for them to sit down at his white butcher-block table. He had already arranged it with place settings, napkins, and utensils. Red sure had gone to a lot of trouble to host them. Their father tended to his food at the same stove where their mother used to cook all their meals. It was a bit of a mind bend for Xavier, if he was being honest.

Red placed the pasta, Bolognese sauce, salad, and sour-dough bread on the table, as well as dressing and Parmesan cheese. Xavier sat down as he took in all the details of the cozy kitchen. Had his father always been this domesticated? Xavier dug into the Bolognese and let out a groan of appreciation. He'd eaten at Italian restaurants all over the globe, and this was on par with the best of them. He remembered this meal and sitting around the table with his brothers and parents. There'd been smiles and laughter ringing out.

Everyone was so engrossed in the meal, there wasn't much talking going on until Red opened a discussion.

Red looked around the table and smiled. "I know a lot has changed, but this used to be your favorite meal, hands down." He nodded toward Caleb. "You used to request it almost every night."

"But it was a Friday night special," Xavier said. The memory was a great one. They had been a real family. And Bolognese had made them all happy, including his mother. A hazy memory of his parents slow-dancing to Prince in this very kitchen popped into his mind. Red had twirled her around until she was dizzy. Xavier felt a little bit of anger rise inside him. Why had his father fumbled his marriage and responsibilities so badly? He was still searching for answers.

"That's right," Red said. "It was family night. We played games and watched movies. And we ate Bolognese and carrot cake."

"And made peanut butter Rice Krispies treats," Caleb added, looking over at Xavier. They had always been

Xavier's favorite. He absolutely remembered standing by the stove and counting the minutes until the timer went off so they could devour them.

"Those were pretty epic," Xavier said. He could almost smell and taste the sweet treat.

"So you've owned this house all these years?" Landon asked. "Even though you weren't living here?"

Red nodded. "I have," he said. "Never wanted to sell it, even though Moose Falls hasn't been my home base for years. Until now."

"So you're back permanently?" Caleb asked as he helped himself to another serving of Bolognese and a thick slice of sourdough bread. "To work at Yukon Cider?"

"I'm back and hoping to plant permanent roots," Red said. "Your grandmother has been trying to get me to work at Yukon Cider for a long time. Only now she's asking me to get involved with Northern Exposure as well."

"But that's True's domain," Xavier blurted out. He couldn't help himself. It would be unfair to bring in Red to micromanage True. "And she's dedicated and hardworking and innovative. Hattie couldn't ask for a better person to run the place."

"Tell us how you really feel," Caleb said, a huge grin etched on his face. "Xavier and True are like two dogs sniffing each other out."

Xavier scoffed. "Charming. You have such a way with words."

"I agree with you about True, Xavier," Red said. "She impressed me when I met with her at the tavern." He held up his hands. "So far I've only agreed to brainstorm with her, nothing else. I don't have any desire to run the place or take her job away from her."

"That's good to know," Xavier said. He felt protective

toward True, and the feeling surprised him. He was ready to go to battle for her. For a long time now, he hadn't allowed himself to feel much of anything at all.

"I came back because your grandmother is dying. I'm determined to help her any way I can." Red's face tightened with emotion. "And of course because the three of you came back. I hope you know that I consider this a chance to get to know my boys—sorry, I mean my three grown sons—all over again."

Xavier didn't have to say the obvious. Second chances were hard to come by in this world, and they didn't always lead to happily-ever-afters. Just thinking about how much work it would take for Red to make amends made Xavier's head ache. His instincts told him that Red was sincere, but it didn't erase the past. It didn't make Xavier any less angry toward him. It didn't obliterate the tears and the heartache and the genuine suffering. And weren't they all just tiptoeing around a major issue? Why had Red been an absentee parent?

After dinner Red waved off their offers to help with the cleanup. Instead he'd led them into the brightly decorated living room. Over hard cider and carrot cake, they played a few rounds of Uno and looked through old albums. Although the dynamic still felt slightly awkward, Xavier was proud of himself for going with the flow. He wasn't going to ruin this for Caleb and Landon. If they wanted to rebuild their relationship with Red, he wasn't going to stand in their way, but for him, doing so would feel like a betrayal of their mother. And Xavier wasn't going to do that, not for anything in this world.

🌲

On the way back to Hattie's house, Xavier had plenty of time to go over the events of this evening in his mind. Tonight had turned everything on its head, Xavier realized. He didn't even want to admit it to himself, but he had begrudgingly enjoyed their time with Red. His memories confirmed that when moments in their family had been good, they'd been very, very good. Knowing he came from more than a dysfunctional family gave him a kernel of peace. But one cordial dinner shouldn't make him forget all this man had put them through with his chaotic behavior and long absences. Had he ever even apologized for smashing their childhood to smithereens? Not that Xavier could remember. Worst of all, Red had broken their mother's heart, which was unforgivable. For a time, Daisy's aura of love and light had been snuffed out. It had taken a long time for her to bounce back. Xavier couldn't give Red a pass, not after everything he'd done.

"Hey! We're back." Caleb's voice dragged Xavier out of his thoughts. His brothers were standing outside the vehicle, staring at him with confused expressions stamped on their faces.

He stepped out of the car and stretched. Thankfully, he'd worn his boots, since the snow went past his ankles. The house was mostly dark, save for a few glimmers emanating from the second floor.

"Where'd you go just now?" Landon asked. "Are you okay?"

"Nowhere. I'm fine. Just a little tired," Xavier explained. There was no point telling them where his thoughts had drifted. They knew how he felt about their father being back in their lives. He didn't want to hit them over the head with it, especially if they were feeling good about the evening. In truth, the three of them needed to keep their eyes focused on their inheritance and meeting the stipulations of their agreement with Hattie. Then they all had to be on the same page about whether to sell or stay.

One year in Moose Falls to make a life-altering decision! This was way harder than he had ever imagined.

Once they entered the house, Xavier immediately noticed the silence, as well as the dim lighting. Even the night when they had returned to Hattie's place from karaoke after midnight, there had been glowing lights setting the place ablaze. And the house had never been this quiet since their arrival.

Xavier checked his watch. It wasn't even ten o'clock. From what they'd observed, their grandmother was a night owl. With her fading health, he worried something might be wrong.

"Hattie," Xavier called out, walking down the hall and looking in the dimly lit kitchen.

"Maybe she went to bed early," Caleb said, shrugging. "No need to worry."

"Upstairs is lit up," Landon said, pointing to the upstairs landing.

"Let's just turn in," Xavier suggested. "We have to get up early tomorrow to meet with the distributors."

Caleb groaned. "One of these days, I'll learn to love sunrise. But I'm sure that it won't be tomorrow."

Just as they reached the landing, the sound of hushed voices and laughter reached their ears. They stopped in their tracks and looked at one another. The voices sounded intimate. Hattie wasn't alone. Before they could beat a fast path to their bedrooms, Hattie came out of her room, her arm looped through Jacques's. Their grandmother, dressed in a black silk robe, didn't see them at first. She was too busy canoodling with Jacques.

Xavier wished he could sink through the hardwood floors and disappear. Landon covered his eyes with his hands.

Caleb's eyes were practically bulging out of their sockets. Xavier cleared his throat to get her attention.

"Oh, my goodness," she said, drawing her robe together. Hattie pressed her hand against her throat. "I—I thought you wouldn't be home for a while."

"Evidently," Xavier drawled, his lips twitching.

Hattie couldn't seem to drag her gaze away from Jacques. She was looking at him as if he were the sun, moon, and the stars. The only word that came to mind was *besotted*.

"How was dinner?" Hattie asked, seemingly unbothered by being caught in an entanglement. There was no way in the world, Xavier thought, this was simply two friends hanging out. Unlike their grandmother, Jacques at least looked sheepish. He wasn't making eye contact with anyone.

"It was nice," Landon said, peeking at Hattie through his fingers. "Good food. Good conversation. It's all good," he said, rambling.

"Well, good night, everyone," Jacques said, heading quickly toward the staircase. He still couldn't seem to look them in the eye, which made Xavier feel bad for the guy.

A chorus of good nights rang out. An awkward silence settled over them once Jacques took off. Should they just pretend not to have noticed they were involved? Or would that make things more awkward?

"So…you and Jacques?" Xavier asked, uttering the first thing that came to his mind.

"Jacques is my paramour," Hattie proudly announced.

"Paramore?" Landon asked with a frown. "The only Paramore I know is the rock band."

Xavier ran a hand over his face. "She means *lover*."

Landon let out a shocked gasp. "Oh, no, no, no, no, no!"

"Stop being a drama queen," Caleb hissed. "They're consenting adults."

"We have a very mature and satisfying relationship," Hattie said, her lips curving into a satisfied smile.

Xavier covered his ears and began chanting, "La la la la. Don't want to hear any of the details. Not a single one."

Caleb was openmouthed. He made sputtering noises. He slapped his palm over his eyes. "I cannot unsee this. It will forever be burned into my eyeballs."

"Now who's the drama queen?" Landon hissed.

Hattie waved her hands at them. "Oh, grow up, boys. How many times must I tell you? I'm dying, but I'm living every day to the fullest."

"So you've said," Xavier responded. "And we think that's wonderful. Honestly, we were just surprised seeing you—"

Hattie winked at him. "In a compromising position?" She let out a throaty laugh. "Maybe I should have been more discreet, but honestly, I didn't think anyone else was at home. Furthermore, I'm not ashamed of our relationship. In the end, love is what matters most."

Hattie loved Jacques. It was obvious in the way she'd looked at him and the passion ringing out in her voice. Xavier was blown away. Despite everything she was going through, Hattie was still finding time for love.

"Jacques seems like a good dude," Xavier said. "We like him a lot."

"And he better treat you right, or he'll have to answer to us," Caleb said in his fiercest voice.

Xavier almost laughed out loud. Caleb was as tough as the Cowardly Lion in *The Wizard of Oz*. He was more about looks than right hooks. Xavier couldn't ever remember Caleb putting his fists up in his entire life.

"That's for sure," Landon added. "We'll be watching Jacques," he said, gesturing toward his eyes with his fingers.

"Oh, goodness gracious," Hattie said. "I appreciate that

the three of you have my back, but everything is splendid. Jacques is a wonderful man."

"They're just teasing. Aren't you?" Xavier asked, sharing a pointed look with his brothers. This really wasn't any of their business. Hattie was a grown woman who was fully capable of making her own choices.

"Of course we were," Caleb conceded. "Jacques is the salt of the earth."

"Well, that's a relief. I'm glad we're on the same page. Good night, boys," a beaming Hattie said, blowing a kiss in their direction.

They serenaded her with a chorus of good nights, heading toward their bedrooms after she walked in the opposite direction toward her own.

"Sometimes Granny scares me," Landon whispered.

Xavier turned toward him and asked, "Only sometimes?"

# CHAPTER ELEVEN

As soon as True's Saturday shift ended, Xavier showed up. He was right on time, which she took as a good sign. Her past was filled with men who thought punctuality was a four-letter word. Garrett in particular had always made her wait around for him. More and more she was beginning to question what she'd ever seen in him in the first place. He hadn't been particularly nice or caring. And come to think of it, his idea of romance had been a six-pack of beer and watching episodes of the original *Star Trek* television series. It was sad thinking back over how much she had put up with in their relationship.

She'd changed since then. True liked to think she wouldn't tolerate such foolishness ever again in a romantic relationship. Maybe the truth was that she had hardened herself to the idea of loving and being loved. She hated being so jaded, but there it was.

True wasn't getting all dolled up for Xavier. If he wanted to pursue her, he needed to realize that she was a regular girl who dressed in regular clothes and put on the barest hint of makeup on a good day. She chuckled thinking of herself as an "as is" date. If she had learned anything from past experiences, True now knew that being completely herself was the only way to go.

Dark jeans and an oatmeal-colored sweater, paired with her Sorel winter boots, was her outfit today. Overnight they had experienced a snow event, which left Moose Falls with eight inches of fresh snow. True loved Alaskan winter weather and the powdery white stuff. A perfect day for True was when Moose Falls was having a snowstorm.

Xavier texted her as soon as she arrived, letting her know he was outside. True had arranged to meet him in the lot so as to avoid any questions from Bonnie or the rest of the staff. Although she viewed this as a meetup rather than a date, she wanted to avoid any speculation or rumors from her staff. In a town this small, it didn't take long for gossip to fly on the wind, especially if it concerned anything related to Hattie Stone, the grande dame of Moose Falls. As heir to Yukon Cider, Xavier was big news here in town. Everyone wanted to know if the famous football player was going to plant roots in Moose Falls.

True heard a lot of talk at the tavern. All three Stone brothers were considered hot commodities. Between Xavier, Caleb, and Landon, it seemed that there was something for everyone. The hot, caring athlete. The charismatic, gorgeous actor. The brainy but adorable scientist. The residents of Moose Falls were in a feeding frenzy. She couldn't really blame them, since pickings were slim here in town. Everyone had known everyone from the cradle, which left little room for romantic prospects, in True's opinion.

Once she stepped outside, True easily spotted Xavier sitting behind the wheel in a large hunter-green truck. She raised her hand in greeting as he rolled down the passenger-side window.

"How's it going?" he asked, grinning at her.

"I can't complain," True said, her pulse racing at the sight of him. If he wanted to make a fortune, Xavier could bottle his charm and sell it to the highest bidder.

"These roads are challenging," Xavier said. "We're not used to all this snow and ice in Arizona."

"I'm so used to driving in these conditions, I barely notice. Why don't I drive?" she suggested. "My truck is over there."

Xavier let out a relieved sigh. "I'll take you up on that offer," he said, appearing relieved. "There's a learning curve on Alaskan driving, but I'm going to figure it out. Let me go park, and I'll meet you over in the lot."

True nodded and headed over to her truck, getting into the driver's seat and putting the heat on blast. January in Alaska was the coldest month of the year. Everyone layered up and wore their most rugged clothes and insulated boots. Days only had about five or six hours of sunlight. Some folks hated this month due to the extreme elements, but True loved it best of all.

The passenger-side door swung open, and Xavier appeared, sliding into the truck beside her. He smelled good, like sandalwood. He rubbed his hands together. "Much nicer in here. It's cold enough out there to freeze our buns off."

True chuckled. An immediate picture of Xavier's buns being frozen popped into her mind. It hadn't escaped her notice that he had a nice pair of cinnamon buns.

"Before I forget, this is for Jaylen." Xavier handed her a piece of clothing. "It's one of my Cardinals jerseys. I signed it for him."

"Oh, my gosh. This is epic," True gushed as she looked at the red-and-white jersey. "Jaylen's going to absolutely love this." What a sweet gesture from Xavier. If he was trying to win her over through Jaylen, he was definitely on the right track. There wasn't much True wouldn't do for her baby brother. She would fly to the moon and back to make him smile. A signed jersey from the Storm was going to cause her brother to do backflips.

"I hope he likes it," Xavier said. "Making kids happy was always one of the best parts of my career."

"So, how much of Moose Falls do you remember?" she asked, dragging her thoughts away from his physical attributes. She could easily stare at him all day.

"Not that much, although snippets come back to me at random moments. We left here with my mother when I was ten, so it's been a while."

"That's a sweet age. My brother is nine." Just thinking about Jaylen made her smile. "How come you never came back for visits?" True asked. Surely if he had, they would have crossed paths at some point in a town this size. She vaguely remembered the Stone brothers as young kids, but she had only been around seven or eight when they'd left.

"No, we never made it back, which sounds odd, but my parents' divorce changed everything." A muscle in his jaw began to bounce around. "Once we left Moose Falls, a lot of ties were severed. We had our new life in Arizona, and my mom focused on acclimating us to our new surroundings. My dad pretty much bailed on us. And no, I've never been okay with that, but I learned to live with having just one parent."

True took a quick look at him, then settled her gaze back on the road. His face reflected a tinge of sadness. A surge of anger toward Red caused her breathing to quicken. How could he have treated his sons so shabbily?

"That must've been difficult for all of you. I can't imagine leaving everything you've always known and being transplanted into a whole new world. Arizona is very different from Alaska." Her heart bled for the ten-year-old little boy whose life had been uprooted due to divorce. Xavier must have been forced to navigate a rocky road to adulthood.

Xavier shrugged. "It wasn't easy, I can tell you that, but neither was hearing the fights going on between our parents. Those memories are seared into my brain. Getting away from all that was a relief."

"But didn't you miss Hattie...and your dad?" she asked, trying to be tactful.

"I don't remember, honestly," he said, his expression shuttered.

True wasn't sure she believed him. How could a person forget something like that? Wouldn't it be imprinted in your memory with all the permanence of a tattoo?

"The other night Red had us over for dinner, and we found out he still owns our childhood home." He shook his head. "It was such a trip being back there. A lot came back to me. Family dinners. Game nights. And even though I didn't want to go, I actually had a decent time."

"That's great. Maybe there'll be some healing between all of you."

Xavier snorted. "I think that aligns with Hattie's master plan."

True wrinkled her nose. "I thought the master plan was to leave Yukon Cider and her other holdings to you and your brothers. Are there more layers to this situation?"

"And I thought you knew Hattie." The sound of his deep-throated laughter filled the truck. "She's sentimental. And she's not just trying to settle her business affairs. She wants to patch up her family." He cleared his throat. "Kind of like a deathbed wish."

"Do you think that's possible? I'm sure Hattie would be over the moon if it happened."

He heaved a tremendous sigh. "Honestly, I don't need that type of pressure. We already have to learn the ropes at the company, which frankly is a lot harder than I imagined. That's about all I can handle at the moment."

Although she wanted to ask Xavier about his agreement with Hattie, True knew that might be overstepping. She was curious, though. Had he signed ownership papers for Northern Exposure, or would he simply inherit the tavern after Hattie's death? Was there still a chance for True to make a bid for the business? Or had the opportunity already slipped through her fingers?

"Well, here's our first stop," True said as she turned down a wooded, tree-lined road. After traveling a short distance, they reached a clearing. True parked and got out of the truck with Xavier right behind her. Seconds later a rushing waterfall appeared. She heard Xavier let out a loud gasp, which was just the reaction she wanted. The roaring, whooshing sound as the water cascaded over the jagged rocks was a musical treat.

"Whoa! This is incredible," Xavier said. The expression on his face was one of reverence and pure joy. His reaction aligned perfectly with how True had hoped he would receive this amazing sight. *He got it!*

"That rush of wind against my face feels good," he said, lifting his chin so he could get the full effect.

The wind from the falls was one of the main reasons True loved this spot. She always felt like she was experiencing a caress from Mother Nature.

"Doesn't it?" she asked, closing her eyes and stretching out her arms to receive the blessing. "So is this bringing back any memories?" she asked. Odds were that he had been to this very spot as a child. But, from what he'd told her earlier, most of his memories of Moose Falls were hazy.

He nodded. "I do recall being here. I remember being

really happy. Maybe we came here in the summer and had picnics." His brows were knitted together as he focused on drawing out the image in his mind.

True could easily picture it since once spring and summer arrived, more folks headed out to the falls. She felt good knowing this place held happy memories for Xavier. Bringing him to this spot had been a good decision.

"The falls is actually where Moose Falls gets its name." Most folks didn't make the connection between the two, but she loved this fun fact.

Xavier let out a low whistle. "I can see why. It's pretty spectacular."

The waterfall, set against a cerulean-blue sky and craggy mountains, provided a stunning landscape. In her estimation, nothing was better than this stunning vista. It really was her happy place, where absolutely nothing could go wrong, and everything was serene. "It's my favorite place in town, other than Northern Exposure."

"You really love that place, don't you?" Xavier asked, his gaze intense as he looked at her.

How could she put into words what the tavern meant to her? As a young woman raising her brother after a tragic loss, the tavern had served as a lifeline. Being hired by Hattie, then rising up the ranks to manager, had allowed her to stay in the family home and provide a decent life for Jaylen. It represented what hard work and dedication could result in if a person gave it their all. Sometimes her goal of owning the tavern felt so lofty and out of reach. She struggled to feel worthy of such an undertaking.

"I'm going to tell you a secret. I've been dreaming of buying the tavern from Hattie for a long time now." She crossed her arms across her chest and said a little prayer that Xavier didn't laugh in her face.

"Why is it a secret? Shouldn't you be shouting it from the rooftops?"

"That's hard for me," True admitted. "Because once I put it out there, I can't take it back. Do you know what I mean? I've cherished this dream for so long that I'll be crushed if I fall flat on my face."

"Have you approached Hattie?"

"No, not yet. With her terminal illness, I didn't want to seem predatory. And it's a little bit more complicated now that she's handing over the reins of Yukon Cider to her three grandsons." She was tiptoeing around a bit, hoping Xavier might give her some intel about the future of the tavern. All she was working with at the moment was speculation. "For all I know she has plans to put the three of you in charge of the tavern as well."

"Hattie is pretty private about her estate planning, so I can't confirm or deny any of that, but I say go for it, no matter what. I'm guessing no one loves the place like you do. That'll work in your favor, along with your passion." He reached out and squeezed her hand. The gesture was intimate and tender. Not to mention he was providing reassurance.

Xavier was right. By hiding her ambitions, she gained nothing. And even though she still wasn't in a position to buy the establishment outright, perhaps she could reach some amenable terms with Hattie. Or dig deeper into business loans that could help her out.

Once they were back in the truck, True turned toward Xavier. "I'd like to broach the topic with Hattie on my own terms, so please don't mention it to her."

He made a zipping motion on his lips. "I wouldn't dream of saying anything. I believe in you. You've got this."

"Thanks," she murmured, buoyed by Xavier's vote of confidence.

True headed toward their next destination, pointing out landmarks along the way. She drove slowly as they approached a "Moose Crossing" sign. She grabbed Xavier's arm when she spotted a moose in the distance. "See. You never know when you're going to come across a moose or two. If you have the misfortune to hit one, you might not survive the collision, because they weigh over a thousand pounds. In general, it's always wise to give them a wide berth."

"Fun fact. Guess I'm not in Kansas anymore," Xavier quipped, his gaze trained on the moose.

"No, you're not," she said, amused by the way Xavier kept turning his head to make sure the moose was in their rearview window. Although the animals were majestic, they weren't to be messed with under any circumstances.

A short while later, she pulled up to the Klondike Ice Rink. This place had been a staple in her childhood. It was an institution here in Moose Falls and not just with kids. Everyone she knew had learned to skate here. Maybe Xavier had as well.

"Ta-da. We're here," True said. She couldn't keep the excitement from her voice. So far, touring Xavier around Moose Falls had been a blast. True loved her hometown the same way she loved chocolate cake, Saturdays, and sangria. Wholeheartedly and without reservation. Maybe Xavier would learn to adore it too. For Hattie's sake she hoped the Stone brothers would stick around town and carry on her legacy.

*Just for Hattie's sake?* a little voice in her head asked. Who was she kidding? She had really warmed up to the idea of Xavier sticking around, even if he inherited Northern Exposure. From the sound of it, he wasn't all that interested in her tavern. That knowledge made her breathe a little easier.

Xavier craned his neck to look at the sign. "Skating, huh?"

*Hmm.* Judging from his comment, the rink wasn't ringing any bells with him.

"Skating, hockey. Whatever floats your boat," she explained. "Let's go inside so you can check it out."

"I'm guessing it's big here in Moose Falls?" Xavier asked as they stepped down from the truck.

"It's hugely popular. I actually learned to skate here and played hockey in high school."

"Hockey? That's very cool." Xavier looked at her approvingly. "I knew you were a badass."

"You got that right," she said as Xavier pulled open the door for her as they approached the building where it was just as cold as outside.

Once they were inside, True inhaled deeply. She loved the smells and sounds of the rink. The swishing noise of the blades against the ice always made her pulse race with excitement. Right before hockey games, she'd loved being on the ice doing warm-ups with the team. Her parents had shown up for every game, cheering her on with unbridled exuberance.

Although she'd thought this would be fun for Xavier, it hadn't crossed her mind that he might not know how to skate.

"So, is hockey a thing in Arizona?" she asked. Although she had never been to Arizona, she knew it was a hot, arid place with little snow.

"Not really. Hockey isn't something I learned how to do there," he explained.

Aha! So he was a novice. Since he was a professional athlete, there probably weren't many sports she was better at than him other than this one. "Are you interested?" she asked, sensing the athlete in him wouldn't be able to say no.

"Sure. I'll give it a whirl," he said, appearing nonchalant.

*What a good sport!* A lot of people were nervous about learning to skate as adults, but clearly Xavier didn't feel that way.

"You're an athlete, so I bet you'll pick it up fast. What size are you?"

"I'm a thirteen." He was looking around the place with curiosity.

"I'll be right back with our skates," True said as she headed off to the skate rental counter.

"Hey, Scotty. How's it going?" True greeted Scotty Hanes, the owner. He had been running the rink for four decades. With a head of silver hair and sky-blue eyes, he was a sweet guy who had an unfortunate habit of being involved in everyone's business.

"That guy you came in with? Is he one of Hattie's grandsons?" He jerked his chin in Xavier's direction. "The football player, right?"

"Yeah, that's him," she acknowledged. What must it be like, she imagined, to be constantly referred to by your career? One you no longer were able to do because of a freak collision on the field.

"He used to be a great player," Scotty said. "Tough break."

She knew Scotty didn't mean any harm, but she wanted him to stop talking about Xavier like he was washed up. Her face felt heated as she brusquely told him their sizes and plunked the money down on the counter.

A few minutes later, True returned to where Xavier stood waiting. She held up his pair of skates and handed them over to him. "I taught Jaylen to skate, so I'm sure that I could teach you as well if you're up to it. Just the basics for today."

"I'm up for anything," Xavier said, bending over and

lacing up his skates. He frowned as if he wasn't quite sure he'd done it correctly.

His comment made her think about kissing him again, something she was definitely up for. She didn't usually go around kissing men she didn't know all that well, but the oldest Stone brother's cool confidence was winning her over. She headed toward the ice after lacing up her skates, holding out her hand to Xavier as he walked tentatively toward the ice. He gripped her hand so tightly, she wondered if he might break it.

"Easy there," she said, loosening his grip. "I'm going to need my hand for the long haul."

"Sorry. I just need to get my balance," he said, holding on to the railing, his legs quivering.

She wondered if she needed to go get him one of the orange cones that kids worked with on the rink. He really didn't seem to have any ability to balance at all.

She turned toward him and said, "Just watch me. Push off on one leg, then the other. Try your best to stay upright." Something told her he might just fall on his butt, but it was a rite of passage when learning to skate.

Suddenly, Xavier zoomed past her, his movements full of agility and power. He skated roughly fifty feet, then performed a turn and headed straight back in her direction skating backward.

"Hey! You said that you didn't know how to skate." She placed her hands on her hips. Not only could he skate, but he resembled a pro hockey player as he zoomed across the ice.

A smile crept across his face. "Nah. I said that it wasn't something that I learned to do in Arizona." He grinned at her, transforming himself from good-looking to drop-dead gorgeous. "I actually learned right here in Moose Falls. Just not at this rink."

"Stinker!" True said, sticking out her tongue at him. "You sure fooled me."

He skated toward her at top speed, stopping mere inches from her. Before she knew what was happening, Xavier reached for her. Seemingly not caring that eyes were upon them, he placed his arms around her waist, pulling her flush against his body. He looked down at her, his eyes twinkling with purpose. "Please kiss me," she murmured. Ugh, she had meant to talk in her head, but she'd spoken her desire out loud.

"Don't mind if I do," Xavier said, his wide grin only enhancing his dark good looks.

He dipped his head down for a kiss. His lips were frosty cold, but within seconds their lips heated each other's up. She felt his hand brushing tendrils of hair from her face before cradling the side of her neck in his palm. Normally she shied away from PDA, but at the moment, she was swept away by the kiss. True parted her lips, inviting Xavier in. For what seemed like an eternity, they stood on the ice kissing. She was lost in it, tumbling, falling into the void where nothing else mattered but this moment. Out of nowhere a loud honking sound rang out, causing them to pull apart and look around.

"It's the Zamboni," True explained. "They're letting us know to get off the ice so they can clean the surface."

"I always wanted to drive the Zamboni when I was a kid," Xavier said, wiggling his eyebrows as if he were still a mischievous child. "That would've been a blast."

"Goals," True said, chuckling at the idea of a pint-size Xavier careening around the ice in a Zamboni. "If you play your cards right, maybe we can arrange that." She winked at him. "The owner is a personal friend of mine."

"Don't play with me, girl. If I can scratch that off my

bucket list, I'll be a happy man." He reached for her mittened hand and clasped it in his.

Once they were off the ice, True took her mittens off and placed her fingers on her lips. They still felt all tingly from their make-out session. This man was quickly endearing himself to her even though the idea of falling for him terrified her. She needed to remind herself to put on her shield of armor before it was too late. Getting too attached to him might blow up in her face.

At moments like this one, True felt as if she didn't have a single defense against Xavier Stone.

# CHAPTER TWELVE

"Last stop on the Moose Falls tour," True announced as they pulled up to a log cabin–style home surrounded by an abundance of trees. Furls of smoke emanated from the chimney, making the home seem cozy. Xavier thought it was a beautiful place, the very image of an Alaskan storybook home snuggled in a peaceful woodland setting. He even caught a glimpse of majestic-looking mountains looming in the distance.

"Where are we?" he asked. He had a hunch it was True's home, but he didn't want to assume she would take him there as part of his Moose Falls tour. If so, he was honored. The place was spectacular.

She drummed her fingers on the steering wheel. "My place. I figure introducing you to Jaylen will score me major points. And you can give him that jersey yourself."

He was pretty blown away that True had brought him home. She was a private person, and he was now being invited into her world. He knew better than to overthink the gesture. True's motivation was clear. She would do anything for her baby brother.

"That's a great idea. Can't wait to meet him."

Xavier didn't know why he felt nervous as they headed inside. So far, today had been amazing. Seeing Moose Falls through True's eyes had been an eye-opener. He now knew what mattered to her most of all in this little Alaskan town. He wanted to uncover everything about this woman, one day at a time. Xavier sensed she didn't reveal herself to most people, so he suspected this was a bit of a big deal.

"I'm home," True called out as she pulled off her boots. Xavier followed suit and yanked his own off before placing them beside True's on the mat. Xavier looked around his surroundings. The immediate impression of True's home was comfort and warmth. True had made a home for herself and Jaylen. Earthy tones. Nothing too fancy. The smell of baking cookies wafted in the air, a sensory delight that caused his stomach to grumble.

Shuffling feet heralded the arrival of an older woman with a kind face and a shock of white hair. "Hey. We're in the kitchen baking cookies. Our last batch is about to come out," she said, smiling at them.

"Hi, Annie. This is my friend Xavier." True turned toward him. "This is Annie Swenson. She's Jaylen's sitter."

"You're one of Hattie's grandsons, aren't you?" Annie asked, her blue eyes twinkling. "She's talked a lot about you over the years."

"Nice to meet you, Annie," he said. Once again here was further proof that Hattie had held him and his brothers in her heart for all these years. He didn't think he could possibly feel any guiltier for being absent from her life. So many questions were burning inside him. How had everything gotten so messed up?

"Annie! The timer went off." A child's voice called out from the kitchen. When Xavier and True walked in, Jaylen's jaw dropped. He began to babble nonsensically. He couldn't take his eyes off him.

"Take a deep breath, buddy," True instructed him, wrapping her arms around the boy.

After a few moments, Jaylen collected himself. "Am I dreaming? Is it really you? The Storm?"

"Hey, man. It's nice to meet you." Xavier held out his hand to Jaylen, who reached up and shook it. "Your sister tells me you're a Cardinals fan."

"More like a fan of the Storm. I mean you," Jaylen said, a wide, infectious grin spreading across his face. Jaylen was a good-looking kid with almond-shaped brown eyes, a head of curly dark hair, and cinnamon-colored skin. He had a slim, athletic build that seemed to lend itself to sports. Right away Xavier could tell Jaylen was fast. He might excel at track, Xavier imagined.

"That's nice to hear," he said. "Hey. I've got something for you." He handed over the jersey. "Just a little something for a super fan."

Jaylen held up the jersey and let out a guttural scream. "This is sick!" he cried out. "Wait till I show my friends. No one will believe it. Thanks so much."

He closed the distance between himself and Xavier, then wrapped his arms tightly around Xavier's waist. The hug made him feel like Superman. Jaylen was holding on for dear life. Xavier couldn't remember the last time anyone had hugged him like this, but it felt good.

"Okay, you're going to have to let him go at some point so he can breathe," True said, smiling. Her voice sounded a bit emotional. Her love for Jaylen was etched on her beautiful face. He felt privileged to witness it and be a part of a special moment.

Jaylen let go and took a step backward. He was gaping

at Xavier with an expression of shock and awe. No one had looked at him like this in a very long time, and he hadn't realized how much he'd missed it. Not the hero worship part, but knowing he was valued and not simply a has-been.

The young boy's eyes were shimmering with excitement. "I can't believe this is really happening. It's like Christmas and my birthday all rolled into one."

Everyone laughed at his expressiveness. True looked as if she was lit up from the inside. Clearly, her brother being so overjoyed made her happy. It felt good knowing he'd done something for her family to bring some happiness their way.

"I've got fresh-from-the-oven chocolate chip cookies here," Annie said, holding up a plate of cookies. "Come and get 'em."

They all sat down at the kitchen table with Jaylen snagging a seat beside him. He jumped up to get milk for everyone and poured a glass for Xavier. True sat across from Xavier, watching the interaction between him and Jaylen.

"So, do you play football yourself?" Xavier asked as he bit into a cookie.

Jaylen dunked his cookie into his glass of milk. "Well, we had a team for nine-man football, but we don't have a coach anymore."

"Nine-man football has become popular in Alaska. It allows for smaller schools to play with nine members rather than the usual eleven," True explained.

"Makes sense," Xavier said with a nod. "Sorry about your coach."

"Me too," Jaylen said, sticking out his lip. "I miss playing football a lot."

True placed her arm around Jaylen. "You're going to be all right. We'll find something else for you to do."

Something else? At that age there was nothing else that

would satisfy a kid who'd had a taste of football. The sport seeped into your veins, and before you knew it, you'd fallen in love with all aspects of the game. Other than his family, Xavier had never felt as passionate about anything in this world as football. Not even Heather.

Before he could properly think things through, Xavier blurted out, "Maybe I can help."

True frowned at him from across the kitchen island. "How?"

"I can volunteer my services as a part-time coach," he suggested. Both Jaylen and True looked at him with disbelief. Annie busied herself at the stove, seemingly uninterested in the discussion. He wasn't sure why his lips were so loose at the moment, but his brain was working overtime trying to find a solution for Jaylen. Little boys shouldn't have to give up sports because of adults not following through on their commitments. The experience could be life altering for Jaylen, just as it had been for Xavier.

Jaylen began jumping up and down and squealing. True shifted from one foot to the other, her unwavering gaze trained on Xavier.

"Xavier, can I speak to you for a moment?" she asked, motioning him to leave the room.

Uh-oh. She didn't sound too happy with him. Had he overstepped in making the offer to coach Jaylen?

"Sure," he said, following behind her as she hotfooted it out of the kitchen.

Once they reached the living room, True turned to face him, letting out a huff of air. She looked extremely perturbed. "You cannot say things like that!" She began to pace back and forth, darting irritated glances at him.

"Like what?" he asked, genuinely confused. "About being his coach?"

"Yes," she hissed, throwing up her hands. "He immediately took it to heart."

"Isn't that a good thing?" he asked, running his hand across his jaw.

True began tapping her foot against the hardwood floor. "Only if you're one hundred percent sure about it. Can you confirm that you're committed?" She folded her arms across her chest.

"Yes, I can," he said. "And I'm a tad insulted that you're doubting my intentions. Not to mention my integrity. I would never dangle a carrot like that in Jaylen's face if I didn't plan to follow through." He was getting a little heated now and feeling the need to defend his honor. It was hurtful knowing she didn't trust him.

For a few beats they stared at each other with neither speaking. Xavier wasn't used to having his honesty questioned.

"I'm sorry that I doubted you." True's shoulders slumped a little. "It's just that I'm very protective of Jaylen. He's faced a lot of disappointments in his life. And it's my job to watch over him, to make sure he doesn't get hurt. By anyone or anything."

Xavier could see the stress and anguish on her face. Her feelings were genuine. His anger quickly dissipated. He couldn't imagine how tough True's road had been. Raising her younger brother had been thrust upon her at a young age. It seemed that her entire world revolved around Jaylen. Could Xavier really blame her for wanting to make sure he didn't pull the rug out from under the kid?

He moved toward her, reaching out and brushing his knuckles against her cheek. "I've coached kids back home in Arizona. It's always been really rewarding for me. So much of my football career was about building my profile. It was all centered around me. Working with kids is as pure as it gets."

True nodded. "So you're all in?"

"One thousand percent," he said emphatically. "I think it's best if I recruit another person, maybe a parent, to work with me. I'm going to have to work around my hours at Yukon Cider, but my weekends are wide open."

True nodded. "I think that I might know just the person. She might be open to it, since you'll be the lead and her daughter really wants to play."

The lead? What had he gotten himself into? He wasn't even sure how football was played here in these wintry elements. Flag football? Nine-person teams? He would need to figure this all out so the kids would have a rewarding experience.

"Are you guys done talking?" Jaylen called out from the kitchen. "I'd love some company in here."

Both Xavier and True chuckled. "Yes, here we come," True called back to him.

"So we're good?" Xavier asked. He made a peace sign with his fingers.

"We're good," True said. "Just don't let him down. That's all I ask."

As they headed back into the kitchen, True's parting words nagged at him. Ever since his injury, that was all he had managed to do. Letting folks down was his superpower. His teammates. His management team. His family.

"So you're going to be my coach?" Jaylen asked as soon as he saw Xavier. "For real?"

Xavier grinned at Jaylen's over-the-top excitement. "I need to work out the details, but yeah, I'm going to be your coach."

"Sweeeeeeeet!" Jaylen shouted, doing a little celebratory

dance that resembled the one Xavier and his teammates often did in the end zone. Xavier got a kick out of seeing Jaylen copying their moves.

"Would you like to stay for dinner?" True asked. "We're having salmon chowder and bison burgers on sourdough buns. You too, Annie."

"My favorites," Annie said. "Count me in."

"Can't say no to that invitation," Xavier said, his stomach grumbling at the sound of her delicious dinner menu. He hadn't realized how hungry he was after touring around town and skating. He'd worked up quite an appetite.

"Hey! Come to my room. I want to show you my football card collection and my posters," Jaylen said, tugging on his arm.

"So you like football, huh?" Xavier asked, allowing himself to be tugged along.

"Oh, you don't know the half of it," True said. "I'll get dinner started while the two of you hang out." She made a shooing motion with her hands.

Xavier cast a look over his shoulder at True before he left the kitchen with Jaylen.

At that exact moment, he realized how much he wanted to prove to True that he was a man of his word. Doing so mattered to him. *She* mattered to him. And he knew pretty soon that Jaylen would matter to him as well.

Despite his best intentions not to dive headlong into any romantic entanglements, he was now swimming in the deep end of the pool.

🌲

After dinner Annie drove Xavier back to the Northern Exposure lot on her way home so he could pick up his vehicle. True's thoughts were full of Xavier as she washed the dishes and cleaned up the kitchen. *He's a good guy.* The thought popped into her head without warning, surprising her. It had been a long time since she had felt that way about anyone. Most people who were close to her would say she was jaded and reluctant to trust. The more time she spent with Xavier, the more she was opening up to the possibility of being with someone new.

Now, after a fun day hanging out with Xavier, she had to tackle something difficult. She hadn't yet mentioned anything to Jaylen about her meeting with the principal or the school's belief that he was academically gifted. Honestly, she didn't know where to start. And she had no idea how Jaylen would react.

She headed toward her brother's room, gently knocking on the door before pushing her way inside. As usual, he was surfing on his computer with his headphones on, no doubt checking out sports clips and stats. True sat down beside him on his bed. His bedroom was decorated in sports paraphernalia and Marvel comic figures. She felt a smile tugging at her lips as a poster of Xavier gazed at her with brooding intensity in his Cardinals uniform.

Yes, the man was hot. Smoking! He was definitely the hottest guy to ever land in Moose Falls, bar none. And she was falling for him like nobody's business.

She looked away from Xavier. This talk was going to be important to Jaylen's future.

"Hey, kiddo. I need to talk to you about something."

Jaylen's brown eyes grew large in his small face. "Uh-oh. Am I in trouble? Whatever it is, I didn't do it." He held up his hands. "I've been framed."

True had to bite her lip to keep from laughing. This kid was always two steps ahead of her.

"You didn't do anything. This time," she said with a

pointed look. She loved her brother to bits, but she wasn't naïve. She knew he got caught up in mischief from time to time. He wasn't an angel. "This is about school."

Jaylen frowned. He put his computer to the side, now completely focused on their conversation. "Did I get in trouble for something?"

She reached out and gently tweaked his nose. "You're not in any trouble. Matter of fact, Principal Dandridge reached out to me about how well you're doing in school."

"Yes!" Jaylen said, raising his fist in the air. "That's what I'm talking about," he said, moving from side to side and wiggling around in a celebratory fashion.

"She said you're academically gifted," True said, tears pricking her eyes. If their parents were still around, they would be so incredibly proud of their baby boy. Jaylen was such a little rock star. She bit the inside of her cheeks so she wouldn't burst into tears.

Jaylen frowned. "What does that mean exactly?"

"It means that you're way above your grade level, and the administration is trying to figure out ways to make sure you're being challenged." She looked down at him. "So we have to make some decisions."

"We do? I'm not sure that I like the sound of this." Jaylen was trying to play it cool, but his lip was trembling.

She placed her arm around him and pulled him close to her. "There's no need to worry. I've got you. The way I see it, promoting you to another grade or two isn't in your best interest socially."

Jaylen vehemently shook his head. His cheeks were flushed. "Nope. I do not want to jump grades. That's not cool. I don't want to lose all my friends." He held up his arms. "I'm doing good right where I am."

She winked at him. "We're on the same page. Also, I'm

not sending you away to a private school in Homer where we can't see each other every day. I need to lay eyes on you and know that you're doing all right. I'm just laying out the options in case that's ever something you're interested in." True drew in a big breath. "In the end I'm always going to do right by you. And you have a voice in this. This is your life."

"I do not, I repeat, do not want to go anywhere." He clutched her arm and rested his head on her shoulder. "I'm happy here with you, True. Please don't ever send me away."

She rustled his curls. "That's never going to happen. Are you kidding me? I'd be lost without you, like a chicken with my head cut off. You're the peanut butter to my jelly. The ketchup to my fries."

Jaylen began to giggle so much, he clutched his stomach. "True! You're so funny."

"And you are my everything," she said, squeezing him. "I'm going to look into getting you a tutor who can work with you on more challenging topics. In addition, I'm going to request that your teachers do the same and test you at a higher level."

Jaylen slapped his palm against his forehead and let out a groan. "So my work is going to be harder?"

"Yes," True said with a nod. "Answer this question honestly. Has the work been too easy? Have you been trying to blend in by not being too smart?"

Jaylen's head dipped down. True grasped his chin and drew it up so that their gazes locked. She knew the answer before he even opened his mouth. Not making eye contact was his tell.

"Sometimes," he answered. "I just want to be like everyone else. It's not good to stand out, and I don't want anyone calling me a brain. Or making fun of me. It's already weird that I don't have parents."

"I get it, but you do have parents. And even though they're not physically here, we carry them around with us every single day," True explained. All kids wanted to fit in, so she completely understood his predicament. But, at the same time, as his parental figure she wanted Jaylen to be proud of his strengths. "First of all, your true friends aren't going to treat you poorly because you're a brainiac." Jaylen made a face. "Secondly, being smart is a gift, and it's something you got from Mom and Dad."

"I did?" he asked, his voice radiating surprise.

"You bet. They were both brilliant," she said. "So moving forward I'm going to need you to promise me something. Okay?"

"All right." He looked at her solemnly. "What is it?"

"Never hide yourself, Jaylen. Hold your head up high," she said, taking his chin and lifting it a notch. "You're the son of Lou and Jessie Everett. They would want you to fly high and soar. Okay?"

He made a thumbs-up sign. "Got it. So, do I get a prize or something?"

True sputtered. "A prize? For what?"

"For being gifted," he said, grinning. "I mean, it is an accomplishment."

Jaylen was nothing if not ambitious.

"You little rascal!" True began to tickle him all over his chest and arms. The sound of Jaylen's laughter and squeals rang out in his bedroom, bringing True pure joy and contentment. Being with Jaylen, raising him into adulthood, making him happy—this, she thought, was what mattered most of all.

# CHAPTER THIRTEEN

As the days went by, with January turning to February, Xavier found himself quickly getting a handle on working at Yukon Cider. Twice a week Hattie would have lunch with him and his brothers in order to check in with them. She was only working a few days a week at the office now, but she was always busy. Hattie met with distributors, the marketing staff, and sales representatives. She was involved in all hiring decisions, from cider makers to the packaging crew members. Xavier liked the time they spent together, mainly because it allowed him to find out more about her and the company. Plus, she always had fun stories from their childhood and Red's. She was a wonderful storyteller, and her recollections actually brought some of Xavier's memories to the forefront. There was only one subject that seemed to be taboo, which was talk of their grandfather. So far, Hattie was mute on the subject.

He wasn't sure whether it was because they were members of the Stone family, but all their co-workers were treating them well. No one treated him like a former NFL player.

They seemed to accept him as he was. It was fascinating learning about the history of Alaskan cider and the origins of the company. There were so many aspects of the company that he found interesting. In reality, this was Xavier's first real-world, nine-to-five job. Before now, his sole employment had been with the NFL. He'd been fortunate to work at his dream job until it all came crashing down around him.

He shook off the bittersweet memories. It wasn't the time or the place to wallow. Xavier needed to focus on the here and now. He and his brothers had struck a bargain with their grandmother that they intended to uphold.

At the moment he, Caleb, and Landon were at the Yukon Cider distillery after attending a meeting with the marketing team regarding new packaging. Xavier loved being here where the hard cider was created. It still seemed miraculous to him, although he and his brothers had been walked through the process numerous times. His grandmother had created all this magic from the ground up. She was an extraordinary woman, a visionary.

"Never in a million years did I think that I would enjoy this type of work experience so much," Xavier said, shaking his head at the discovery. He really enjoyed the camaraderie among the staff and brainstorming to problem solve. Although he was a newbie at this type of job, no one made him feel useless.

"Right? This is an art form. And a tasty one at that." Caleb took a swig of the pear-cranberry cider. "This one is amazing."

Landon's eyes grew wide. "We're not supposed to be sampling the merchandise. It's against the rules," he chided.

"Just a little sip," Caleb said. "I'm playing catch-up for all the years when we missed out on hard ciders." He raised the cider to take another taste.

Xavier reached over and took the hard cider away from him. "Let's play by the rules, all right? We represent Hattie here at the company. If you mess around, that's all our reputations on the line." He hadn't realized until this moment how much he cared about Hattie's reputation and legacy. It mattered.

"It's a lot like working in the lab, to be honest," Landon said. "Without all the backstabbing and stealing of scientific formulas." He let out a snort. "If I weren't intent on clearing my name, I could get used to this."

It was nice to see Landon back on his feet and ready to fight to get his reputation back. He had been in a funk for such a long time. His baby brother had earned his reputation as a scientist through hard work and the pursuit of academic excellence. A Presidential Scholar. MIT. No one had the right to take away his scientific discoveries and label him a thief. Xavier trusted that his brother would win out over all the lies.

"Whatever you decide to do," Xavier said, "we support you."

Caleb put up his fists. "And if you need any muscle... Xavier can handle that."

All three of them laughed, knowing Caleb was a lover, not a fighter.

"It's nice knowing you guys always support me," Landon said, blinking back tears. "I'd be lost without the two of you."

"Brothers Stone," Xavier said, holding up his fist as his brothers did the same, and they bumped knuckles. "Forever and always."

"So... you never really told us about your date with True," Landon said.

"That's right," Caleb said with a nod. "Are you holding out on us?"

Xavier let out a chuckle. "Not at all. I didn't know that you would be all that interested in the details."

"Do you even know us?" Landon asked, looking at Xavier with an incredulous expression.

"It was an awesome day. She took me skating," Xavier said. He felt the corners of his mouth stretching into a grin. "I'm telling you guys, you've got to get back on the ice," Xavier gushed. "There's something about the rink that feels so energizing."

"I might break my neck," Caleb said, making a face. "It's been years since I've hit the ice."

"But it all comes back to you," Xavier said, lightly grabbing Caleb's arm. "It's like riding a bike."

"I thought you didn't like the cold?" Landon asked with a frown. "Rinks are freezing."

"That's right," Caleb said, eyeballing Xavier. "What's changed? You were the one complaining about coming to cold-ass Alaska. Isn't that what you said?"

"I may have," he said. "But being back here is way more interesting than I imagined." He let out a chuckle. "Hey! Maybe I like small-town Alaskan living."

Caleb and Landon shared a look full of meaning.

"What's with that look?" Xavier asked, swinging his gaze back and forth between his brothers.

"This is about True, isn't it? You really like her, don't you?" Caleb asked, peering intensely at Xavier.

He avoided Caleb's probing gaze. His brother could read him so easily. "It's too early to make a declaration like that. We haven't really known each other for long."

"You like her," Caleb and Landon said at the same time, nodding with conviction.

"So tell us more about this date the two of you went on," Landon said, rubbing his hands together. "I fully admit that I want to live vicariously through you."

"Speaking of which, you really need to get out more and stick your toe in the dating pond," Caleb said to Landon. "I

can be your wing man. I promise you we'd have a lot of fun."
He wiggled his eyebrows.

"I think we have two very different ideas of fun," Landon
said, quirking his mouth.

Xavier was intent on downplaying the time he'd spent
with True. If he didn't, Landon and Caleb would be in a
feeding frenzy with him as the bait. "I wouldn't call it a
date. We hung out. Went skating." He felt a smile stretching across his face as memories of their kiss filled his head.
"She took me to this amazing waterfall we used to go to
when we were kids."

"I remember that place," Caleb said, his eyes lighting
up. "We used to have picnics and race around in the field of
flowers. It was pretty cool," he gushed.

"Yeah, we sure did," Xavier said. "Forget-me-nots and
wildflowers." He could picture them now in his mind's eye.
Their mother had laced the flowers through her French
braids and danced to Earth, Wind and Fire.

"As usual, I've got nothing," Landon said, letting out a
frustrated sound. "Not a single memory except the gingerbread cookies."

"I'm sorry about that," Xavier said, clapping Landon on
the back. "But on the upside, everything that we do over the
next year is making new memories. Hopefully, ones you'll
never forget."

Landon's face lit up the same way it always had since
they were kids. "I hope so."

"So, what do you think so far about Yukon Cider?"
Xavier asked, feeling the need to check in with his brothers. This was what they needed to do throughout the year
so they were all on the same page about the future. As the
contract stipulated, their decision had to be unanimous, or
they would forfeit Yukon Cider.

"It's fine," Caleb said with a shrug. "But to do this for the rest of my life? I don't see myself in this role. No disrespect to Hattie, but I still want to act, and I can't pursue an acting career here in Moose Falls."

*Acting.* It was all Caleb had ever wanted. He was as passionate about an acting career as Xavier was about football and Landon was about being a scientist. They still had almost a year to make their decision, but from the onset, Xavier hadn't believed that all three of them would agree to stay and run Yukon Cider.

"I like it here," Landon said, "but it's too soon to make any decisions. I'm a bit homesick, to be honest. I miss Mom."

Caleb let out a sigh. "Yeah, it's strange not seeing her and knowing she's thousands of miles away from us." He made a face. "And she wasn't thrilled about this adventure either. She hates Alaska and Moose Falls."

Xavier's chest tightened at the mention of their mother. She had always been at the center of their world, so it was only natural they would all miss her. And it stung a little bit that they had come here against her wishes. In the end, he had realized that she was letting her own personal feelings get in the way of something that could be life altering. He didn't think she hated Alaska or Moose Falls either. For Daisy, this place served as a trigger, since her marriage had fallen apart here and she had left under strained circumstances.

"She's only a FaceTime call away," Xavier said, trying to sound reassuring. "Maybe we should call her tonight."

"Do you think she's still salty about us coming to Moose Falls?" Landon asked.

"I think she was just scared," Xavier answered. "Of all the bad memories and the way we left. The divorce was messy. We still don't know all that went down between our parents after all these years." He shook his head. "Us coming back here must feel a bit unnerving. Like she might lose us."

"That could never happen," Landon said. "She's the center of our world."

Daisy Stone had always been their rock. Xavier's ex-fiancée had always griped about him putting his mother on a pedestal, but Heather hadn't understood the ties that bound them all together. She'd barely been on speaking terms with her own parents, so he'd taken her criticism with a grain of salt. Love and mutual respect weren't bad things.

"Oh, by the way," Xavier said, trying to sound casual, "I forgot to tell you guys that I volunteered to be a football coach for local kids. I start today."

Caleb and Landon gawked at him.

"You did what?" Caleb asked, his voice raised.

"When did this happen?" Landon's tone radiated concern.

Xavier made a hand motion for them to settle down. "It's not a big deal. True's brother had a coach who bailed on the team, so I volunteered to step in. I managed to get one of the moms to be my assistant coach, so I'm not doing this solo." He looked back and forth between the two. "I cleared it with Hattie, and she thinks it's a great way to get to know more of the Moose Falls community."

Both of his brothers let out throaty laughs, which only served to annoy him. It was as grating as nails on a chalkboard. What was so funny about volunteering his time with young kids? They were acting like two jerks.

Caleb shook his head. "Oh, man. You are definitely falling for True. You've got it bad!"

Landon nodded, seemingly in agreement with Caleb's assessment. "Just make sure you're seeing things clearly," Landon added. "You just got back on course after all the drama with your ex." He twisted his mouth for emphasis. "We don't want to see you torn apart again."

Xavier felt himself getting heated. This was familiar territory with his brothers. They had often accused him of being easily manipulated in relationships, particularly with Heather. He'd always been so eager to please his ex-fiancée, even if it meant jumping through hoops to make her happy. Maybe he should have heeded the warning signs back then, but he was entitled to mistakes. He and True were just getting to know each other, but now his brothers were making him question everything. Was he already falling back into old patterns?

"Just make sure this is what *you* want, Xavier. Clearly, True has you wrapped around her little finger," Caleb muttered.

"That's not true. Don't even start with that mess," Xavier said, bristling. "Giving back is one of the few things I can still do when it comes to football. Nobody seems to want my skills in the NFL, so why shouldn't I volunteer my services? This has nothing to do with True. It has to do with me." He was breathing heavily through his nose, and although he knew that he needed to calm down, he was annoyed and furious.

Xavier stormed out of the room, ignoring the pleas of his brothers to stay and talk it out. Just when he was beginning to feel positive about being here in Moose Falls, Caleb and Landon had to throw grenades at him. He wasn't the same man he used to be. Clearly, that wasn't something his brothers understood.

He had learned so much during his relationship with Heather and the wounds he'd suffered due to her selfishness and deceit. Xavier had no intention of being used by a woman ever again, but he knew True was different. She was the furthest thing from his ex.

So far, so good, Xavier thought as he stood in the gymnasium looking out at the assembled group of children. Twenty-five kids had shown up for practice, although around five admitted they had only come to meet a famous football player. Honestly, he struggled with the notion as of late. Fame was such a fleeting concept. He hated that it mattered to him, but was he still a celebrity without the glare of the lights and cameras and *Sunday Night Football*?

He had spent a lot of time contemplating whether he could truly be happy without being a famous athlete playing on an elite team. So far, he hadn't come up with an answer. Maybe that was one of the things he would discover about himself in Moose Falls.

"As some of you might know, I'm Xavier Stone. You can call me Coach Stone," he said. "And this is Lisa Jardine, Alicia's mom. Coach Jardine to all of you."

Lisa beamed from ear to ear. "Hey, guys. I'm excited to be coaching with the Storm. I mean Coach Stone," she said, quickly correcting herself and causing the group to erupt into giggles. Xavier knew she'd used his football name as an ice breaker, and he didn't mind it.

"How many of you have played football before?" Xavier asked. He looked at the raised hands. Only a few members of the group had any football experience. It was kind of nice starting with a blank slate. That way he would easily be able to see if anyone had raw abilities and any leadership qualities. Even at this age, there would be team captains, scrimmages, cool team apparel. There was so much involved in youth sports that would fire these kids up. Memories of his own experiences flooded him. Despite what his brothers thought, this was a worthwhile endeavor.

"We're going to start out with some drills so we can begin conditioning your bodies. When the weather permits, we can practice outside, but for now, we can practice right here," Xavier said. This might be a workout for him as well, considering he hadn't been keeping up with his grueling gym workouts. To this day, he was plagued by random head-aches where he needed to lie down in a dark room. He had blind spots in his peripheral vision on the left side. Those were his limitations, and he hoped they didn't interfere with his ability to coach these kids.

"We've got waters in a cooler for after we finish up," Lisa said. "I hope everyone remembers to drink water throughout the day so you're properly hydrated."

For the next hour, Xavier put the kids through their paces. Some of the players really rose to the occasion and showcased skills and lots of heart. He was impressed. When he looked toward the bleachers, his heart leaped at the sight of True. She was sitting there watching all the action unfold-ing. She waved at him, causing a funny feeling to lodge in his chest. He walked over while the kids finished up practice by running laps.

"Hey there. How's it going?" he asked, stopping a few feet from the bleachers.

"Hey, Xavier. I hope you don't mind me watching the practice."

He jammed his hands in the pockets of his sweatpants. "Of course I don't mind. I appreciate the support."

"How are things going?" she asked, holding out a packet of M&M's to him. "Everything seems to be running smoothly from up here."

He took the packet and shook a few into his hand before giving them back to her. His fingers brushed against hers in the process, giving him a rush of awareness. "Good, I think.

So far the kids are responsive and energetic. I've got a good feeling about this group. From what I can see, they're great kids. I'm happy to be mentoring them."

She popped a handful of candy in her mouth, crunching and swallowing before she spoke. "I know all of them, and they're pretty sweet. Thanks again for helping out. I know they're over-the-moon happy about being coached by the Storm. Trust me, your being here is big news in Moose Falls."

There it was again, that strange feeling in his gut when someone called him the Storm. Was he really still that dude? Or was that yet another thing he needed to let go of? But, if he wanted to make a comeback as a football announcer, he needed to embrace that persona.

"I should get back over there," Xavier said, darting a glance in the direction of his new players. They were still running laps. A smile tugged at his lips at the sight of a few of them laboring to make the last go-round. He imagined they would all sleep well tonight out of pure fatigue.

"Hey, I promised Jaylen pizza after practice. Care to join us?" True asked. "There's a place here in town called Last Frontier Pizza." She brought her fingers to her mouth, kissed them, then raised them in the air. "Best pizza you'll ever have."

"Are you asking me on a date?" His voice had a teasing quality, but he wasn't totally kidding. He wanted to spend more time with True, whether it was over pizza or at an ice rink or at Northern Exposure.

True quirked her mouth. "Yeah, I don't usually bring my little brother on dates, but we can call it that if you like." She made a funny face.

Xavier chuckled. Jaylen was a cool kid, and so far, they were getting along really well. Although Xavier wanted to spend one-on-one time with True, he didn't mind her little brother being there. If their relationship continued to blossom, he knew that aspect would be important to True.

"I would love to join the two of you," he said. "I've been hearing a lot about reindeer pizza, and I can't wait to try some."

True wrinkled her nose. "It's a huge specialty item here in Alaska, but I'm not a fan. My favorite is pepperoni."

He liked hearing what she liked and what she didn't like. True was like a puzzle, and he was putting the pieces together one by one, creating a picture of one of the most interesting women he'd ever met. Xavier was filing it all away for future reference. It scared him a little bit how much he was starting to care about True. He wasn't sure he wanted to feel so invested in any woman. That's when a person opened themselves up to getting hurt.

"Gotcha," he responded. "Mine is sausage with anchovies, but I'll eat any kind of pie."

"Oooh, anchovies might be a deal breaker," True said, wrinkling her nose and laughing.

He laughed at her expression. "I'll meet up with you after practice."

As he walked back over to his team, a random thought crossed his mind. For a woman like True, he might just permanently give up the anchovies.

# CHAPTER FOURTEEN

True didn't think she had ever seen Jaylen look at anyone with such pure hero worship as the way he was staring at Xavier at the moment. They were sitting at a booth at Last Frontier Pizza after having ordered three large pizza pies—sausage with anchovies, pepperoni, and reindeer. She was surprised that Jaylen could even manage to eat with all the stars in his eyes, but he was stuffing his face with pizza fast and furiously the way most nine-year-old boys did. Xavier was keeping up with her brother's pace as the pieces of pizza were rapidly disappearing right before her eyes. He could keep his anchovies, though! In her opinion they ruined a perfectly good pizza.

It was safe to say Jaylen and Xavier were getting along really well. Her little brother beamed as Xavier heaped praise on him for a successful football practice. This, she realized, was what had been lacking in Jaylen's life. A male figure, preferably a cool one, whom he could admire and learn from. So many thoughts were running through her mind. Was it safe for Jaylen to bond with a man who might not be sticking around Moose Falls? Perhaps she was really asking herself if she could trust Xavier with her own heart as well as her brother's.

"I'm full," Jaylen pronounced, pushing away his plate. All he'd left behind were crumbs. She hoped Jaylen didn't have a bellyache later on, because he had devoured the pizza as if it were an Olympic sport.

Xavier grinned at him from across the table. "I guess that I'm the winner, because I'm still not full." He reached for another slice, folded it in half, and proceeded to take a huge bite. True had never thought a man eating pizza could be sexy, but here he was looking like eye candy.

"You're a beast," Jaylen said, laughing so hard, True worried he might break a rib.

"I'll take that title," Xavier said. He made a growling noise like an animal, causing Jaylen to laugh even harder.

Jaylen turned toward True. "Is it okay if I go play pinball?" he asked. "I'm trying to break my personal record."

"Go for it, but we're leaving in about fifteen minutes or so," True said, glancing at her watch. "It's getting late."

"No problem. Feel free to hold hands or whatever while I'm gone," Jaylen said slyly before walking away. He flashed them a thumbs-up when he was a few feet away.

True let out a groan. "Sorry about that. I think he's trying to make you a member of our family. In case you didn't notice, he thinks you hung the moon."

Xavier let out a hearty laugh. His eyes trailed after Jaylen. "He cracks me up. Honestly, he reminds me a bit of myself, although I'm not sure I had his confidence." He turned his gaze back to True. "You're doing an amazing job raising him."

Warmth filled her insides at the compliment. As much as she loved the tavern, bringing up Jaylen was her life's mission. Her true calling. "I appreciate you saying that. Being the stand-in for my parents is the hardest thing I've ever done or ever will do. Nothing else is as important to me."

"I wish Red had felt that way about fatherhood," he said. "I'm still trying to find a way to ask him the hard questions about why he vanished from our childhood," Xavier admitted.

True could hear a wistful tone laced in his voice. "That must be frustrating," she acknowledged. "I can't imagine leaving Jaylen in the lurch like that."

"Neither can I. You're devoted to him." Xavier's gentle smile washed over her like a warm rain, giving her goose bumps in the process.

"But it's still important to have your own personal goals totally unrelated to Jaylen," he said gently. "Trust me, he'll grow up happier knowing you didn't sacrifice your dreams for his benefit."

"Oh, I know," she said. "I always talk to him about wanting to run Northern Exposure and making it my own." She lightly heaved her shoulders. "So even if those aspirations don't come to fruition, he'll always know that I tried to reach for the brass ring."

"You really need to be open with Hattie about the tavern. Be completely honest and vulnerable with her. Give it your best shot, otherwise you'll always regret it," Xavier said, reaching for the last slice of reindeer pizza. "This stuff really is amazing, by the way. Completely addictive." He was eating with such gusto, True had trouble keeping her eyes off him. He made eating pizza look like an art form.

She knew what he was giving her was sage advice. It was time to put on her big-girl panties and speak her dream into existence. She and Hattie had a solid bond, and their relationship was based on mutual respect and affection. Why shouldn't True make a play for Northern Exposure? After all, the tavern was her baby. The worst thing Hattie could say was no and that she was leaving it in the hands of her grandsons or Red. Yes, those words would sting, but at least True could let go of this dream and chase another one.

She drummed her nails on the table. "Okay, so if I do that, you've got to talk to Red." They locked gazes.

He drew his brows together, appearing startled. "About what?"

"Umm…about everything. The past. How he dropped the ball with you and your brothers when you were kids. The animosity that still lingers between you. Why you haven't seen him over the years. Need I say more?" She arched an eyebrow.

Xavier let out a low grunt. "I guess it's time. Past time, really. It's just that…I've made it this far in my life without hashing everything out with him. I'm not sure that I can handle what he might have to tell me. Or how I might react."

"But getting it off your chest could help you in ways you can't even imagine."

He slowly nodded. "You're right." He placed his palm over his chest. "There's this weight that presses down on me from time to time. I used to think it was tied in with being a professional athlete and the huge expectations that were placed on me, but it didn't go away when I stopped playing." His eyes were glimmering with an intensity that made her shiver. He was being real and raw with her, immediately making her feel more connected to him. There was something crackling in the space between them, and although she couldn't put a name to it, it felt intense.

On impulse, she reached over and gripped his hand, lightly squeezing it. "You've got this, Xavier. And so do I."

He leaned across the table, and she met him halfway,

brushing her lips against his. Anchovies be damned, she thought, as she opened her mouth to him. Xavier reached around and cupped the back of her neck in his hand, pulling her closer. His lips were sweet and a little bit salty. As the kiss deepened, True forgot all about time and place. There was only the two of them in this moment, lost in their fiery connection.

"Ahem!" The loud clearing of a throat abruptly ended the kiss. As they pulled apart, True saw Jaylen standing beside the booth. And although she really wanted to pull Xavier by his collar and draw him back into the kiss, she knew that would be pure madness. Jaylen didn't need a front-row seat to her and Xavier smooching up a storm.

"Sorry to bust up this make-out session," Jaylen said with a grin, "but you did say fifteen minutes."

"Good timing, buddy," Xavier said, holding up his palm for a high five.

"Yeah," True said, her voice coming out in a rasp. "Really good timing."

A few days later, True walked into My Cup of Tea, the best tea shop in Moose Falls, and immediately scanned the establishment for Hattie. She had taken Xavier's advice and reached out to her mentor about having a meeting about Northern Exposure. Much to True's surprise, Hattie had been thinking along the same lines—that they needed to check in with each other regarding the business.

"Hey, True. Hattie beat you here," Delilah, the owner, said, nodding toward a table by the window.

"Thanks," True said as she quickly walked toward Hattie. Teatime with Hattie was something True immensely enjoyed. Every month Hattie invited her to partake in this lovely ritual. Being alone with her mentor afforded her the opportunity to pick the older woman's brain and to soak up all her knowledge like a sponge. Now, more than ever, True realized the importance of doing so. Time was fleeting, with Hattie's illness looming over them.

Hattie was waiting for True at their usual table, wearing an elaborate cream-colored tea hat. As always, she looked regal, as if she were a grand duchess or a queen. Some people were just born with it, the ability to command attention no matter where they were or what they were doing.

But, as she drew closer, True noticed cracks in Hattie's facade. Her friend put on a good act, but she wasn't looking well. Dark shadows rested under her eyes. Her top appeared several sizes too big. Tinges of yellow colored the whites of her eyes. True had to draw a deep breath to collect herself. She wasn't used to seeing her friend like this.

"What a delight to see you at our favorite meeting place," Hattie gushed. "And don't you look lovely in that shade of purple."

Wanting to look nice, True had dressed in a lavender pantsuit that she'd found at the back of her closet. She'd been saving it for a special occasion such as today. She had to look and act sharp in Hattie's presence.

"I'm thrilled to be here," True said, bending down to kiss Hattie on the cheek. "You look splendid yourself." She sat down in the velvet chair across from Hattie.

Hattie gave her the side-eye. "Don't lie to me, girl. We know each other too well for that. I look like five miles of bad road. Isn't that right? There's only so much makeup can hide."

True didn't know how to respond. The situation was breaking her heart. Hattie was such a strong woman, but dealing with a terminal illness could break the most resilient person.

Somehow True found the words. "Oh, Hattie. I wish you weren't going through this."

Hattie patted her hand. "I know. Let's have some tea and scones. That always makes everything better."

Just then Delilah came over to their table with two pots of freshly brewed tea. "I brought both your favorites. Chamomile for you, Hattie, and lavender for you, True. I'll be right back with the finger sandwiches and other treats."

True did the honors and poured tea into both of their teacups. For the next few minutes, they sipped tea and indulged in cucumber sandwiches, scones, and petits fours.

"So, my sweet girl, what did you want to discuss with me?" Hattie asked. It wasn't her nature to beat around the bush. Normally True loved how Hattie got straight to the point, but at the moment, she was a bundle of nerves.

True crossed her hands in front of her and fiddled with her thumbs. "For a long time now, I've wanted to make Northern Exposure my own." She watched as Hattie's eyes widened. "I truly love that place, and it would be such an honor to buy it from you. I know you're planning to leave some of your holdings to your grandsons, so perhaps you have another vision for the place. But I can't help but feel that no one will ever love the place as much as I do." She splayed her hands on the table. "Now I'll be honest. I don't have all the money in hand at the moment, but I'd like to work something out with you that's fair for both parties. I'm also investigating loans." Finally, she stopped talking and took a deep breath. "That's it in a nutshell."

Hattie daintily lifted her teacup to her mouth, then took a long sip before speaking. "I admire your pluck and vision. I always have, True. It's evident how much you love Northern

Exposure. To be honest, I had no idea you had these dreams, and I wish you'd told me a long time ago."

"I should have," True admitted, "but sometimes it's hard to attach words to our dreams. It's scary."

"I understand, my dear. Believe me, I do," Hattie said, nibbling on a treat. "The tricky part is that because of my illness, I'm in the process of turning my holdings over to my family members. Forgive me, but I can't get into the specific details. That being said, there may be a way you can make an offer. I'll look into it, True. You have my word." A smile lit up Hattie's face. "Red has been telling me all about your brainstorming sessions. He's very impressed by your ideas."

"He's very creative, Hattie. You must be thrilled to have him back."

"I'm excited for my grandsons now that they're all back in Moose Falls along with Red. I truly believe healing can happen if everyone works hard toward that goal." Hattie made a tutting sound. "I'm not naïve. Red has problems that have affected his ability to be a father and a husband. Those might not have gone away. But I still want him to be a part of my legacy and to give him another chance."

From the sound of it, Red's issues had not only impacted his ability to be a father to his sons and a husband. They had also altered his ability to function within the Yukon Cider empire. Red's absence from the executive ranks of the company had always puzzled True. Things were starting to make sense now.

"I won't make you wait long for an answer, True. Time is not on my side these days." Hattie's lips trembled, a slight vulnerability in her armor.

"I'm so sorry," True said. And she deeply meant it. Life without Hattie Stone would be like a carnival without rides. Moose Falls would feel lackluster without Hattie or her shimmering sparkles.

Hattie patted her hand. "Don't be sad. I'm not afraid to die, just as I've never been afraid to live. What bothers me are the lost years between me and my grandsons." A sigh slipped past her lips. "I'm never going to get that time back, and even though we're making memories now, I fear they'll never be enough to satisfy me. I want to see their children come into the world and watch as they find their soul mates." She let out a chuckle. "I want to dance at their weddings and watch them grow into the best versions of themselves."

True swallowed past the lump in her throat. Tears misted in her eyes. If she could, True would give Hattie all these moments on a silver platter.

All of a sudden, she heard the clearing of a throat. When she swung her gaze up, Xavier was standing there looking down at them. With a sprinkling of snow dotting his dark hair and jacket, he looked as handsome as ever. Along with him came the smell of sandalwood and a light citrus aroma.

"What brings you here?" Hattie asked, her hand dramatically laid against her chest.

Xavier scrunched up his forehead. "Seriously? What do you mean? You invited me."

Hattie scowled at him. "Take a seat. You're not subtle at all," she muttered.

Clearly True wasn't in on what was going on between Xavier and Hattie, but she had a hunch that it involved her. Xavier wouldn't have known Hattie was here unless she'd told him, and he didn't really look like the type of guy to frequent teahouses.

Delilah quickly came over and placed a teacup and saucer in front of Xavier. "What kind of tea would you like?"

"I'm not really the tea-drinking type," he explained, looking sheepish.

Delilah laughed. "Are you sure you're Hattie's grandson? Tea flows in her veins."

"Have some tea," Hattie barked. "It's good for the soul."

Xavier regarded his grandmother with a mixture of confusion and awe. "Okay, how about black tea?"

"Coming right up," Delilah said before walking toward the kitchen. It didn't escape True's notice that Delilah had to bite her lip to stop herself from laughing at the Xavier–Hattie show.

"So, what's the deal, Hattie? Why did you want me to come down here?" He looked over at True. "Other than the lovely company, of course."

"Likewise," True murmured, pouring more hot water into her teacup.

Xavier let out a pained sound and looked at Hattie with a horrified expression. "Ouch! Did you just kick me under the table?"

Hattie buried herself in her teacup, then stuffed a pastry in her mouth. She was avoiding all eye contact, which wasn't like her at all. Delilah walked up and placed Xavier's teapot in front of him. "Enjoy," she said in a chirpy voice before walking away.

Clearly, Hattie Stone had put her matchmaker hat on.

"If I'm not mistaken, Hattie is trying to play matchmaker between us. Isn't that right, Hattie?" True asked, shooting her friend a pointed look.

The older woman sputtered. "That's ridiculous. I—I was simply trying to let Xavier see some of the hot spots in Moose Falls. I don't meddle."

He eyed his grandmother skeptically. "News flash. I don't have any problems getting women. Matter of fact, I get lots of ladies."

His tone radiated cockiness. True folded her arms across her chest and stared him down. "Oh, really. Do tell."

"I didn't mean it like that," he said, quirking his mouth.

"So what did you mean?" True asked. He was coming off like a Casanova, and she didn't like it one bit. That was the last thing she needed in her life.

"I meant that I don't need any help in the romance department," he explained. "Not in an arrogant way or anything. Just speaking facts."

True loudly sucked her teeth. Great! She was falling for a womanizer.

Hattie looked back and forth between them. "My spies were right. There's something brewing between the two of you." She held out her arm. "I've got goose bumps. And for the record, I don't have a single objection to the two of you getting together."

True felt her cheeks flushing. The last thing she wanted was for Hattie to know True had the hots for her grandson. She hoped to be taken seriously as a businesswoman, and she didn't want Hattie's opinion of her to change.

"Spies?" Xavier asked in a raised voice. "What is this? Spy games?"

Hattie rolled her eyes. "You're being silly, Xavier. You should be happy that someone is trying to help you after your disastrous engagement to that awful woman."

*Ouch!* Hattie wasn't pulling any punches. And judging by the expression on Xavier's face, he was far from thrilled with her comment. This was classic Hattie. She could be as blunt as a sword.

"Well, tell me how you really feel," Xavier drawled. He reached for a finger sandwich and popped it in his mouth. True sensed he did so in order to stop himself from responding to his grandmother. Better to fill one's mouth with food rather than pop off to the grande dame of Moose Falls.

Hattie reached for her purse and leaned on the table for

support as she stood. "Great meeting, True. I'll call you shortly." She leaned down and kissed Xavier on his temple. "Don't be too mad at Granny. I only want the best for you."

Seconds later Jacques appeared, looping his arm through Hattie's and escorting her out of the tea shop. True could see that Hattie was leaning heavily on Jacques. Time was definitely not on her side.

"She sure knows how to make an exit," Xavier said, shaking his head. He picked up his teacup and took a tentative sip. "It's not half bad," he concluded. He then proceeded to add heaps of sugar and milk before bringing the cup once again to his lips. "Aah," he said. "Much better. So, is Hattie always like this?"

"She's a trip, if that's what you're asking," True said. "But she's got more heart and loyalty than anyone I've ever known. I hope she didn't hurt you with her comment about your ex, and I know it might sound messed up, but she's coming from a place of love."

"I'm not hurt. To tell you the truth, she's growing on me, sharp tongue and all. It's hard to fathom that we've only been reconnected for a few weeks now, 'cause it kind of feels like forever."

She let out a tightly held breath. "That's nice to hear. Hattie wants to be close to you, Caleb, and Landon. That's what this whole inheritance is about. Bringing you back home so she can spend her final days with you." A random tear slid down her face. Xavier reached out and wiped it away with his thumb.

"Hey, don't cry. It's going to be all right. Everything's good."

She sniffed back the tide of tears. "I'm not crying," she protested. "There's just something in my eye."

Xavier didn't say anything, but his gaze was intense as he stared at her.

"What?" she asked after a few moments of silence.

"I want to take you out, True. I know we're both busy, but let's make time for each other. You make Moose Falls way more interesting."

"Are you asking me on a date?" True asked, mirroring Xavier's words from the other day.

"Yes, I am, and no offense, but this time without Jaylen."

She felt a grin tugging at her lips. "I think he'll be okay with that considering he's trying to play matchmaker just as hard as Hattie. Not sure which one of them is worse."

They both looked at each other and said "Hattie" at the same time. Both of them knew she had the potential to be far worse than True's little brother. She was going to cut Hattie some slack because she wanted to see things in her world settled due to her illness.

"So when can we go out?" Xavier asked, leaning across the table. "I need some True time." He reached out and laced his fingers through hers. She couldn't remember ever holding hands with a man like this. It was warm and comforting. Reassuring.

"We're having an event at Northern Exposure on Friday night. There's going to be live music and dancing, as well as the unveiling of Yukon Cider's newest flavors. Are you up for it? I think you'd have a good time."

"Say less," he said, holding up his hand. "Since you're bringing out the new line, it's a business obligation for me to be there," he said with a wink.

"I won't be working for the whole night, so we can hang out once I'm off the clock." Suddenly she felt so awkward. He had asked for a date, but was hanging out the same thing? Man, she was out of practice. *Just relax and play it cool*, she reminded herself.

"Sounds good to me," Xavier said.

She reached for a blueberry scone and took a bite. The flavors burst on her tongue, causing her to let out a moan of appreciation.

"And bring your brothers along," she suggested. "The three of you are celebrities here in Moose Falls, in case you didn't realize it. You'll be good for business."

Xavier scoffed. "Okay, but they are not horning in on our date. I'm not sharing you."

*Whoosh.* Sometimes he said things that made her weak in the knees. She was falling for this man like a ton of bricks. And even though she had a few reservations, he was showing her that he was a good man. She couldn't judge him by his past or her own train wreck of a relationship with Garrett. So far he hadn't given her a single reason not to trust him. But there wasn't a safety net anywhere in sight!

*Lean in*, a little voice whispered. *Choose happiness. Don't let fear win.*

That's exactly what she was going to do. She was done with living in the past. It was too heavy of a burden for her to carry around. What would it feel like, she wondered, to have this weight lifted off her shoulders?

From this point forward, she was choosing joy. She was choosing Xavier.

# CHAPTER FIFTEEN

By the time Friday night rolled around, Xavier was raring to head over to Northern Exposure so he could meet up with True. Despite the gnarly weather, Alaskans went out and about conducting their business and living their lives. The heavy snow might make driving these roads a bit trickier, but Xavier had been getting a lot of practice in with Jacques. Bless his heart, he was a really cool dude with a big heart. And now that Xavier knew Jacques and Hattie were an item, he could see all the dozens of ways they showed their love for each other.

He should be so fortunate. If he could find a love like what they had, he would consider himself the luckiest man on earth.

The other day True had pointed out that Hattie's condition seemed to be worsening, and it was something he had been trying to ignore. The moments shared between them would be fleeting. No one knew what tomorrow might bring, and even though Hattie thought she might have months and months left, there were no guarantees. No matter what, he needed to make the most of the time he had left with his grandmother. There was still time to make memories.

And Hattie wasn't the only one he wanted to make memories with.

When he wasn't with True, Xavier found himself missing her. For him that was huge. He knew what it meant. His heart was on the line now. And it made his insides feel all tangled up. His emotions were all over the place. He wanted to fall in love again, yet he wasn't sure he could ever fully trust anyone. His heart had been kicked around so badly by his ex-fiancée, it felt as if he might never fully recover from the trauma. But yet he wanted to love and be loved.

Every romantic relationship in his adulthood had involved him being used for some purpose or another. Mostly it had been for financial reasons. As an NFL player, his lifestyle had been lavish, until he'd lost it all. He'd been played for such a fool that he almost didn't trust himself not to go down that road again. But it wasn't fair to True to be so jaded. She'd done nothing wrong, and he couldn't place all of his baggage on her shoulders.

Furthermore, he didn't have anything True could use him for. He was rebuilding his income from disastrous levels. If they sold their Yukon Cider holdings in a year, he would be financially sound. But, at the moment, he wasn't exactly rolling in it the way he had been during his time in the NFL.

Regardless, True wasn't like any other woman he'd ever known. There was a realness about her that resonated in every one of their interactions. She wasn't shallow or fake. If nothing else, he was beginning to learn how to spot a quality woman.

"You're on your own tonight. I've got a date with True," Xavier informed his brothers as he pulled into the parking lot of Northern Exposure. He looked around for a spot, noticing that the lot was already packed with vehicles. After a few minutes, he spotted an available spot not too far from the entrance. A large flashing sign out front advertised "Friday Fun Night." Xavier chuckled. It was kind of corny, but it seemed to be working to pull in a crowd.

Caleb rolled his eyes. "We'll be fine. I thought we'd never get here with you driving at granny speed. Did you forget where the gas pedal is?"

Xavier looked over at Caleb. "The roads are slick. I'm not trying to end up in a ditch. But next time feel free to drive, since you haven't gotten behind the wheel much since we've been here."

"I for one appreciate the fact that you're a safe driver. Did you know that fatal accidents in Alaska have decreased by twenty percent in the last few years?" Landon asked.

"Of course we didn't know that," Caleb responded as they exited the car and headed toward the tavern. "Landon, I mean this as a compliment. Your mind is a national treasure."

Landon grinned. "Thanks for saying so. What a cool compliment," Landon said, holding out his hand so his brother could high-five him.

"If you meet any ladies tonight, I wouldn't drop all that knowledge on them. Keep it light," Caleb advised. He slapped Landon on the shoulder. "Know what I'm saying?"

"I think he gets it," Xavier said, quickly seeing the crestfallen expression on Landon's face. He didn't need to be constantly reminded that he didn't have skills with women. "You pretty much hit him over the head with a sledgehammer."

"Sorry," Caleb muttered, not sounding sorry at all. "I was trying to be helpful."

"It's okay," Landon said. "I'm not like the two of you. Women don't gravitate toward me." He shrugged. "I don't have that special Stone magnetism."

"That's a load of crap!" Xavier said. "You just haven't met the one yet. That special person who's going to appreciate everything you bring to the table."

He'd heard his youngest brother described as a hot nerd by women. For some reason, Landon didn't understand his appeal. Caleb, on the other hand, reveled in his.

Caleb nodded. "What Xavier said. You're the coolest smart guy I know."

"Aww, you love me. You really love me," Landon teased, leaning against Caleb, who pushed him away.

"Personal space, bro," Caleb muttered. "I'm not the touchy-feely type."

"That's not what I heard," Landon said, causing Xavier to crack up while Caleb rolled his eyes.

Once they were inside the building, Xavier left his brothers behind and focused on locating True. The tavern was packed, which was making it difficult to spot her.

All of a sudden, he saw her, causing his heart to lurch inside his chest. She was dressed in a denim jumpsuit that hugged all her curves. He stopped in his tracks for a moment to admire her without her noticing him. She was the most stunning woman he'd ever seen, and that was saying something. His profession had put him in the orbit of countless beautiful women—but True was in a league of her own. Her beauty was matched by her personality and heart. A rare woman indeed.

"You came!" True called out as soon as she spotted him making his way through the crowd toward her. Her voice oozed excitement that couldn't be faked, and she was lit up like pure sunshine. She was just as into him as he was into her, he realized. This was the first time Xavier had gotten this type of confirmation from True. Up to this point, he was only hoping her feelings mirrored his own.

"Of course I did. I've been looking forward to tonight," he said, pulling her into a secluded corner so prying eyes couldn't see what he was about to do. He placed his hands on her back, gently pulling her toward him. The curves of her body fit perfectly against his chest, almost as if she were meant to be there.

"Hurry up and kiss me," she urged, standing on tippy-toes so she could beat him to it. Her lips tasted fruity as they pressed against his. Xavier liked the way she took control of the kiss as her tongue explored his mouth. She was holding on to his jacket for leverage.

When she broke away from the kiss, he couldn't help but feel that it was ending way too soon. He could do this all night.

True said, "I've got to take care of a few things in back, but then I'm off the clock."

"I'll keep myself entertained till then. The music sounds pretty good."

"Save me a dance. By the way, Red's here," she said, nodding in the direction of the stage. "Did you two ever talk?"

"I haven't had a chance yet," Xavier said, knowing he was bending the truth. Every time he'd picked up his phone or run into Red at the Yukon Cider office, he had chickened out. He still didn't know how to put his feelings into words. *Hey, Dad. Why did you bail on your three boys?*

True swept her hand across his cheek. "Now may not be the right time to hash everything out, but you can certainly tell him you'd like to talk."

"I guess," he said, shifting uncomfortably from one foot to the other.

"Sometimes the hardest thing to do is face down the past, but I believe in you, Xavier Stone. You've got this." She placed one last smoldering kiss on his lips before dashing away.

And with those simple words, True made him feel that he could do anything. Leap tall buildings in a single bound. Climb Mount Everest. Dunk on LeBron James. Eat all his lima beans.

If she could talk to his grandmother about wanting to buy Northern Exposure, he could talk to his father about the past.

True made her way toward the bar, winding her way through the throng of people to get to her office. She paused along the way to greet regulars. It was nice to see familiar faces as well as newcomers and tourists.

"Sophia!" she called out to her friend, surprised to see her out on the town. As a single mother of a four-year old, Sophia Brand didn't get out much. Tall and shapely with long auburn hair and almond-shaped eyes, Sophia was a former beauty queen turned photographer. She was a sweetheart and had mad skills with a camera. "It's so good to see you."

"You too," Sophia said, pulling her into a tight hug. "Patience made me come out tonight. She said I was getting too stuck in my ways."

Patience was Sophia's older sister. They had all gone through school together and been the best of friends. After the plane crash, True's life had become all about raising Jaylen and working at the tavern. Sadly, she wasn't as close to the Brand sisters as she'd once been. It hit her all at once how badly she missed them. They were both fun and supportive women.

"I think Patience is hoping to get a glimpse of the Stone brothers. Word on the street is that they're extremely easy on the eyes." Sophia's eyes twinkled with excitement. "I vaguely remember them from when they were kids."

True nodded and let out a little laugh. "I can definitely

vouch for their good looks. They're the eye candy Moose Falls desperately wanted and needed."

Sophia laughed along with her and fanned herself with her hand.

True looked around the tavern, then back at Sophia. "And if I'm not mistaken, Caleb Stone is eyeballing you at this very moment."

"Where? Can I look?" Sophia asked.

"To your left by the stage. He's wearing a light blue shirt," True said, watching as Sophia discreetly turned her head in Caleb's direction. After a few beats Sophia looked away.

"So. What do you think?" True asked, knowing Caleb's striking looks were hard to ignore.

Her friend lightly shrugged her shoulders. "He's handsome, but he just winked at me. Kind of cheesy, don't you think? And wasn't he the one from the reality show?"

Suddenly True felt protective of Xavier's brother. "Yes, he was on a reality show, but I believe those programs manipulate situations. I don't know him that well, but he seems like a solid guy."

"I'm not really looking at the moment, but I'm sure Patience will love him," Sophia said. "By the way, I love what you've done to the place," she gushed, looking around her. "It's been a while since I've been in here."

"Thanks, Sophia. It's been a labor of love." And it had been. Long hours, working her way up the ranks, and being away from Jaylen during her shifts had all taken a toll. But True's sacrifices were beginning to pay off.

"It really shows. If you ever need a photographer to take shots of the tavern, I'm your girl." Sophia was brilliant in her profession. She had won several awards for capturing Alaskan wildlife on film.

"That's a definite possibility. I'll be in touch," True said, her mind spinning with ideas for a photo shoot. "If you can, spread the word to your clients and any tourists you might come across about our events. I'd appreciate it."

"I sure will," Sophia promised.

"Well, enjoy yourself tonight. I've got to take care of a few things in back. It's so good to see you," True said, patting her old friend on the shoulder.

As she continued through the crowd, a feeling of accomplishment swept over her. Many guests had stopped in for dinner and stayed for the festivities. Every time she heard Northern Exposure being touted for its culinary fare, she considered it a triumph. Things were shifting and evolving, all for the better, despite a few hiccups.

Once she sat down at her desk, True quickly finished up her paperwork, then typed up a few notes for her online calendar. If she didn't do it now, she might forget to record these important upcoming dates. Seeing Xavier had given her a rush. He made her weak in the knees and caused her heart to flutter. She was nervous about having another date with Xavier. She'd been dateless for quite a while now, and frankly, she wasn't sure she had ever been any good at it. After the Garrett fiasco, she'd turned inward, firm in her belief that she wasn't good with relationships. They were too hard, she reasoned. Love was elusive. But now, thanks to Xavier, she was reevaluating her position.

*One man's foolishness shouldn't stop the party.* Words to live by from Hattie's mouth. Hattie-isms. The woman was a precious resource. True wished that she had a mini-size Hattie to put in her pocket so she could get pearls of wisdom whenever she needed advice. The very thought of it made her giggle.

Footsteps echoed right before Bonnie stepped into True's office. "We have one of our biggest turnouts that I can remember."

True grinned. "It's fantastic, and it shows that special events reap big rewards. I can't wait to tell Hattie." This was confirmation that Northern Exposure was still on the right track. By hosting more events, hiring live bands, and featuring new drinks and food items, they would keep customers lining up outside their doors. She made a mental note to thank Red for his suggestions and input on this event.

"You doing okay?" her friend asked. "I know today can't be easy."

"So far, so good," True lied. The seven-year anniversary of her parents' death was rocking her to the core. She had been distracting herself with this event as a way of not thinking about the tragedy. She needed to keep a stiff upper lip. Otherwise she might just fall apart. And she didn't want Xavier to see her in that light. Or for anyone else to, for that matter. She had been keeping it all in for so long that she was almost afraid to succumb to the pain.

"What's up with you? You look as if you've been crying." True couldn't ignore her friend's red-rimmed eyes. They told a story of their own. Bonnie was a happy-go-lucky person, so seeing her in this state was worrisome.

Bonnie shrugged. "Tucker and I had a fight. It was pretty bad. We both said things we shouldn't have." Bonnie's lips were quivering as if she might just burst into tears.

"Oh, no. Is it fixable?" True asked. Tucker was such a great guy, and he was devoted to Bonnie. As far as True was concerned, they were the perfect couple.

"Don't know. He asked me to marry him." Bonnie grimaced. "Can you believe that?"

True grabbed Bonnie's arm. "Oh, my goodness. That's wonderful. Why were you fighting? I figured you would be happy-dancing after a proposal."

Bonnie twisted her mouth. "Because I said no. Not now.

Not ever. I'm not the marrying kind. And he was foolish not to see that."

True's heart sank. Bonnie was allowing her past experience to cloud her vision. She had already written her story well before meeting Tucker.

"You told me not to let Garrett influence my relationships with other men. But isn't that what you're doing? Allowing the past to dictate your future?"

"True, it's complicated," Bonnie said with a huff.

"But you two love each other. Isn't that what matters most?"

Bonnie grabbed True by the shoulders and peered into her face. "Sometimes that's just not enough."

With that, she turned and left the back office, leaving True stunned. All her life she'd believed that love was enough. Despite her terrible experience with Garrett, deep down True had held on to hope that love prevailed. Wasn't that what all the romantic ballads promised? *Love will keep us together. Ain't no mountain high enough.* Love was the end game. Wasn't it?

Her friend was living proof of the power trauma could have over a person. Bonnie's turbulent past with a violent partner had made her believe she wasn't worthy of a happily-ever-after. True wasn't sure Bonnie could trust in the fact that Tucker loved and adored her. He'd put his best foot forward and proposed to her, yet Bonnie still was skeptical of their connection.

By the time True made her way back to the main floor, her head was pounding along with the beat of the live band. She didn't even need to look for Xavier. He made a beeline straight toward her. She managed a smile and grabbed him by the hand, pulling him in. "Want to dance?" she shouted over the din.

"What?" he shouted back, pointing at his ear. "It's too loud."

She decided to simply tug him by the hand toward the makeshift dance floor. The band was playing an upbeat tune that was energizing the crowd. As soon as she turned around to face Xavier, the music shifted to a slow song. Xavier gently placed his hands on her hips, and she leaned her body flush against him. True rested her head on his chest and began swaying to the music in time with his movements. He reached down and grasped her hand, interlocking their fingers. He dipped his head down and brushed his lips across her forehead. His mouth was by her ear, and she heard him singing along with the song. It was one of her favorites— "Kiss from a Rose" by Seal. Such sweetness.

Never had she felt so protected resting in a man's arms. Even though this was a heavenly sensation, her thoughts kept going back to her parents. Life would be so different if they were still living. Her world would feel so much fuller. She could have benefited from their wisdom and unconditional love. Most of the time, she was strong about the tragedy that had devastated her world, but this year was different. All she really wanted to do was curl up in a little ball and cry a bucket of tears.

She was clinging to Xavier so tightly that she wondered if he sensed he was her human life preserver at the moment. He was so resilient and solid. True wanted to absorb some of his strength so she didn't feel so fragile. She was so close to breaking.

A few minutes later, True motioned to Xavier that she didn't want to keep dancing. He frowned down at her but quickly led her off the dance floor.

When they made it to a semiprivate area Xavier ran his hand across her cheek and looked into her eyes. "You seem a bit rattled. Are you okay?"

At the moment she didn't have the strength to pretend everything was all right. She wasn't okay. Not today of all days. It felt as if her heart were sitting outside her chest, raw and exposed for all to see.

"Not really. It's been a hard day," she admitted, surprising herself by being so open with Xavier. She had been putting on a huge smile ever since waking up, and her face felt like it was on the verge of cracking.

"Want to talk about it? I'm a good listener," Xavier said, his voice soft and tender. She wasn't sure how he did it, but he made his voice sound like a caress.

A ragged sigh slipped past her lips. "It's the anniversary of my parents' plane crash. They've been gone for seven years. Sometimes it feels like just yesterday, and then at others, it seems like an eternity since I've seen them, talked to them, been held by them."

"I'm sorry. I can't imagine how bad that must feel."

"It feels like someone keeps jabbing me in the center of my heart with something sharp." She bit the inside of her cheek. "Everyone says the pain will lessen, but it just morphs into another type of pain. Not less, just different."

He was listening to her with a single-minded focus that endeared him to her. Xavier wasn't phoning it in. He truly seemed to care.

"It's funny, because Jaylen was only two years old, but he's felt the loss acutely. Even though they say kids that age don't hold on to memories, Jaylen remembers them. It's uncanny how he can recall details. How they looked. The things we did. Songs they sang."

"Love imprints itself on you."

*Bam!* His words resonated so deeply with her. That was exactly how she felt about her parents. They had been so special and loving and devoted. The brand of love they had heaped upon their children had been epic. And their lives being cut short had always seemed like a nightmare she couldn't wake up from.

She had surprised herself by telling Xavier about the devastating event that had shaped her life. The loss of her parents wasn't something she talked about. Everyone in Moose Falls knew about the tragedy already and respected her boundaries. Just reflecting on the plane crash felt traumatizing. Although she was struggling on this sad anniversary, Xavier was making the situation better simply by being with her and listening. Speaking the words out loud served as a release after holding it in for such a long time.

True took a steadying breath. A few more hours and this awful day would be done, and she wouldn't have to mark this date for another year. She just had to find a way to make it through the rest of the night.

# CHAPTER SIXTEEN

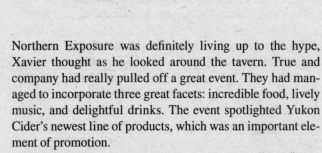

Northern Exposure was definitely living up to the hype, Xavier thought as he looked around the tavern. True and company had really pulled off a great event. They had managed to incorporate three great facets: incredible food, lively music, and delightful drinks. The event spotlighted Yukon Cider's newest line of products, which was an important element of promotion.

"I think I'm going to test out the limited edition blackberry cider," True told him, grabbing one from the server as he made the rounds with the complimentary drinks. "Hattie said the flavor was her idea and based on her childhood memories of summers in Alaska."

"I'm right there with you." He winked at her. "This is definitely work-related research."

True gingerly sipped on the hard cider, then smiled. "I like this one."

After a moment, she said, "You know what's funny? I very rarely drink, even though I manage a tavern and promote the Yukon Cider brands. But tonight I wanted to feel no pain."

"Is it working?" he asked, genuinely curious. He'd enjoyed his share of drinks in his clubbing days, but he had never done so in order to block out pain. And although True seemed to be marking this particular date, he imagined the loss resonated every day as she went about the business of living her life.

"Not really," she admitted with a shrug. "I'm still thinking about them and how unfair life is. I know it's a crappy thing to think, but why them? Why my parents? They were good people."

"It's normal to question such a tremendous loss, True. It would be strange if you didn't ask. If it makes you feel better, I used to ask why my parents had to split up."

"But you were a kid."

"Nah, this was just last year," he said, hoping the joke would land. When he saw a smile tugging at her lips before morphing into a full-fledged grin, triumph flared inside him. If only for this moment, he'd given her a sliver of joy.

"You crack me up," True said, shaking her head.

He was watching True carefully. Since he knew she wasn't a social drinker, these hard ciders might hit her like a ton of bricks even if she consumed just a few of them. He didn't want to treat her as if she weren't a fully grown and capable adult, but at the same time, she was in a vulnerable state.

Xavier loved watching her in action now that she was off the clock and the assistant manager had taken over. There was a huge difference in her demeanor when she wasn't working versus on the clock. His gaze trailed her as she flitted around the tavern, chatting up old friends and greeting people. They took another spin on the dance floor, then hung out with his brothers for a bit. True was lively and engaging, even though he knew she was hurting. When she spotted

Red, True gently pushed him in his father's direction, letting him know none too subtly that they needed to talk.

"Hey, Red," Xavier said, walking up beside him at the bar. "How's it going?"

"Hey, Xavier. I saw you earlier on the dance floor, but I didn't want to be a third wheel. The two of you look great together, by the way."

"Thanks. True would pretty much make anyone look great next to her."

"Well, you look happy. It looks good on you."

Being with True made him feel joyful. His father was right about that, but he didn't want people in Moose Falls to immediately pair them off and put pressure on them as a couple.

"We're just getting to know each other right now. Taking it slow."

"Slow is good," Red said with a nod. "Nothing wrong with taking your time."

Now came the hard part. For so long Xavier hadn't wanted anything to do with his father. He hadn't exactly been receptive to any of his overtures. But now, he needed to lay some issues to rest. True was right. He needed to get it off his chest so he could move forward.

"I wanted us to talk. Not now, of course, but sometime soon. There are things I need to ask you. Things I need to say to you."

Red's expression was open and inviting. "I'm ready whenever you want to talk, son. There's nothing you can't ask me." Their gazes met and held. Red's eyes radiated understanding. He must have known this moment was coming. After all, it had been brewing for two decades.

"I'm going to hold you to that," Xavier said. Red had just opened the door for Xavier to press him on things Xavier had always wondered about, and as a result, he was experiencing a mix of emotions. Relief. Anticipation. And pure terror about opening such a huge can of worms. His daddy issues served as an emotional hot button. It was way past time their conflicts were hashed out.

"Okay, son, go find your lady. We can talk later." Red placed his hand on Xavier's shoulder. "I think she's looking for you." Red was grinning as he looked past Xavier at a spot in the distance.

Xavier turned around, spotting True standing by his brothers. She was talking animatedly and using her hands, pausing every few moments to look in his direction. Knowing she was checking in on him caused his pulse to race. She was cutting through all the walls he had set up after Heather.

Caleb and Landon were laughing at something True had said to them. Seeing the three of them getting along and socializing warmed Xavier's insides. His brothers had a history of not liking the women in his life. Their relationship with his ex-fiancée had been a hot mess.

He walked up behind True and placed his arms around her waist. He could feel Caleb and Landon's eyes glued to his every move.

The crowd was beginning to thin out when the band made an announcement for the last song of the night. "One last whirl?" True asked, holding out her hand.

"How can I say no to that?" he asked, following her. The floor had only a few couples dancing, lending an intimate air to their slow dance. When the music started to fade out, everyone considered it a cue to leave the floor.

"So, I'm going to call an Uber. I shouldn't drive," True said to him.

Definitely a good call, considering she'd stumbled a few times on the dance floor.

"You have Ubers here?" he asked, sticking out his tongue in a teasing gesture.

"Hey, buddy. Don't act as if this is some backwoods town. Moose Falls is a tourist destination thanks to Yukon Cider." She snapped her fingers. "This is one happening Alaskan town."

"Okay, I get it," he said, holding up his hands. "Moose Falls is where it's at."

She nodded approvingly. "I hope you're falling in love."

"Uh, what?" Her comment completely knocked him off-kilter. *Falling in love?* The very thought of it made his stomach tense and his pulse quicken.

"With Moose Falls, of course." Clearly she was in a teasing mood. He let out a relieved breath. For a host of reasons, he didn't want to think about falling in love. Just being with True and allowing himself to feel romantic toward a woman was significant progress.

"It's growing on me," he said, surprising himself with the admission. Moose Falls was nestling its way into his heart, right along with his grandmother, Yukon Cider, and True. "I'm not sure that I'll ever get used to the cold, but I'm dealing with it."

"I hope you tell Hattie that," she said. "That would make her so, so, so, so happy. Am I saying *so* too much?" she asked in a loud stage whisper. Yep, she was tipsy.

Suddenly, in his mind the plan changed. He would drive True to her place so she would have her vehicle parked outside her house in the morning. He didn't want her passing out in an Uber. The car ride service was generally safe, but he didn't want True to take any chances.

"So, how about you scrap the Uber and I'll drive you home?" Xavier asked True.

"But what about my truck?" She looked totally confused.

He was thinking the hard ciders were really catching up to her. Thankfully, she had the good sense to know she couldn't get behind the wheel in her condition.

"I'll drive it, and my brothers can follow behind us and give me a ride back to Hattie's."

She grabbed his arm. "Oh, that's so nice of you. Oops, I said *so* again." True placed her hand over her mouth.

Xavier looked around the tavern. Where the hell were his brothers? They were nowhere in sight, and the crowd had thinned out considerably in the last half hour or so. Xavier figured they would be fairly easy to spot. He picked up his phone and called them. Neither one picked up. Maybe they couldn't get a signal in the area. He glanced over at True. Her eyes were starting to close. He needed to get her home where she could sleep it off.

This woman was precious to him. And he would do everything in his power to protect her. He placed his arm around her waist after helping her into her parka and grabbing her purse from her office. He made one last futile attempt to locate his brothers before realizing the vehicle they'd driven wasn't in the lot. Minutes later Xavier and True were on the road heading toward True's place. Rather than going to sleep or passing out, True became really animated and started singing at the top of her lungs.

"Girls just wanna have fun," she sang, rocking her head to the beat of Cyndi Lauper's hit song.

"Of all the songs to be playing right now," Xavier muttered. "Talk about life imitating art."

"They just wanna. They just wanna." True continued to belt out the lyrics at an eardrum-shattering volume.

True was a spectacular woman, but she wasn't a singer by any means. Every time she tried to hit a high note, it reminded him of nails on a chalkboard. He started to chuckle. It was kind of nice to know True wasn't perfect after all.

"Xavier. Stop the car!" she shouted with an urgency that sounded alarming.

"What? Why?" he sputtered. "What's wrong?" He wondered if she was going to be sick. Xavier spotted a safe spot to pull over up ahead, and he steered the truck to a shoulder.

"There's a full moon," she said, wrenching the door open and hopping outside the truck in knee-deep snow.

"True!" Xavier called out. "What are you doing?"

All he heard were howls, and they sounded more human than animal.

With a groan, Xavier jumped out of the truck and headed after True.

🌲

Morning came in with the full force of a blinding snowstorm, with thunder, lightning, and coastal flooding all combined. True slowly opened one eye, then the other. She let out a low moan. Her head was pounding. Her stomach was churning. What in the world was going on? The last thing she remembered was being at Northern Exposure. With Xavier. He had been taking care of her and sticking by her side. She had been determined to drown her sorrows in hard ciders. More flashes came back to her. Little snippets from last night. Bonnie having been proposed to. The live band. Xavier slow-dancing with her. Drinking way more than she should have. How many cranberry ciders had she consumed? She peeked under the covers to find she was only wearing a T-shirt and a pair of undies.

Sounds emanated from the kitchen, and the smell of freshly brewed coffee rose to her nostrils. It couldn't be

Jaylen. He wasn't due back from his sleepover until this afternoon. Heavy footsteps emanated from down the hall. Closer and closer they came until Xavier was standing on the threshold of her bedroom. "Good morning. Rise and shine," he said with a sparkling grin.

True let out a groan. *Kick up your heels. YOLO.* Famous last words. As a result, she found herself in an awkward situation with her boss's grandson.

Words bubbled up from her throat. "I just want to let you know I do not do this. Ever!" True tightly clutched the sheets to her chest. Panic was causing her to breathe heavily.

"What do you mean?" Xavier leaned against the door frame with a cup of steaming coffee in his hand. He was wearing the same button-down shirt he'd sported last night, except it was unbuttoned, giving her a glimpse of his incredible chest and abs. Holy smokes, he was one sexy man, which may have contributed to this entanglement.

She motioned to him, then back to herself with her hand. "This...hookup. I don't just have random...encounters with people I barely know."

Xavier covered his mouth with his hand, but True could still see a big, fat smile on his face. "We didn't."

She let out a squeak. "We didn't?" True asked as the weight of the world eased from her shoulders.

"No, we did not. I slept on the couch." He looked ridiculously hot smirking.

"Oh, thank God," True said, closing her eyes as relief swept over her.

"That was rude. In some parts I'm considered quite a catch." She swore he puffed out his chest as he said it.

She quirked her mouth. "I'm sorry if I offended you, but...not sorry. Did I undress myself?" she asked, holding her breath as she waited for his answer.

"Yes, and I'll have you know that I turned my back to give you privacy. When you were finished, I tucked you in."

True let out a relieved sigh. It would have been slightly creepy if he'd undressed her when she was tipsy.

"Now that we've gotten that out of the way, where can I place your coffee?" Xavier asked, holding it up in the air.

*Sweet.* She couldn't think of the last time someone had made her coffee. It felt nice to be taken care of, which was clearly what Xavier had done last night. She had a hazy memory of him placing a blanket over her before kissing her good night on the forehead. So much of the latter portion of the evening was fuzzy.

"Right here," True said, gesturing toward her side table. She watched as Xavier made his way over to her bed, his movements full of power and grace.

She reached for the cup and blew on the java before taking a first sip. Mmm. The coffee was amazing, brewed to perfection.

"Are you hungry? I make a mean cheddar and onion omelet."

At that exact moment, her stomach grumbled. "I am, which is surprising considering I feel like roadkill."

"That's understandable. You downed a lot of ciders, all while trying to show me which ones were the best." He tried to hide his chuckle but failed miserably. She didn't blame him, considering she'd been a woman on a mission. She had a vague recollection of him trying to slow her down without overstepping. Of course, she'd done as she pleased and kept downing hard ciders.

"I don't even really drink," True confessed. "I guess I'm a lightweight." She chuckled uneasily. "I hope I didn't make a fool out of myself."

"Don't worry. Most of your antics happened after we left the venue."

True let out a squeak. "Antics? There were antics?"

He slowly nodded. "Nothing too wild, but you did howl at the moon. You had me pull your vehicle over so you could do it. And you suggested skinny-dipping in the lake."

Yikes. They would have frozen their buns off and gotten hypothermia. Good thing one of them had been able to make good decisions.

She covered her face with her hands. "I really don't want to do a walk of shame tomorrow at work. My reputation around town is pretty spotless. Not that I should care about what other people think, but I do," she admitted, feeling sheepish. She hated that she did care about town gossip and her reputation. She wasn't a sheep or a follower. And she truly believed in living life without inhibitions. Carpe diem! On the other hand, True didn't want to lose all the hard-earned respect she had cultivated in Moose Falls.

"You're not alone in feeling that way. As a professional football player in the public eye, I spent a lot of time worrying about what everyone thought about me. To be honest, it felt overwhelming at times," he admitted.

"I can imagine," she murmured. She wanted to ask him about the fallout from his injury and the engagement that crashed and burned, but she didn't want to seem like she was prying. Maybe if their relationship continued, he would feel comfortable sharing that type of information with her.

"But don't worry, I'm the only one who witnessed your bad-girl side." Another smirk tugged at his lips.

True crossed her hands prayerfully. "Oh, thank God for small mercies."

Xavier sank onto the bed. "I know it was a hard anniversary, True. Losing your parents was a gut punch." He reached out and patted her blanket-covered leg. "It's okay that you wanted to escape reality last night. Just as long as you don't make it a habit."

"I won't. I wouldn't. Seriously, even though I run a tavern, I don't drink. That's probably why it hit me so hard." She let out the sigh she'd been holding in for the last few days. "At first I thought these anniversaries would get easier, that I would get used to not having them around. But there's still this ache inside me that never goes away. And now I'm afraid it never will."

Xavier bit down on his lower lip. "The thing is, I've never had to deal with that type of loss. That soul-sucking sort of devastation. But when my dad pretty much walked out of our lives, it was a massive heartbreak. For a long time, I pretended that I was okay with it, because if I admitted that it broke me, my brothers might not have survived the heartache. And my mom too. She was so busy trying to make a life for us as a single mom, I couldn't place my burden on her shoulders."

"But you were a little kid," True said in a soft voice. "That must've been agonizing."

"A kid who had to grow up fast." His eyes mirrored his emotions, giving True a real sense of what he'd been through.

Just thinking about a pint-size version of Xavier grappling with his father's desertion caused her to tear up. As much as Jaylen's childhood had been impacted by the tragic loss of their parents, at least he would always know that they had always been there for him.

"That's not fair. I try to make sure that despite all he's lost, Jaylen has a robust childhood."

Xavier nodded. "It wasn't all bad. I had an amazing mom. Caleb and Landon are still my best friends even when they're working my last nerves. And I ended up finding my calling at an early age with football. That was a gift."

True wanted so badly to ask him what his calling was, now that his football career was over, but she held her tongue. Something about the way he spoke about his career made her think it wasn't over. At least not for Xavier. He was still wrapped up in his identity as a football player. She sympathized with how difficult it must be for him to start over after losing it all.

"Why don't you get dressed and meet me in the kitchen?" Xavier suggested. "You're about to have the best omelet of your life."

"Promises, promises," True murmured as she watched Xavier walk out of her bedroom. She took a moment to fan herself after noting that Xavier looked just as good walking away as he did coming toward her. She stood and stretched before making her way to the bathroom for a quick shower. As the hot water washed over her, True closed her eyes and basked in the sensation. Despite the sadness of yesterday's anniversary, she felt happy. She hadn't dealt with her pain in the best way, but thankfully Xavier had stayed by her side. He was a natural protector, which was something they had in common. Her heart was opening like a flower in springtime. Although she didn't want to allow herself to hope due to her past romantic disappointment, she had a feeling that Xavier was something special.

# CHAPTER SEVENTEEN

The smell of cheese, onions, and eggs hung in the air as True walked into her kitchen. Xavier was standing by the stove with his sleeves rolled up. His arms were muscular and strong. He was humming a familiar tune as he cooked up a storm. She placed her coffee cup on the counter, then walked over toward Xavier.

"Smells good. Can I help?" True asked, peering over his shoulder to get a peek at his culinary delights.

"No, you cannot. Bring over a plate. It's all done. Breakfast is ready," Xavier said, nodding in the direction of the plates he'd placed on the table. True grabbed both plates and made a beeline to the stove. Xavier placed the omelet and hash browns on both plates. She placed them down on the table, sitting back down and waiting for Xavier to join her.

Within seconds he'd made his way over to the butcher-block table with two glasses and a bottle of orange juice. He'd thought of everything, True realized. She could get used to this.

"Whoa. That is one incredible view," Xavier said as he

looked out the bay window right next to the kitchen table. He sank into the seat across from her, but his gaze was focused on the magnificent mountains.

"That view was the main reason my folks bought this house. They couldn't believe an Alaskan mountain view could be right on their property." True cast her gaze at the view of the mountains. It truly never got old. "My mother used to say it was the perfect way to greet the day."

"I can see why they loved it." He turned toward her. "And why you stayed on here after you lost them."

"I was trying to honor the life my parents chose for us, and I didn't want to uproot my brother after such a catastrophic loss," she explained. "It proved to be the best decision. It wasn't just a house. It's always been a home. A haven for us." Just saying those words out loud choked her up. Xavier was so easy to talk to. She spilled her guts to him every time they were together. That was rare for her. She wasn't a person who easily trusted others with her closely guarded emotions.

Xavier took a pause on eating to respond. "When we went to my dad's house for dinner, I had that same feeling about our childhood home. Even though things got chaotic at times when we were kids, there was a lot of love in that house. After all these years, I still felt that love. It was in every nook and cranny."

From the sound of it, Xavier was beginning to realize that his childhood here in Moose Falls hadn't been perfect, but love had been in abundance.

For a moment they just sat and enjoyed the meal without talking. True had always known that this was the true mark of whether people were comfortable in each other's presence. One didn't need to fill the silence with words.

"This omelet is the best I've ever had," True said, placing

another forkful in her mouth. The cheese and the onions were blended perfectly, she realized. And there was a slight tangy taste. Dijon mustard?

"My mom taught me how to make an omelet when I was twelve. As a result, I became a short-order cook for my brothers," he said, chuckling. "All they wanted to do that summer was eat omelets."

She loved hearing stories about Xavier's childhood and growing up with his brothers. Their being so close was clearly rooted in their childhood. One day she hoped to meet the incredible woman who had raised them into such fine men.

True looked down at her empty plate. She hadn't left a single morsel. "Thank your mama for me. She taught you how to make a slamming omelet."

"She would be pleased to hear that, although she would grill me about you." He let out a laugh. "My mom is the inquisitive type, especially when it comes to her sons."

"Will she be making an appearance in Moose Falls?" True was filled with curiosity about Mama Stone, the woman who'd raised three magnificent men and been married to Red. True would bet her last dollar the woman was incredible.

He made a face. "I'm not sure about that. She never came back to Moose Falls. Not even once." He grabbed his glass and gulped his orange juice.

"Well, from what you've said, it wasn't the most pleasant parting. I'm guessing she's reluctant to face all those memories."

"That's for sure," Xavier said, his face contemplative. "I'm not sure she's ever gotten over the divorce, and that makes me sad for her. I'd love for her to find someone to walk through life with, now that she's finished raising us."

"I'm sorry. I'm glad she has the three of you." True imagined that Xavier, Caleb, and Landon were their mom's entire world. Having them away in Alaska had to be difficult.

Xavier glanced at his watch. "Okay, I should scoot before Jaylen comes home. Practice is at four."

Even though nothing had happened between them, True preferred that her little brother not create any scenarios in his mind about Xavier spending the night. That way he wouldn't slip up at school or practice by talking out of turn about her love life.

"I appreciate that," she said. "Can you get a ride? I'd drop you off, but I want to be here when Jaylen gets home. I'm not sure he remembered his house key."

"No worries. I just texted for an Uber." He winked at her. "This ain't no backwoods town. Remember?"

She vaguely recalled saying that line last night. It was surprising how comfortable Xavier made her feel about last night's goings-on. She had acted the fool by drinking too much, but he seemed to understand the level of pain she'd been in. She'd learned how futile it was to try to dull pain with alcohol. With each and every day, Xavier amazed her more and more with his compassion and integrity.

As she waved to him from the doorway as he stepped into his Uber ride, she reflected on how much her attitude had changed regarding this wonderful man. He had gone from being an unwelcome interloper in Moose Falls to someone who had nestled his way into her heart. And although the idea of falling in love with him should have terrified her, all she was feeling was excitement at the possibilities stretched out before her.

Xavier couldn't stop thinking about last night. Seeing True in such a vulnerable state had only served to strengthen his feelings for her. She had shown him a wide range of emotions—grief, tenderness, humor, gentleness. Once she had fallen asleep, Xavier had placed the covers on her and tucked her in before flipping the lights off and leaving the room. She was lightly snoring and cuddled up on her side. She looked so peaceful and content. Beautiful. He had closed the door behind him and grabbed a blanket so he could bunk on the couch.

In a perfect world, Xavier would be spending a leisurely day with True, but having made the commitment to coach Jaylen's still unnamed team, he was determined to fulfill his promise. As soon as Xavier spotted Jaylen at practice, he casually looked around for True, hoping she had tagged along with her brother. Although a few parents sat in the stands, True wasn't one of them. He hoped she was doing something relaxing after the emotional upheaval of last evening. A bubble bath. A mani-pedi. He needed to find a local florist and order her a spectacular bouquet.

After all the kids trailed in—minus a couple who'd dropped out after a few intense practices—Xavier and Lisa called the team over to get started.

"So, ladies and gents, we've got a surprise for you, courtesy of Yukon Cider." Lisa held up a black-and-red water flask. "Pretty snazzy, huh?" She flipped the flask around, showcasing the fact that their individual names were emblazoned on the back. Every player had one with their name on it. The group immediately let out a roar.

"Let's take a moment to thank Coach Stone for putting this in motion," Lisa said, clapping enthusiastically. "He's the GOAT!"

Before he knew what was happening, the kids began to

swarm around him, giving him hugs and offering profuse thanks. They began chanting, "GOAT."

This, he thought, was worth every moment of the time he was investing in this team. These children were amazing. They weren't angels by any means, but they had so much heart and soul. They were showering him with gratitude, and it was a little bit overwhelming. When was the last time he'd experienced this type of gratitude? He honestly couldn't remember.

Kids had the purest hearts, and they didn't hesitate to show their love. Just being around them lifted him to the stratosphere.

"Okay, okay. I get the message, and it's appreciated." He clapped once. "Let's get down to business. We need to find a team name and vote on it so everyone has a say. Team names are important."

"Very important," Lisa chimed in. "It'll be our identity. For instance, if we call ourselves the Turtles, folks are going to assume we're pretty slow."

The kids must have found the comment hilarious, because giggles broke out among the team.

"What about the Wolverines?" suggested Alicia. With her sandy-brown hair and blue eyes, the little girl was her mom's mini me.

"That's cool," Jaylen said. He lifted his hands and let out a howl. Several of the kids followed suit and let out howls.

"The Mavericks."

"The Mighty Moose."

"Pride of Alaska."

"Yukon's Finest."

The names were being thrown out fast and furiously. Lisa was jotting them down on a pad of paper. Once all the names had been tossed out, Xavier handed everyone a piece of paper and a pencil. When Lisa collected the papers a few minutes later, they added up all the votes.

"We've got a winner," Lisa announced. The kids were watching them with anticipation in their eyes. "Coach Stone, why don't you do the honors?"

Xavier raised the pad of paper in the air and said, "The winning name is...the Mavericks." He turned the notebook around so the team could see *Mavericks* written out in bold ink. Some of the kids started jumping up and down, hollering and hooting. A few kids seemed crushed that their name hadn't been chosen. Xavier took a moment to check on those kids and lift their spirits. After the team name decision and celebration, Xavier lined them up for drills—blocking, tackling, catching and throwing passes, handing off the ball.

Everything seemed to be going seamlessly until all of a sudden, right before his eyes, a scuffle broke out between the members of his team. "Hey," Xavier called out as he rushed toward the dustup. Lisa was right on his heels, ready to step in. With their names on the jerseys, it was easy to identify the culprits.

To his surprise, one of the boys was Jaylen. Xavier pulled him by his jersey while Lisa did the same with Tai, the other kid involved in the fracas. Tai was one of Jaylen's closest friends, so it was perplexing to see them throwing hands at each other.

"He started it," Tai shouted, pointing at Jaylen.

"Did not!" Jaylen shouted back. He folded his arms across his chest and glared at Tai.

"Did too. You were the one who got physical!" Tai yelled back.

"Well, you ran your mouth," Jaylen said, shouting even louder.

"Enough! You two need to be separated. Come with me, Tai," Lisa instructed, leading him to the other side of the gymnasium. Xavier pulled Jaylen off to the side.

"Hey, what's going on? This is about football, not fighting," Xavier said, frowning down at Jaylen. This seemed completely out of character for him.

"He said something about True!" Jaylen put his head down. "I couldn't not do anything about it."

"Really? What did he say?" Xavier knew enough about Jaylen to realize he wasn't a kid who started brawls. He was respectful and kind, a rule follower. And, according to True, he had a mighty high IQ.

"He said she was hot," Jaylen mumbled. Xavier had to lean in to hear him properly.

Tai hadn't told any lies as far as Xavier was concerned, but Xavier knew most kids didn't want to hear that kind of stuff about their sister.

"That's definitely not cool. He crossed a line. Sisters are off-limits."

"Right? He should have kept True's name out of his mouth," Jaylen said, swinging his gaze up to look at Xavier. "So you understand why I socked him?"

*Don't laugh*, he urged himself. He needed to be the adult here and not revert to his childhood self. Jaylen needed to understand that he couldn't solve any problems in this world with his fists.

"No, I do not," Xavier said in a firm voice. "You crossed a line as well. We don't put our hands on folks. You two are friends and teammates."

As much as he'd once wanted to deck his teammate Chazz after rumors surfaced about him and Heather, Xavier had resisted the urge. Cooler heads had prevailed. To this day he wondered if he should have punched him.

Jaylen stuck his lip out. "I thought he was my friend. Until today."

"I think you should give him a chance to apologize. He made a mistake. Trust me, Jaylen. You're going to make mistakes in your life. If you're lucky, you'll be forgiven."

"What if he doesn't apologize?"

"Well, he'll still be your teammate, and you two have to find a way to practice together. But I think you two can work things out." Xavier patted Jaylen on the shoulder. "You've got this!"

Xavier brought Jaylen back toward the group. Tai came back as well with Lisa by his side. Jaylen and Tai tentatively began moving toward each other. As Xavier watched, they shook hands and exchanged a few words. Xavier let out the breath he'd been holding. There was no place on teams for hostility or grudges. He knew that from personal experience.

Being teammates was sacred. Or so he'd always thought. Bitterness slid through him, cutting him like a knife. He had worked so hard to stuff those dark memories down. Betrayal was a hard thing to forget...or forgive. His had been on a massive scale, and it had involved his teammate and the love of his life. Xavier had believed he was finally working his way through the situation until this very moment when it all came back to him again.

Could a person ever get over such a devastating betrayal? Would he ever move past losing his career, his financial stability, and the woman who had promised him forever? Unlike what he had just told Jaylen, sometimes a person couldn't just work things out. Of course, his situation was much more intense than the squabble between Tai and Jaylen, but he still felt like a hypocrite.

At the end of practice, he spotted True as she waited with the parents to pick up their kids. He waved at her from a distance and watched as Jaylen ran over to her side. True seemed to be waiting for Xavier to head over, but he stopped himself. As the coach he needed to keep a discreet distance from True so the other kids didn't think he was biased toward Jaylen. He was also in his head about the past, and he needed time to shake it off.

He stayed in the gym until every kid was accompanied by a parent or guardian. On the drive back to Hattie's place, he put the radio on blast and allowed himself to decompress. He pushed the past down into the black hole where it belonged. Coming home to Moose Falls had been the first step in a new chapter in his life, one he was determined to make into a success. Although meeting True had been serendipity, he couldn't allow himself to forget that being here was a means to an end. He'd never envisioned settling down here, no matter how much he was enjoying his time in Alaska.

He still had things he needed to accomplish in Arizona. He wanted to show the haters that he still had potential. If he focused really hard, there was still a chance he could get his old life back.

Xavier Stone wasn't a washed-up football player. Not by a long shot!

# CHAPTER EIGHTEEN

True couldn't shake the feeling that Xavier had been avoiding her after Jaylen's practice. He had waved at her from a distance, which was nice, but she had expected him to come over to her. They had grown much closer over the past week, confiding in each other about their romantic disappointments and their families. She had been so wrong about the man, it was ridiculous. He had been through heartaches and trauma just like her. It taught her a huge lesson about judging people simply by what you thought you knew about them.

Maybe Xavier was playing it cool. He could potentially raise eyebrows among the parent set if he paid her too much attention. That wouldn't be fair to Jaylen or the rest of the kids. She let out a sigh. Now, all of a sudden, she was wondering if his coaching Jaylen's team had been a good idea. She didn't want to have to hide their relationship from everyone.

Who was she kidding? In a town this size, she was sure most folks had caught wind of their dating situation.

Her phone pinged. A smile twitched at her lips when she saw it was from Xavier.

I'm baking cupcakes for Hattie's birthday. Wanna come over?

She waited a few minutes before responding.

What flavor?

Chocolate.

And the frosting?

White cream frosting and sprinkles.

Score. I'll be there as soon as my shift ends.

Yay. A simple text and an invitation from Xavier made her want to happy-dance, serving as further proof that she was falling in love with him. All thoughts of Garrett were fading away to the point where it felt like he'd been a part of another life. Had she really been in love with him? Sobbed over him? It truly was a thing of the past.

Life was showing her the things that truly mattered the most. Sometimes it seemed as if she was seeing everything with heightened clarity and not through a filmy haze.

True loved being at Northern Exposure. She loved the sights and the sounds and the chatter. She loved the smell of down-home Alaskan cooking emanating from the kitchen. She loved her co-workers and the customers. Honestly, there wasn't a single aspect of being a tavern manager that she didn't like. But now, at this very moment, all she wanted to do was head over to Hattie's house so she could bake cupcakes with Xavier.

Within the hour she was at Hattie's door after leaving Northern Exposure and making a quick stop to pick up

Godiva chocolates as a birthday gift for Hattie. When True rang the doorbell, Jacques let her in the house. He helped her with her coat, then stood by as she took off her boots and placed them on the mat. "Xavier is waiting for you in the kitchen," he announced with a smile.

"Where's the birthday girl?" she asked, looking around the foyer for a sighting of Hattie.

"Paul took her to the ceramic shop so she could paint a pot for her birthday."

She frowned. "Paul?"

"Sorry, Red," Jacques said with a shake of his head. "I seem to be the only one who still calls him by his birth name."

"You've known him a long time," True surmised. Jacques and Hattie had been besties for decades, and according to town gossip, they were now more than friends.

"Since the day he was born. I'm hoping he and his sons can reconcile. Honestly, that's what Hattie desires more than anything else."

She could hear the sincerity ringing out in Jacques's voice. "That would be such a blessing for the whole family," True said.

"I truly believe it can happen," he said, beaming. "Now wouldn't that be something?"

*Yes, it would*, she thought. The Stone family deserved closure.

When True entered the kitchen, Xavier and his brothers were standing by a large kitchen island surrounded by bowls, spoons, and a mixer. The smell of chocolate wafted in the air.

They were all wearing aprons and covered in flour and chocolate. Xavier had a white smudge on his nose that made him look a little bit ridiculous.

"Reinforcements!" Caleb shouted as he spotted her. "I'm

tagging out," he said, ripping off his apron and tossing it on the counter. "Thanks, True," he said as he left the kitchen.

Landon dipped his finger in the bowl and raised it to his mouth, licking it.

Xavier let out a groan. "Come on! We're baking here. Keep your fingers out of the batter."

"I'm out too," Landon said, smirking. "I'm the worst baker in the family." He took off his apron and handed it to True. "Have fun!"

"Is it something I said?" True cracked as it became just her and Xavier in the kitchen.

Xavier walked toward her with a grin on his face. He took the apron from her and tied it around her waist, leaning in close as he did so. He tipped his head down and brushed a kiss against her lips.

"Mmm," she murmured against his lips. "You taste like chocolate."

"I snuck a taste when Caleb and Landon weren't looking."

She reached up and wiped the smudge off his nose. "Let's go make these cupcakes before your grandmother comes back."

"That's what I'm talking about," he said, clapping once.

True made her way over to the counter and surveyed the cupcake operation. She wouldn't be exaggerating to describe it as a hot mess. Batter was on the counter, along with a white powder resembling flour. Sticks of butter were melting. And there wasn't a single baked cupcake in sight.

"I see why you needed help," she said, chuckling. It felt kind of nice that she was the one he'd reached out to for it.

Xavier held up his hands. "Not my fault. My brothers held me back. They were goofing around and not focusing on the task at hand."

"Well, let's get some in the oven before Hattie returns."

True took the cupcake liners and began placing them in the baking tin. Xavier took the hand mixer and began to work the batter until it was completely smooth. True looked toward the oven as it pinged, indicating the temperature was set for baking.

Together, they spooned the batter into the liners, and then Xavier opened the stove and placed the cupcakes inside. True held out the whisk and asked, "Want to share?"

"I'll never say no to cake batter," Xavier said, quickly closing the space between them. He leaned in and licked the whisk, his tongue darting in and out. *Have mercy*, True thought as she watched him.

She had never considered licking batter a sexy act, but Xavier was changing her mind. Was it getting hot in here? she wondered as her cheeks heated. Xavier was making her feel a little weak in the knees.

"Your turn," he said, handing it back to her. True, aware of Xavier's intense gaze, made quick work of licking the whisk clean. Xavier took it from her, their fingers brushing in the process. She felt a jolt at the skin-to-skin contact. Xavier's eyes widened. Clearly he was feeling it too.

"Can I get you some tea? Lemonade?" Xavier asked.

"I'd love a lemonade," she said, sitting down on a kitchen stool. Seconds later Xavier was pouring them each a tall glass of lemonade. She took a sip, relishing the tart taste of the drink.

"So now I know you like lemonade," he said. "That look on your face gave you away," he said with a laugh. "Just curious: What do you know about me?"

"I know that you were engaged," True blurted out. She let out a shaky laugh. "Sorry. I Googled you."

He frowned. "Seriously? Did you go online and check my background?"

She shrugged. "Honestly, I just wanted to know more about the grandsons Hattie was giving the keys to the kingdom to." Now it all seemed so silly. She was slightly embarrassed about it and wishing she hadn't gone down that road.

"Yes, I was engaged. We broke up. But I guess you saw that online too," he said, his tone slightly sharp.

True's heart sank. "You sound upset."

"Just surprised," he said with a shrug. "I would have told you myself if you'd asked. It's part of my past, though, not my present. There's way more to me than my bio and the things that went public about my engagement to Heather."

Now she felt horrible. Maybe she should have just kept her mouth shut. Curiosity had gotten the better of her, and she'd gone down a Google search rabbit hole.

"This was before you came to town, Xavier," she explained, hoping that this fact made him feel better. "I was curious about the Stone brothers. Can you blame me? You're going to be running the tavern in all likelihood, aren't you?"

He held up his hands. "Hattie hasn't made her plans public, so it's not something she wants us to discuss."

"Sorry for snooping," she said, feeling the need to apologize.

"It's okay. I get the need to check me out. But now you have to tell me something about your love life so we're even."

"That's fair. But you haven't really told me anything." She shrugged. "I just read some articles."

Xavier quirked his mouth. "Her name is Heather. She's a model. I loved her, and she said that she loved me." A vein jumped around on his forehead. "Until my life and career fell apart. Bottom line is, she was running around behind my back with my teammate, a dude I thought was my friend. She never wanted me. Heather craved the limelight and a football player husband."

"She's an idiot," True told him. "There, I said it. I'm sorry you had to go through that when you were already mourning the loss of your career."

"Thanks. It wasn't the best year of my life, I can tell you that."

"You really loved her. I can tell." His eyes and his voice said it all.

"I did."

"My version of Heather was Garrett. My ex. He ghosted me in the middle of our relationship." She ducked her head. "It's mortifying to admit, but I thought we were in love until he disappeared on me with no explanation. Nothing. Then he randomly popped up with another woman as if we hadn't even been dating for a year."

"He sounds like a narcissist," Xavier said matter-of-factly. "You're better off without him."

She raised her forefinger in the air. "Facts," she said. "For a while I wondered what I'd done to warrant a disappearing act, but now I know it was definitely him and not me."

"Because if it had been you—and I do not think for a minute it was—why wouldn't he act like a normal human and tell you face-to-face? That should show you he has mad issues that have absolutely nothing to do with you."

"And your ex? Cheating with your friend? That's a low blow."

"Right?" he asked. "At least step out on me with some-one who's not sporting the same NFL jersey."

Just then the buzzer dinged, and Xavier got up and moved over to the stove so he could check on the cupcakes. "They look done," he said, reaching for the oven mitts.

"Aww, we're cooking with gas now," True exclaimed as Xavier pulled the first batch out. All of the twelve cupcakes looked perfect and emitted a heavenly aroma that made her mouth water.

"Just in time," Xavier said as voices emanated toward the kitchen.

"Let me go head her off at the pass so your surprise isn't ruined," True said. "I'll keep her occupied."

Xavier winked at her. "Much appreciated. Hattie deserves a sweet surprise. I'm finding out that she has a heart as big as the state of Alaska."

True couldn't help but notice the way Xavier glowed as he talked about Hattie. Whether he realized it or not, he had love for Hattie in his heart. Seeing that love radiating from her grandson would be the perfect birthday gift for Hattie.

"This is a grand birthday," Hattie pronounced from the head of the mahogany dining room table. With presents, flowers, a sushi dinner, and cupcakes for dessert, they had put on quite a shindig for Hattie. She deserved each and every kindness bestowed on her.

"Make a wish!" Landon called out as Hattie blew out her candle.

Everyone clapped as the flame went out. "I have nothing else to wish for," Hattie said, her eyes misting over. "I have everything in the world a woman could ask for, especially now that my boys are back."

Xavier put his arms around his grandmother and kissed her on the cheek. Seeing her so happy meant everything to him. It was astounding how much he cared about her—this woman who'd been nothing more than a memory for almost twenty years. Over the past weeks, they had grown close to the point where he couldn't imagine his life without her in it. Just looking around the room made him happy. True had stayed for the festivities, and she fit in seamlessly with his family. Hattie adored her while his brothers hung on her every word.

Caleb even pulled out his saxophone and began playing jazzy tunes like a professional musician.

"My talented grandson," Hattie exclaimed, clapping after he finished his songs.

Caleb grinned and bowed. He really enjoyed performing. Xavier knew there was a part of his brother that still sought out the accolades and the spotlight. Xavier didn't think that particular desire had been snuffed out. Or ever would be.

Shortly after Caleb put away his saxophone, Xavier found a moment to sit quietly with Hattie. In all likelihood, this would be the last birthday she celebrated. Just acknowledging that fact rocked him to his core. The loss of his grandmother was going to hit like a land mine.

"Thank you for all this," Hattie said, smiling as she looked around the room at the balloons and celebratory banners.

Xavier had that feeling humming around in his chest, the one he always had when he'd done something good for somebody. "It's well deserved, Grandmother," he told her.

Hattie let out a gasp. "That's the first time you've called me that since you've come back to Moose Falls."

Xavier nodded. "It is. I had to warm up to it. Hope that's okay."

"It's more than okay. That's the best birthday present you could ever give me." She held his hand, but her grip wasn't her usual tight squeeze. She looked tired. Hattie hated people asking her all the time about her health, so he usually didn't inquire. But, at the moment, it was a question he couldn't avoid.

"How are you feeling?" he asked, looking into her eyes for an honest answer.

Hattie sat up tall. "Right as rain. Why? Don't I look good?" she asked, batting her eyelashes.

"You always look beautiful, but your color is a bit pale. How about a glass of water?"

She raised a hand to her throat. "I'd like that. It is a bit warm in here." She fanned herself. Just as he stood to get the glass of water, Hattie began to sway in her chair.

"Hattie!" he called out, catching her before she could slump to the floor.

The next half hour passed in a chaotic blur. He shouted for someone to call 911 while he tried to revive her. Hattie came to after a few minutes, but she was clearly in distress.

Everything happened fast, with Red insisting that Xavier ride with Hattie in the ambulance. His father's face was strained and full of fear. Xavier agreed, with Jacques, True, and his brothers all promising to meet him at the hospital.

On the way to the hospital, Xavier held tightly to his grandmother's hand and spoke to her in a soothing voice. She murmured a few words to him, but she appeared disoriented. Hattie looked pale and weak.

The ride in the back of the ambulance was terrifying for Xavier. For the first time, it truly hit him that they were losing her. Maybe not today or tomorrow, but her life was ebbing away. Months. Weeks. Not even Hattie's doctors knew for sure.

When they arrived, Hattie was whisked away to an examination area where he couldn't accompany her. Instead, he was led to a family members' waiting room where he paced back and forth, filled with nervousness and a heavy weight on his chest. Hattie had to make it through this. He wasn't ready to lose her, especially since they had just reunited.

Ten minutes later True rushed in, her cheeks tearstained, her hair windswept. She raced toward him, her expression frantic.

"Your brothers and Jacques are right behind me," she said. "Red too, I think."

He pulled her into his arms and hugged her tightly. True was exactly what he needed in this moment of uncertainty. She was giving him strength just by being here. When he finally let her go, she asked him, "What's going on? How is she?"

"They took her in the back and said they'll come out to give an update as soon as they can," he explained.

True's face crumpled, and she let out a moan. "She looked so still at first, as if she wasn't breathing. I'm so worried, Xavier." Tears began to stream down her face.

"Everything's going to be all right." He placed his arm around her shoulders and drew her close to his side. With True being so upset, it gave Xavier something to focus on other than Hattie's condition. He wasn't the only one who adored his grandmother. True's connection with her was deep and meaningful.

"How do you know that?" she asked, wiping away tears from her cheeks. "I want so badly to believe she's going to pull through, but life doesn't always work out the way we want it to." Xavier understood her fears. She'd lost so much in her life. More than most people, True knew that sometimes life went haywire and bad things happened. And she had no control over it. Xavier knew a little about that as well.

"I don't know for certain," he admitted. "I'm sorry. People used to say that to me all the time after my injury, and I hated it."

"Because everything wasn't all right?" she asked, peeping up at him from under wet lashes.

"Not by a long shot," he said. "But mostly I hated it because they had no clue if everything would work out, but they kept telling me it would."

True let out a snort. "Some comfort you are!"

He laced his fingers through hers. "I'm right here with you, True. So whatever you need, just tell me. I know Hattie's my grandmother, but she's the closest thing to a mother you have. I understand how this must feel."

"Xavier, I'm scared of losing her. Just the thought of losing someone close to me is unbearable. And I know she's terminally ill, but this is all happening so fast. I'm not ready to say goodbye."

"I know this is triggering for you because of your parents," he said. "You're frightened. And that's okay. It's just a measurement of how much you love her." He leaned over and pressed a kiss on her temple. "She's an easy woman to love." He was wearing his heart on his sleeve right now about his grandmother.

True leaned her head on his shoulder. "She really is."

All of a sudden, Caleb, Landon, and Jacques appeared in the waiting room. Xavier looked past them to see if Red was on their heels, but he was nowhere in sight. Apparently, they had gotten a little turned around on the way with the directions due to Jacques being a nervous wreck. Between Xavier and True, they caught everyone up to speed on the situation. Everyone had their role in supporting one another. Jacques buoyed their spirits by telling amusing Hattie stories while Caleb ran to get coffee for everyone. Landon spouted facts about Alaska's moose population and how it was the official state animal.

Xavier pulled Caleb aside. "Where's Red?" he asked. He had almost slipped and used the D word.

Caleb scrunched up his face. "He wouldn't come with us. It was strange," Caleb said, scratching his jaw. "He said that hospitals make him uncomfortable." He shook his head, looking disgusted. "Jacques tried to convince him to come, telling him that we would all be together, but nothing would sway him."

Xavier let out the breath he'd been holding. What would they tell Hattie when they went back to check on her? That her own son couldn't gather the strength to see her?

Red was proving once again that he couldn't be counted on. *Fool me once, twice, a hundred times.* Xavier wasn't going to open his emotional vault to a man who always ran away at the first sign of trouble or human frailty. Wasn't that what his mother had said? That every time she had needed him as a husband or a father, Red had left her in the lurch.

Xavier wasn't interested in being played for a fool, not by anyone in this world, especially his father.

# CHAPTER NINETEEN

True stood right by Hattie's family as Dr. Akash came to the waiting room and updated them on Hattie's condition. At this point, she was one of the Stones, united in their concern for their matriarch. She couldn't have felt closer to Hattie if she were her own flesh and blood. All that mattered was Hattie's well-being.

"Hattie is stable at the moment," Dr. Akash announced. "We gave her some IV fluids, and we'd like her to stay overnight for observation."

Everyone collectively let out a sigh of relief. Hattie was going to make it.

"Was it her blood sugar again?" Jacques asked. The poor man looked distraught, but he was trying to hold it together by supporting everyone else. Red, on the other hand, was nowhere to be seen.

"No, it wasn't a blood sugar issue. It's important to understand that at this stage in her illness, her body doesn't have the strength it used to," the doctor explained. "I don't want to sound indelicate, but her body is giving out."

"So, did you give her any instructions post discharge?" True asked.

He winked at her. "I know better than to tell Hattie how to live her life. I'll do whatever I can to extend her life as long as possible and keep her pain-free, but she is terminal, and I can't change that."

When they made their way to Hattie's room, she was sitting up in the hospital bed looking alert and irritated. "I want to go home! I've got a meeting in the morning with a new distributor. Jacques, help me up!"

"Hattie, I can't do that. You need to stay put," Jacques said, gently pushing her back down on the bed. Hattie tried to get up, but the slight pressure Jacques was exerting kept her in place. True imagined she didn't have the strength to put up much of a fight. Although she looked better at the moment, Hattie still appeared to be in a weakened state.

"Where's Red? He'll take me home," Hattie said defiantly. True exchanged a glance with Xavier, who didn't seem pleased with his father's disappearing act. A vein was jumping around above his eye. This couldn't be good for his strained relationship with his father.

Everyone seemed at a loss as to how to deal with Hattie. They watched as Jacques inhaled a deep breath and stood up straight, his shoulders erect. "Hattie Stone. You need to listen up and listen good." His voice bristled with authority. "Everyone in this room loves you. And that includes me. You scared us to death back there at the house." He reached out and gripped her hand. "We want the very best for you. Always. What you're going through is unimaginable, but we're trying to support you the best way we can, so knock off the foolishness."

Hattie was gazing at him with wide, shocked eyes. True's jaw dropped. Jacques had always been so genteel and mild mannered, always agreeable and catering to Hattie's wishes.

True imagined this was the first time he had ever told her how things were going to be.

"Sometimes life tells us to be still. This is one of those times," Jacques said in a decisive tone that brooked no disagreement.

Hattie sputtered. "Some birthday this turned out be!" She sank back into the hospital bed and stuck her lip out.

"I'm going to ask them to bring in a cot so I can stay with you," Jacques said, raising Hattie's hand to his lips before placing a kiss on it. Hattie looked like she might swoon. They really were adorable.

"Oh, Jacques, that's awfully sweet of you," Hattie said in a syrupy-sweet voice. "Give me some sugar."

Jacques leaned in and placed a kiss on Hattie's lips. True wasn't sure if she had ever seen anything so adorable in her whole life. True stepped back to give the couple some privacy and motioned for the Stone brothers to do the same.

"Crisis averted," Xavier murmured. He wiped his hand across his forehead in a gesture of relief.

"Who knew Jacques had it in him to take on Hattie?" Caleb asked. "He's a boss."

"Love can move mountains," Landon said, earning him a chorus of groans. He grinned at them, clearly proud of himself.

True looked at the clock hanging on the wall. "Yikes. I've got to scoot to pick up Jaylen at Tai's house."

"On that note we're going to head out," Xavier said. He grabbed True's hand and held it as they said their goodbyes to Hattie and left the room. True couldn't remember the last time she'd held hands with someone. It was highly underrated and a seriously romantic gesture. She noticed the way Hattie, Jacques, Caleb, and Landon looked in their direction with huge smiles on their faces. To True, it felt like they were giving them a stamp of approval.

Once they were in the corridor, Xavier pulled her toward him so they were facing each other. "Can I tag along with you?"

"Sure, but we're not doing anything exciting other than dinner, homework, and some TV time before bed. Kind of boring."

He placed a kiss on her forehead. "Nothing is boring when I'm with you," he said, flashing her a pearly smile.

"Aww, that's so corny, but I love the sentiment." She pulled him down toward her and planted a kiss on his lips. Her lips didn't linger long since they were in a hospital hallway with people milling about, but she gave it plenty of sizzle.

"Let's go," she said as the kiss ended, and they linked their hands as they walked toward the exit.

At moments like this, she felt coupled up with Xavier, although neither one of them had said anything to make it official. When had anything in her life ever been so right? So seamless? At times it seemed as if she'd known this man for a lifetime.

True was falling hard for him. She had avoided thinking about her feelings toward Xavier and what they meant. Love had never been good to her in the past. She had always fallen flat on her face in relationships after giving her all to someone.

But what if this time was different? Xavier wasn't anything like the others. He was honest and sensitive, and he had been through his own romantic drama with his ex-fiancée. He had come to Moose Falls to carry on Hattie's legacy. Although she had never asked him directly, she assumed he would stay in Alaska to run the company after Hattie's death. She didn't know exactly what kind of agreement he and his brothers had made with Hattie. Honestly, it wasn't her business. But she knew that if he ended up leaving Moose Falls, her heart might never recover, because it now belonged to him.

Three days had passed, with Hattie now out of the hospital and making noises about getting back to work. Xavier, Caleb, and Landon agreed to pitch in to do extra work in order to lighten her load. Rest was what their grandmother needed even if she resisted being away from Yukon Cider for a little bit. *Maybe she could take up knitting*, he thought, chuckling to himself. She might throw something at him if he suggested it.

During his lunch break, Xavier ducked out of work to buy his grandmother some flowers at a local florist shop. He left with a large bouquet of forget-me-nots. Although Hattie put up a strong front, she was a mushy marshmallow on the inside. The flowers would make her smile and forget about being cooped up.

When he arrived at the house, Xavier stopped short when he caught sight of Red pacing back and forth in the foyer. At the sound of his approaching footsteps, his father whirled around, his expression sheepish.

"Xavier," he said in a clipped tone. Xavier could see the guilt etched on Red's face. At least he had the decency to feel bad about bailing on Hattie. Being MIA for days and not answering your cell phone was toxic behavior.

"Where have you been?" Xavier wasn't bothering with pleasantries. Honestly, Red didn't deserve them. Xavier reminded himself to breathe. Just the sight of his father raised his blood pressure. To be standing here in Hattie's house after leaving her in the lurch during a medical crisis was mind-blowing.

"I know that I should have been at the hospital," Red said in a halting tone.

"It's been days now. You haven't even checked on her. She could have died," Xavier said in a trembling voice that showcased his own fears. Hattie's condition had appeared perilous. Red had been right here in the house when she had fallen ill, so he'd seen how dire a situation it was. There wasn't a single excuse he could make to justify his actions.

"I checked in with Jacques. He got me up to speed on Hattie's condition," Red said feebly. He was looking all over the place, anywhere but directly at Xavier. "I know that's not the same as being there with her."

"Why can't you look at me?" he asked in a raised voice. "The last time we talked at Northern Exposure, you knew I wanted to get some things straight with you."

Finally, his father met his gaze. "And I'm still more than willing to answer any questions you might have. I want us to be close."

Xavier scowled at him. "You did another disappearing act on us. How can I trust you after that?" His childhood had been filled with vanishing acts, times when Red promised to show up and didn't. Graduations. Plays. Football games. Science fairs. The list went on and on.

"My first instinct was to take off out of fear and anxiety, but I didn't go anywhere, son. I just stayed away from the hospital until I could gather myself." He let out a moan. "I have my own demons I'm battling, going all the way back to witnessing my father's death. Going to the hospital was a trigger of sorts."

"And what about bailing on your kids?" he asked. The anger was boiling up inside of him like a tea kettle on the stove.

Red drew a ragged breath. "I'll never stop wishing that I'd been stronger. I felt like a failure as a dad after the divorce. After all, I'd been running away from the hard stuff all through our marriage, never stopping to think about Daisy's feelings. And then I lost her, along with my children." He clasped his hands together. "I was depressed for years and barely functioning. I left Moose Falls because I couldn't bear to be here after losing my family."

"You didn't lose us! We wanted you in our lives, but you couldn't even be bothered to see us."

"Xavier, I know I've let you down time after time, but things are different now." He clenched his jaw. "*I'm* different now."

Xavier wanted so badly to believe him so he could begin to heal the brokenness inside himself. Even though he'd tried to tell himself that he didn't need a father in his life, it wasn't true. He remembered vividly the draft day when he'd been chosen as the number one pick by the Cardinals. Although his mom and brothers had been in attendance, he'd looked around the room and seen all the other players with their dads. In that moment he had felt such anger amidst the joy of being selected by Arizona. He wasn't sure that fury had ever been extinguished. Without him truly knowing, the feeling had festered.

He let out an explosive sound. "That's not true! You just proved that by not showing up for Hattie when she needed all of us." He took a few steps toward Red, easily swallowing up the distance between them. "Can't you see how scared she is? How overwhelming this situation is for a woman who's used to being in control? She's your mother."

"I know that!" Red said fiercely, his dark eyes glittering with anger. "It's what I've always done when things get difficult. I run, Xavier. I'm not proud of it, but it's the truth. Only this time I stuck around. I'm still here. Don't you see that I'm not the same man I used to be?"

Xavier shook his head, consumed by disappointment. He had allowed himself to hope that all these years later, things would be different, but Red was still stuck in the past, repeating old mistakes. This wasn't a person who had turned over a new leaf. And Xavier felt stupid for falling for his changed-man routine.

"I hear what you're saying, and it's a damn shame. You're still the same selfish man who stood your children up when they yearned to have you in their lives."

"Xavier, give me a chance to—"

"To what? Break my heart all over again?" He let out a brittle laugh. *Been there. Done that.* If he was learning anything at all from the past, it was to not repeat old mistakes. No matter how much he ached for a relationship with his dad, he wasn't sure he could handle being disappointed once again. Wasn't that why he had pretended not to care as an adult? Deep down he'd feared this very thing.

Red placed his hand on Xavier's arm. "I'd never want to hurt you, son."

Xavier shrugged him off. "That's all you've ever done." Painful memories rose, reminding him of old hurts.

Red winced. "You have no idea how sorry I am about that. Tell me what I can do to fix this." His voice had a pleading tone.

Hurt unfurled in Xavier's chest. For so long he'd stuffed it down, but now everything was threatening to burst out of his chest. "There's nothing you can do." With those parting words, Xavier turned and headed up the staircase to see his grandmother. By the time he made his way to Hattie's bedroom, Xavier was emotionally exhausted. Dealing with Red was full of ups and downs. Just when he thought they could cut through some of the issues that were causing a divide between them, his father showed him that he was still emotionally unavailable. If Red could abandon Hattie in her time of need, Xavier knew he could do it to him as well.

He tapped on Hattie's door, pushing the door open when he heard her inviting him in. She was sitting up in the bed with a pad of paper on her lap and a pen in her hand.

"Xavier! You're such a welcome sight," Hattie called out as she beckoned him over to her bed.

"I brought these forget-me-nots to lift your spirits." He handed the bouquet to her.

"For me?" she asked, pressing her hand to her chest. "These are lovely," she gushed, bringing the flowers to her nose and inhaling their scent. "Aah, these are my favorites," she said, closing her eyes. "They remind me of Jack, my husband. He used to give them to me on my birthday and our anniversary. Most romantic man I've ever known."

"I'm not sure I was ever told what happened to him other than he died young." His mother hadn't told them much of anything about their family roots. And according to Red, he had seen his father die.

"He was taken from us well before his time," Hattie said, emotion clogging her throat. "My Jack had an adventurous spirit. He didn't feel alive unless he was doing something to challenge his own existence. That's what he used to say. So he climbed Mount Everest, trekked in the Himalayas, flew a seaplane." She slapped her leg and said, "He even swam with sharks, believe it or not. I tried for a time to get him to stop living on the edge, as they say, but he wouldn't hear of it."

"How did he die, if I may ask?" Xavier was trying to be as delicate as possible, but he was consumed by curiosity about his thrill-seeking grandfather. Clearly his death had heavily impacted his father.

"Mountain climbing in Alaska. It wasn't even as challenging as some others he completed, but a simple misstep on a ridge ended his life." She let out a tremendous sigh. "I was a widow at thirty-five years old. The love of my life died chasing something he loved more than his own family." A note of bitterness clung to her words.

"I doubt that's true," Xavier said. "Sometimes there are things that get in our blood, and we just can't seem to shake them." He empathized with Jack. Football had seeped into his bloodstream years ago, and he still couldn't seem to let it go. He wondered if anything could ever make him feel the same way.

"Like football?" Hattie asked, staring at him like a sharp-eyed hawk. When he nodded, she shook her head. "It's been your lifelong passion, hasn't it? I'm glad you're coaching the youngsters so you can still do what you love in some capacity."

Coaching the Mavericks was rewarding. But was it enough to quell his desire to be back in the thick of the camaraderie, the competitiveness, and the glory? It was worlds apart from the NFL.

"Maybe Jack shouldn't have had to choose." What would he have done if someone had asked him to make a choice between love and football? Even now he couldn't get the sport out of his heart and mind. His grandfather had simply been doing something he loved.

"It may be hard for you to understand, but since he was a father and husband, I wanted him to make different choices for me and our son." She dabbed at her eyes with a tissue. "That's all water under the bridge," she said with a wave of her hand. Xavier sensed that she didn't discuss Jack's death very much due to the fact that it was painful.

Hattie fiddled with her fingers. "My hearing is still pretty good. I heard you and Red shouting at each other after he visited me. Don't be too angry with him for disappearing when I went to the hospital. At least this time he didn't leave town," she quipped. "He's been doing that for years."

"How can you joke about him not supporting you?" Xavier asked, his frustration threatening to boil over. "He's a grown man."

"Oh, Xavier, I've learned to accept him as he is. I'm flawed as well. I need to apologize to you for allowing my health issues to deter me from visiting you. With dialysis treatments it was very complicated, but I deeply regret it." Her voice was filled with deep sorrow. Tears pooled in her eyes, causing Xavier to put his arms around her in a tight embrace.

"I understand. You were going through a lot. We would never hold that against you," he said. "And my mom could have brought us back to see you, so it's not all on your shoulders."

"Red has changed for the better, that's all I know." She let out a ragged sigh. "Some people have limitations that don't allow them to deal with the hard stuff. It boils down to the luck of the draw. We're either born with backbone, or we're not."

He scoffed. "That sounds like a cop-out." He placed the flowers in a vase on Hattie's bedside table. "So some folks just get to avoid the hard stuff? And what about the people they hurt along the way?"

"Xavier, you know firsthand about not having a father present during your formative years. Red had that as well. He had the added misfortune of being at the mountain that day waiting for his father to descend. He saw way more than any child should." Hattie shuddered and closed her eyes. "He didn't sleep or eat for weeks. And you're right. Passing on hurt is a terrible thing. You and your brothers didn't deserve that."

Xavier couldn't believe his ears. Why hadn't anyone told him this before? Neither of his parents had ever breathed a word about Jack, his untimely end, or the fact his father had borne witness to it. A traumatic event in a child's life might scar him forever.

Maybe Xavier really didn't know a single thing about his father. But the truth was, he needed to find out, otherwise he would be half the man he wanted to become. Perhaps today had been a huge step in that direction. Red had been painfully honest with him, and despite his anger toward his father, Xavier needed him. He was a missing part of his story. The heavy weight on his chest was beginning to ease up. They would both have to work on their relationship, but for the first time he believed they could reconcile.

"On another note, you and True? Is it serious?" Hattie asked.

"It might be. Honestly, I'm not sure," he answered. "I don't kiss and tell, but I confess I'm pretty smitten." He wasn't sure how it had happened so quickly, but he had fallen for True. He couldn't pretend with his grandmother. What they had was the real thing, and with each and every day, he was realizing that he needed her in his life. She made him happy. He couldn't predict the future, but he knew True being in it would make his better.

She wagged a finger at him. "Don't hurt that sweet girl. She's tough on the outside, but on the inside, she's soft as butter."

He had no intention of hurting True, but he was just as vulnerable as she was. His heart could just as easily be broken.

"Kind of like someone else I know," he teased. For the first time, he realized how he enjoyed having strong, independent women in his life. His mother. Hattie. True. Bold, unique women who were loving and fierce.

Hattie let out a cackle. "I'll proudly wear that badge of honor. Now, could you go downstairs and make me a mimosa before Jacques comes back from the store?"

"Absolutely not," Xavier said, laughing so hard it made his sides hurt.

Everyone needed a Hattie in their lives, he realized. And although their time together would be shortened by her illness, he intended to make the most of each and every day they spent together.

# CHAPTER TWENTY

The cold Alaskan air whipped against True's face as she held the reins of the dogsled tightly in her hand. Although she had done this dozens of times, mushing never got old. Thanks to her childhood friend Rocky Aldean, this dogsledding adventure had been made possible for her and Xavier. Rocky was the owner of a dogsledding outfit in town called Klondike Adventures. A former Iditarod racer, Rocky lived and breathed dogsledding and made his living showing tourists the beauty of the sport.

Xavier had just had his turn holding the reins, and they were now almost back at the starting point. True steered the dogs toward the fenced-in area by the cabin, calling out "Whoa" as their command to come to a stop. Despite the frigid temperatures, Xavier seemed to be having a great time. Mushing was a sport that caused pure adrenaline to race through your veins at every twist and turn on the trail. Not only was it stimulating, but the landscape was breathtaking. Sure, she was a bit biased, but Xavier had commented on it all morning.

"This might be the coolest thing I've ever done," Xavier told True. "And I've done some pretty cool things in my life." He proudly puffed his chest out.

"I'll bet you have, hotshot," True said, grinning at him. Decked out in his most durable winter gear—hooded parka, gloves, hat, fur-lined winter boots—Xavier was ready for the elements.

He frowned at her. "Hey, I thought you weren't going to call me that anymore."

She placed a mittened hand over her mouth. "Oops, sorry. I can't seem to quit it." She impishly grinned at him, knowing he would take it in stride. For good measure, she placed a kiss on his frosty lips.

"Okay, lovebirds. I hope you had a good time," Rocky said as he took the reins from True. "Make sure to leave us a good review online if you did."

"I had a blast," Xavier said. "The cold didn't even bother me. Almost," he said, making an exaggerated shivering motion as he stepped down from the sled.

"We'll make an Alaskan out of you yet," Rocky said as he got off the sled. He clapped Xavier on the shoulder and chuckled. "There's hot cocoa in the cabin if you'd like some. I'm going to take the dogs inside and warm up for a bit before my next client arrives."

"Thanks for everything, Rocky," True said, hugging him. "You're the best."

"Anything for you, True." He held his hand out to Xavier. "Nice to meet you, Xavier. Treat this lady right. She's a diamond," he said with a wink.

"Will do," Xavier agreed, nodding for emphasis.

True felt as if everyone who came across her and Xavier automatically paired them up as a couple. It was both exciting and nerve-racking. True didn't want to assume that she and Xavier were going to ride off into the sunset with each other, but she did feel hopeful.

They headed inside the cabin, where it was warm and cozy. Other customers were hanging out, drinking cocoa, and keeping warm. She and Xavier helped themselves to hot chocolate.

"Moose Falls has a lot going for it," he said, looking around him. The cabin was all light wood and stone, with updated furnishings and rustic artwork. It was the type of place that immediately made you feel at home.

"Doesn't it? I knew it was growing on you," she said, playfully poking a finger in his chest. He grabbed her hand and clasped it.

Xavier was grinning, showcasing a perfect smile. "Okay, at first I was a bit skeptical, but this town is full of wonderful things. The falls might be my favorite, but there's so much more, starting with Yukon Cider." His eyes lit up as he spoke. "The factory is a magical place as far as I'm concerned. Friendly folks who make this amazing elixir called hard cider." True let out a giggle. "And then there's Northern Exposure. I've never walked in there without feeling like I'm among friends. So many people here in Moose Falls have treated me like I'm an old friend. I know it's in large part due to Hattie since they often call me Hattie's grandson, but it's a wonderful feeling, let me tell you, especially after finding out my football team didn't really value me."

"I'm so sorry you were treated poorly, but everyone here adores you," True gushed. She could tell by the look on his face that her comment made him happy. She wasn't exaggerating either. Everywhere she went, townsfolk were singing Coach Stone's praises. He was rapidly becoming one of their own.

"Moose Falls definitely has its charms. But you, True

Everett, are by far the biggest selling point." He raised his cup of cocoa in the air, and as soon as she did the same, they clinked cups. "To Moose Falls," Xavier said, with True echoing his sentiments.

"So, are you sold?" she asked, nervousness trickling through her veins as she waited for his answer. She wanted him to be all in on Moose Falls...and her by extension. Other than ownership of the tavern, this was what she wanted most at this moment.

"I'm getting there. Maybe just one more kiss would seal the deal," he said, cupping her face between his hands and leaning in. His woodsy scent immediately filled her nostrils. Xavier placed his mouth over hers, his lips fiery and intense. True kissed him back for all she was worth, wishing this moment could go on and on. How easy it was to lose herself in these moments with Xavier. As the kiss soared and deepened, she realized no one had ever made her feel this way before. This was more than a kiss. True's heart felt as if it might fly straight out of her chest at any moment. This was love. She loved this gorgeous, special, complicated man. And she had never felt so vulnerable yet triumphant at the same time.

If a kiss could convince him to stick around and become a permanent resident of Moose Falls, then True would kiss him until the stars were stamped from the night sky.

🌲

By the time Xavier made it home from spending the day with True, he was exhausted and dealing with one of his headaches. He just needed to get off his feet for a little bit, take a few pain relievers, and lie down until it went away.

Today had been amazing. Their connection was growing

stronger by the day. He hadn't imagined himself connecting romantically with anyone in Moose Falls. In and out—that had been his mindset about returning to his hometown. But spending time with True and Jaylen made him question things. Would it be so bad if he ended up here as one of the owners of Yukon Cider? He would be working side by side with his brothers. Spending time with his grandmother before she passed. Settling down. Maybe?

He'd dreamed that dream with Heather, and everything had blown up in his face.

*She wasn't the one.*

*She wasn't even close.*

He sank onto the bed and placed his hands behind his head and crossed his legs. Xavier let out a moan of appreciation. This mattress was incredible. Soft yet supple. He reached for the remote and turned on the *Sports Zone*. Just because he wasn't playing at the moment didn't mean he shouldn't keep up with the league and the various teams. That way when he was ready to wage his comeback as an NFL announcer, he'd be up to speed on all the teams and new players. Nothing was going to hold him back. Everyone in the NFL had written him off, but Xavier knew he could defy the odds and make his presence known in the industry. After being sidelined with his injuries, Xavier had a hard time getting his calls returned, A few of his buddies had been loyal, but so many of his teammates considered him a has-been. Maybe he'd been paranoid, but it had felt as if they had considered him damaged goods. But he still had a shot at a comeback. Sure, he wouldn't be playing football, but he would still be in the football world! Announcing games would be a piece of cake for him.

"Now this is the wedding of the year," Michael Strahan announced from the television screen. "Supermodel Heather

Denton and Cardinals wide receiver Chazz Garcia tied the knot over the weekend in a glamorous black-tie event at the Royal Palms Resort." Pictures of the couple decked out in their wedding finery flashed across the screen. Xavier's insides twisted. Heather and Chazz looked like a picture-perfect celebrity couple with their Colgate smiles and deliriously happy expressions.

Al Michaels let out a low whistle. "Fancy. Looks like everyone in the world of football was there."

"Except maybe his former teammate Xavier Stone," Strahan quipped. He flashed his gap-toothed smile.

"Ouch! That's gotta hurt when your friend marries your ex-fiancée," Michaels said, shaking his head. "With friends like that..." Both men laughed as if it were the funniest joke in the world.

Xavier felt as if he had been sucker punched in the stomach.

"We wish the couple well," Strahan said. "Now back to those trade rumors coming out of the New England Patriots camp."

Xavier turned off the television and sat still on the bed, not moving a muscle. His thoughts went into overdrive. Although he'd gotten wind that Chazz and Heather were together—Heather had been cheating on him with Chazz during their relationship—he'd never imagined that they would make things official. They had both wounded him so much, and the hits kept coming.

Just when it seemed as if things were finally going his way, this news broke, dragging him back to a past he'd rather forget. Heather and Chazz were married! He couldn't even wrap his head around this turn of events. This was what it felt like to be stabbed in the back, he realized. It hurt way worse than he could ever have imagined. Hadn't they already twisted the knife in by getting together in the first place behind his back?

If he hadn't heard the news from such reputable sources, Xavier wouldn't have believed it. Chazz had been his best friend in the league. Matter of fact, Xavier had been the one to suggest to his coach that he recruit Chazz as the Cardinals' second-round pick. Although Chazz had a reputation for being difficult, Xavier had sung his praises. Not only had Heather cheated on Xavier with Chazz, but now they'd gotten married. Just like everything else in Xavier's life, his relationships with two of the most important people in his life had crashed and burned. He didn't think he still loved Heather, but the betrayal still hurt worse than being cut by the Cardinals.

Something was bothering him. True. She had been asking a lot of questions about whether Hattie had left him and his brothers the tavern. He didn't want to think it, didn't want to let it get into his head, but he wondered if she'd been using him.

His heart protested. True wasn't like that. She wouldn't use him like other women had in the past.

But did he really know her after such a short time? What if she thought he could sway things in her favor with Northern Exposure? No, he was being an idiot! He was allowing his mind to play tricks on him based on the past. Seeing the news coverage about Heather and Chazz's nuptials had messed him up big time.

By the time he went down for dinner, Xavier thought his head might explode. The more he tried not to think about the *Sports Zone* report, the more he thought about Heather and Chazz walking off into the sunset with each other. *Good guys finish last. There's a sucker born every minute.* And he really had no one to blame but himself after allowing

Heather and other women in his past to walk all over him. The commentators—all men he respected—were making a joke out of him. That stung something fierce. Xavier Stone was now being served up as a punch line.

His brothers were already seated at the table, and as he entered the room, their eyes were on him. He couldn't shake the feeling that they'd been talking about him. Xavier walked over to the sideboard and filled his plate with an assortment of food—lasagna, vegetables, bread, and salad. With the daily spread being offered at Hattie's home, he needed to be running the laps with the Mavericks every practice.

"Hey, you okay?" Landon's expression was strained. "We heard the news."

Xavier slid into his seat. "You watch the *Sports Zone*?"

His brothers looked at each other, then back at him.

"Oh, it wasn't just on there. I saw it on at least five other channels," Landon said with a grimace. "I guess it's big news on all the celebrity outlets."

Great! Just what he wanted to hear. He wondered how many other networks and columns had added him as the joke of the week.

"Tough break," Caleb said. "We're here if you need to talk."

"I'm fine, guys," Xavier said, trying to act nonchalant.

"What happened?" Hattie asked as she entered the room on Jacques's arm before filling a small plate with food. "I hope you didn't drop the ball with True. She's a keeper. The two of you would make some pretty babies," she gushed.

"Don't ever say that again. It's creepy," Xavier muttered.

Hattie forcefully placed her plate down on the table as she took a seat. "So what's going on? Don't keep me in suspense. I've been cooped up for days."

Xavier sat back to let his brothers explain. He didn't even

want to say the words out loud. They would taste bitter in his mouth.

"His ex-fiancée married his former friend and team-mate in a huge star-studded ceremony." They all turned in the direction of Jacques, who had just delivered the piping-hot tea.

"Seriously, Jacques?" Xavier asked, scowling at Jacques. "I thought we were cool."

Jacques patted him on the shoulder. "Sorry, but it's all over the news. No point in holding it in."

"Good riddance," Hattie said in a raised voice. "It's fortunate you didn't walk down the aisle with that one. Thank your lucky stars. Your traitorous friend did you a huge favor."

"Ouch. Tell me how you really feel," Xavier said, shooting her a surprised look. At times he forgot that Hattie could be brutal in her observations. He was grateful to have her in his corner.

Xavier knew Hattie was right about his ex, but he was still rattled. It reminded him of how reckless he'd once been with his heart and how he hadn't even seen the blind side coming. Had he changed since then? Was he savvier about protecting his heart? Or was he still capable of being played for a fool?

Was True capable of being another Heather? His heart told him no, but his head was telling him anything was possible.

Hard questions whirled around in his head. Why couldn't he just separate True from all the bad stuff in his past? The way True made him feel was unlike anything else he had ever known. It scared him to admit it, but he was in love with her. Real, true, abiding love. She had come into his life like a random blizzard in Arizona. He hadn't been prepared to feel so much so soon. He wasn't sure he could handle it if

True turned out not to be the woman he thought she was. His heart wouldn't be able to deal with another betrayal.

"I give them six months tops," Caleb said. "Don't worry. You'll have the last laugh."

Xavier knew everyone was trying to make him feel better, but he didn't think their tactics were working. Sometimes a person just needed to sit in the discomfort for a while in order to process everything. The timing couldn't be worse, though, since he was knee-deep in a relationship with True. If someone had asked him a few days ago, he would have said he didn't have a single doubt about her. But now . . . he would have to be a fool to not question it all.

After dinner, he went back upstairs and made a call to his agent, who answered on the second ring. Gordon Baker had been with Xavier since the day he had been recruited by the Cardinals. As loyal as they came, Gordon was the only one who had steadfastly remained in his corner after he'd lost it all and hit rock bottom. He was a good dude who genuinely cared about Xavier and always sought out opportunities in the industry for him to explore.

"Hey there, Xavier. How are you? What's shaking in Alaska?" Gordon's deep baritone voice came across the miles loud and clear. Xavier put the call on speaker and sat down on his bed.

"Hi, Gordon. Things are good here. I just wanted to get back to you. Sorry, I know you've left a few messages for me, but things have been a bit hectic here."

"That's okay, X. From what you've said about Yukon Cider, I imagine there's a huge learning curve." His laughter rang out on the other end of the phone.

"That there is," Xavier said. "So what's going on?" He knew Gordon well enough to know there was something business-related to talk over.

"As you know from our discussions, several major networks are looking to bring on some on-air talent. Fresh faces. Athletes. For the first year or so it would mostly be weekend gigs, which would work out with your arrangement with Hattie to be at Yukon Cider during the week," Gordon explained. "You check off the boxes as far as I'm concerned. I think hiring you would be a no-brainer, especially now."

"What do you mean, especially now?" Xavier asked, confused about what Gordon meant. Was there a spike in interest in washed-out football players?

Silence greeted Xavier on the other end of the phone. Gordon cleared his throat and continued speaking. "I hate to be insensitive, but with all this hoopla surrounding Heather and Chazz's wedding, your name is back in the news. Although it's their wedding, this is causing a chain reaction where everyone is buzzing about you. People remember the on-field collision and your medical issues, plus your engagement to Heather. It's causing a bit of a feeding frenzy."

Xavier put his head in his hands. What a world! For almost two years now, no one had wanted to lift a single finger to help out when he'd been at his lowest point. No interviews. No compassion. He had been written off as a failure. And now, simply because of the wedding, his name was back in the spotlight.

"I don't know, Gordon. It feels a little unauthentic." He didn't want to capitalize on one of the most agonizing moments of his life. Not to mention that he cringed at the thought of being mentioned along with Heather and Chazz.

"Like my grandmother used to say, strike while the iron is hot. And you're on fire, my friend. The thing about fires is that they can sometimes go out without warning, so time is of the essence," Gordon said with conviction. His agent was one of the best in the business, always shooting straight from the hip. Xavier trusted his professional judgment.

"What do I need to do?" Xavier asked. This was the chance he had been waiting for, an opportunity to redeem himself. A shot at redemption.

His conscience was bothering him about bailing on the Mavericks, but he would find a top-notch replacement to lead the team. The team's greatness wasn't about the Storm being their coach. He was hosting a team-building event at the bowling alley for the Mavericks, and he would have to hide his emotions from the kids. He couldn't allow guilt to swallow him up. This was his shot at a career comeback. He'd be a fool to pass on the opportunity.

"There's a round of interviews happening next week in Los Angeles. You need to be here and place yourself front and center. I can line up some on-air interviews for you as well to beef up the interest."

"Okay, I'll do it," he said, battling a sickening sensation in the pit of his stomach. Xavier was saying yes to something that would be beneficial for him, but he knew the fallout would be messy.

"I'll send over the details. And I'll be in touch," Gordon promised. "Talk to you soon."

When he disconnected from the call, Xavier began to pace back and forth along the length of the room. The call with his agent had left him on edge. If he was hired for one of these on-air positions and it became a full-time gig a year from now, he was basically indicating that he wanted to sell Yukon Cider rather than stay on and run the company. That decision could cause shock waves throughout Moose Falls. And within the Stone family.

What would Hattie and his brothers think? Red? And most of all, True. A part of him knew that if he left, it would be the end of them, of what they were building together. That knowledge threatened to burn a hole in his chest, but he was in self-protection mode at the moment. He had no confirmation that True had strong feelings for him. His romantic history had shown that he had a shocking lack of insight where relationships were concerned. For all he knew, he was simply a means to an end for True. Although it gutted him to think such things, he had to be realistic.

He had to put himself first so he could get back what he'd lost. If he listened to Gordon, he could be back on track financially in a few years. He would be rehabbing his image and taking steps toward rebuilding his old life. Leaving Moose Falls and letting True go wouldn't be easy, but it was what he needed to do so he could move forward with his life. If only his heart could be as practical as his head.

# CHAPTER TWENTY-ONE

True knew right away that something was going on with Xavier. He wasn't acting like his usual self with her. Ever since he had arrived at the bowling venue, he had barely said two words to her. He'd been hanging out with Jaylen and their team, bowling, and carefully avoiding her. Honestly, she had no idea what she'd done wrong, but she was hoping his mood would change by the end of the night. Normally they had so much fun together. She felt a disconnect between them that seemed to have come out of nowhere.

His attitude scared her a little bit, because it reminded her of Garrett and how his interest in her had changed so rapidly. Just the thought of going down that road again made her feel uneasy. *No*, she reminded herself. Xavier was different. He wasn't a little boy playing games. He was a man, one she had fallen head over heels in love with. And he cared for her, was falling in love. Surely that wasn't something that could shift so easily.

She wanted to pick Xavier's brain tonight about Northern Exposure. Hattie hadn't yet circled back to her about her pitch, and she was wondering if she should draft a written proposal and send it to Hattie. Xavier had been so encouraging about her plans all the times they had discussed Northern Exposure. He made her feel that she could do anything. Be anything she wanted. A veritable Wonder Woman!

Maybe something had happened that she didn't know about. Was his mother all right? Hattie? Maybe someone back in Arizona.

Now she just had to put her big-girl panties on and pull Xavier aside so they could talk. Just days ago they were enjoying the experience of a lifetime at Klondike Adventures. Even though he hadn't said the words to her, True believed he was falling in love, if he hadn't already fallen as she had. Was it all in her head? How could she have gotten everything so wrong?

True found a quiet moment to approach Xavier when he wasn't surrounded by kids. She had watched him from a distance, enjoying the easy rapport he had with the Mavericks and the parents. Honestly, there wasn't a single person he came across who wasn't charmed by Xavier, including herself.

She tugged on his sleeve, her breath catching when he turned around to face her. He was still the finest man in all of Alaska with his chiseled features and rugged frame. "Hey, I haven't had a moment alone with you all night. Is everything all right?" She didn't see the point in dancing around the issue. Xavier was giving off unapproachable vibes, which didn't gel with his personality. From the first day they'd met at the tavern, he had been inviting and friendly, even after the ghost pepper incident.

"Hey, True. I'm good," he said, his expression shuttered. His eyes weren't emitting any warmth. He was greeting her like an acquaintance, not someone he cared about.

So she hadn't been imagining things. Something had shifted between them.

Hmm. He was giving off so much frost, it felt like an arctic storm had passed through Moose Falls.

"What's going on? You seem really distant." She wasn't going to play coy. If past experience had taught her anything, she'd learned to speak her mind so she didn't have any regrets later.

"I just have a lot on my mind, to be honest." He sounded so sad, as if the weight of the world rested on his shoulders.

Maybe he was worried about Hattie or reconnecting with his father. Was she being too hard on him? Too insensitive? The world didn't revolve around her, and there could be dozens of things he was worried about. Real-world problems that had nothing to do with her.

"I'm sorry, but you can talk to me about anything, Xavier. I'm here to listen, the same way you're always here for me." She was watching him carefully to see his response. True detected a glimmer of a reaction. Maybe her words were getting through to him. "Matter of fact, I wanted to get your advice about the tavern. I haven't heard back from Hattie yet after our meeting."

True watched as Xavier's mouth hardened right before her eyes. "Just so you know, Hattie isn't leaving us Northern Exposure. It's going to Red." There was no mistaking the terse tone of his voice.

Why was he making a point of telling her this? And why hadn't Hattie told her when they met up? "I'm so confused. You didn't mention that to me when I told you that I wanted to buy the tavern."

"Hattie wanted the terms of our contract to be confidential, so I respected that. Matter of fact, I remember telling you that I couldn't talk about Hattie's plans, and I really

shouldn't have told you this information about the tavern."
He let out a sigh. "Just keep it under wraps, please. I'm only
telling you so you know who to focus your energies on. And
it's not me."

There was a sharpness to his voice she'd never heard before.
He was angry at her! She could feel it vibrating in his voice.
His jaw was clenched so tightly, she thought it might snap.

His anger was why the vibe between them had been so
off. But she had no idea why or what it was all about. Tension crackled in the air between them. She placed a hand on
her hip. "And you're angry at me about wanting to buy the
tavern?"

He made a face. "I'm just not a fan of being used."

Her jaw almost hit the floor. "You cannot be serious," she
said, her throat feeling as dry as sandpaper. "I don't know
where all this is coming from," she said, sounding as confused as she felt.

True couldn't believe what she was hearing. This wasn't
the Xavier she knew and loved. What had gotten into him?
She hadn't done a single thing to deserve such an accusation.

"Honestly, I'm not even sure at the moment if I'm sticking around Moose Falls. There's an opportunity that's come
up in California that would be really great for my football
career. I fly out in a few days to be interviewed."

His career? She'd thought he had accepted that his football career was over. From the sound of it, Xavier was still
clinging to that NFL lifestyle and making moves to get out
of Dodge.

"But Hattie will be so sad if you leave. And what about
the Mavericks?" *And so will I*, she wanted to say, but a huge
lump was sitting in her throat. Hattie deserved to have all
three of her grandsons back in Moose Falls with her. And
Jaylen and his teammates would be devastated. How could

Xavier even consider doing this? On some level she recognized that he had the right to make his own life choices, but the ripples of his decision would affect so many people.

She noticed his jaw tremble as he spoke. "Nothing was guaranteed. No promises were made about permanently staying in Alaska."

"And what about us?" she asked, pushing the words out of her mouth.

Xavier looked away from her. "I just can't see us doing long distance, True. It would be too hard."

As much as this was hurting her, she couldn't shake the feeling that he was running away from their relationship. Nothing made sense. He was acting like a wounded animal trying to protect himself.

"You're putting up imaginary roadblocks, Xavier. I've only ever wanted to be with you for you. I never tried to use you. Not once." She took a deep breath. "I know what it's like to feel as if you can't risk putting down your walls. It's scary to believe in people. But I believe in you, Xavier. I love—"

Before she could finish the sentence, Xavier cut her off. "True, I've got to get out of here. I can't do this."

"Of course you're going to run away. I shouldn't be surprised. Like father, like son." She spat the words out so fast, anger fueling her sharp words.

A slow hissing sound escaped Xavier's lips. He shook his head at her. "Nice, True. Really nice."

As he beat a fast path away from her, hot tears burned her eyes. With a quick look to make sure Jaylen was occupied, she made a beeline to the ladies' room, where she proceeded to sit in a stall and sob. How had this happened? She had been completely blindsided by Xavier's change of heart. Maybe she had read everything between them wrong. If so, she needed to let romance pass her by for the rest of her days.

Somehow she managed to get home without breaking down again. Jaylen talked a mile a minute about his bowling scores and how he had beaten Coach Stone. She put on a smile, laughed at his jokes, and sucked up her heartache. No matter what was going on in her world, it was her responsibility to make sure Jaylen's life was free of strife and drama.

Once they got home, True took a shower, got into her PJs, and curled up on her bed. She felt completely broken. This time was different from the Garrett breakup. Her pain right now was so gut-wrenching, as if something had been violently ripped away from her. She felt tears coming on again, and even though she tried to stem the tide, they pooled in her eyes.

Just then, Jaylen came to her room to kiss her good night. He stood by her bed and looked down at her with a troubled expression etched on his nine-year-old face.

"True, what's wrong?" Jaylen reached out and ran his hand along her cheek. He was such an affectionate child, always wanting to provide comfort and love. She wasn't sure what she had ever done to deserve him.

"I'm just a little sad," she admitted. There was no point in pretending nothing was wrong, since Jaylen already detected the telltale signs of her being upset.

"Is this about Xavier? Did he do something to hurt your feelings?" Her brother was peering into her face as if seeking truthful answers. His beautiful brown eyes oozed compassion. Jaylen was her little empath. He knew her so well and picked up easily on her emotional state. Clearly, she wasn't doing a very good job at masking her feelings.

*Okay, suck it up*, she told herself. She had traveled down this road before, and she'd made it through the storm. But that had been different. What she felt for Xavier was epic. A love story. Or so she'd thought.

She blinked back tears, willing them not to stream down her face. The last thing in the world she wanted was for Jaylen to be angry at Xavier. He was his beloved coach and friend. She didn't want to take that away from him. Xavier continued to be the strongest male figure in his young life. They shared such a beautiful friendship, and it hurt just knowing it would fade out when Xavier left town.

"Xavier and I aren't going to work out," she told him. "But it's no one's fault," she quickly added. "Sometimes people just meet each other at the wrong time for it to be right."

Jaylen nodded as she spoke, resembling a wise old owl. She had always believed that her little brother was wiser than his years. "Don't be sad it's over. Be glad it happened."

True burst into laughter. "That is so corny."

Jaylen giggled along with her. "I know, True. I'm a corny kind of kid. But you made me that way."

"Naaah," she said.

"Yaaah," Jaylen insisted.

"Do you know how much I love you?" True asked. She wrapped her arms around his neck and hugged him. True wanted to stretch this moment out so she could protect Jaylen from all the slings and arrows of life. One day he might have his heart smashed into smithereens, and there wasn't a single thing she could do to prevent it.

"I have an idea," Jaylen said. "To the moon and back, right? I'm a pretty lovable kid."

"I can't argue with that. Now off to bed." She made a shooing motion with her hands. "Scoot. I'll make you chocolate chip pancakes in the morning."

He let out a whoop of excitement and began to dance around in a celebratory fashion.

"Okay, no more stalling. Bedtime," she said, trying to

keep a straight face. Jaylen's exuberance was such a gift. Although she still had an ache in her soul about Xavier, her little brother made everything better. In the end, he was her true love story.

Jaylen placed a kiss on her forehead and pulled the covers over her so she was tucked in, completely reversing their roles. "Night, True. I love you."

"Love you back. Don't forget to brush your teeth," she said, laughing as he let out a loud groan. She watched as he padded out of the room. Jaylen's sweet words and endless support served as a pick-me-up.

As she drifted off to sleep, thoughts of Xavier flitted through her mind. Not the Xavier from a few hours ago, but the one she'd fallen in love with over the past few months. The funny, sensitive, warm Xavier who had come into her life like a blazing comet. The one who supported her dreams and always seemed to have her back. The man who seemed to know who he was and where he was going. She didn't know what had happened to that guy, but she wished with all her heart that he would come back.

# CHAPTER TWENTY-TWO

To say he was in a funk had to be the biggest understatement of the century. Xavier woke up feeling like roadkill, and he hadn't had a single drink last night to explain the way his body felt. He'd had trouble falling asleep last night as his encounter with True replayed in his mind. His behavior had been cringeworthy. He should have been kinder and gentler, but he'd been so frustrated and angry. He had allowed fear to take over.

All he'd wanted to do was untangle himself from the situation, but he'd made a mess of it.

Accusing her of using him had been so over the line, but he'd truly wondered if that was the case. She'd been absolutely horrified by the accusation, and he couldn't say that he blamed her. Xavier wasn't sure how he could ever face her again.

In a few days, he would be flying to California for one of the most important meetings in his life. Maybe creating this exit plan from Moose Falls was the right decision. Gordon seemed to think one of the networks hiring Xavier was pretty much a done deal. If he was offered a position, everything would move very quickly, according to Gordon. Xavier would have one foot in Moose Falls and the other in California.

*You're putting up imaginary roadblocks.* True's words were stuck in his head. Was she right? He had been in a tailspin after the news coverage about the wedding. His focus had been squarely on all the mistakes he'd made in the past with relationships and how he no longer wanted to be played for a fool.

*What about us?* True's question had almost brought him to his knees despite his nonchalant façade. Why hadn't he pulled her into his arms and told her that they were going to be fine? He had allowed his own personal demons to ruin what they'd been building. He was too ashamed to face her. True was better off without him!

A knock on his office door dragged him from his thoughts. The door slowly opened to reveal Landon standing in the doorway.

"Caleb and I flipped a coin to see which one of us would ask you if you're doing okay," Landon said. "You don't look so hot."

"Thanks," Xavier said dryly. He knew he looked a bit raggedy with stubble on his cheeks and bags under his eyes. He'd hoped his professional business attire would lend him a more polished look, but his brothers saw past all that.

"I've been better," he admitted, his eyes downcast. "True and I won't be seeing each other anymore." Just saying those words out loud caused a stabbing sensation in his chest.

"Why not?" Landon asked, looking stricken. "You two are so great together. We haven't seen you this happy since...ever."

"I don't want to get played again. The worst part of

falling in love with someone is finding out that they've been using you. Been there, done that. Not doing it again."

Landon frowned at him. "I'm not sure why you think that about True, but she strikes me as being very genuine. You're just letting the news about Heather mess with you."

"And you think it's a coincidence that True zeroed in on me?" He let out a snort. "She probably Googled me and realized that I was a sucker."

"From what I remember, you homed in on her just as much. You told us repeatedly that she was a good person. How can that have changed?" Landon was staring at Xavier with a look of shock and disappointment. In other circumstances it might break his heart, but the situation with True was already accomplishing that feat. He was completely broken in a way he'd never felt before. The Heather situation had been mortifying due to the involvement of Chazz, but he hadn't felt this overwhelming love for his ex-fiancée.

Landon was a softie who always wanted to believe the best about people. It was astounding considering the way his colleagues at the laboratory had betrayed and scapegoated him. He still believed in people despite all he'd endured.

"I envy you." Landon looked at him wistfully.

Xavier scoffed. "Is that right? Why on earth would you envy me?"

"Because you're in love. And True loves you back. I'd give anything to have that."

"Why do you think she loves me?" he asked. His heart began to thump wildly in his chest. True had been about to tell him she loved him when he cut her off. Why had he done that? Out of fear and uncertainty about her motives. A knee-jerk reaction to the way he'd been made to feel in past relationships.

Xavier wanted to believe True was in love with him, but

they had never spoken words of love. He had been reluctant to believe her feelings for him were so powerful.

Landon gaped at him. "Are you kidding me? It's all in her eyes, bro. The way she looks at you is so full of love, it's almost blinding."

Had Landon seen what Xavier hadn't? If so, it made him wonder if he'd gotten it all wrong. Maybe he had allowed his own issues to mess with his head.

"That doesn't mean we walk off into the sunset together, Landon." His voice sounded gravelly to his own ears. Knowing True wouldn't be a part of his future gutted him. When had the idea of being with True become so important to him? Why did he feel as if something sharp were lodged in his chest?

"What's stopping you?" Landon asked. His eyes were full of questions and a bit of innocence that came from never having been truly heartbroken before. His brother meant well, but he had never been in Xavier's position. He didn't know how helpless a person felt when they were in love. The highs and the lows. The hope and the fear. But there was so much beauty too, moments he had shared with True that he would never forget. They were imprinted on his heart.

"Landon, I have an interview in California next week for a sports commentator gig." He held up his hand before his brother could say anything. "I was planning to tell you and Caleb earlier, but I kept putting it off. I'll still honor my commitment for the year, but if I get the job, I'll be in Los Angeles on the weekends."

Landon had a stunned expression on his face. "Why can't you let it go, Xavier? Maybe it's time to dream other dreams."

He had been asking himself that same question ever since his career-ending collision. After all this time, he was still grappling for answers. How could he put it into words so Landon would understand?

"It's been my whole world ever since I first walked onto a field. I've never been any good at anything else. At least with this gig, I can talk about football." *I'll matter*, he wanted to say. *I won't just be a has-been, used to be, almost was.*

"But you don't even enjoy that side of it. The glare of the lights. The interviews. The trash talk. Have you really thought this through?"

"Who am I if I'm not a football player? The Storm? At least if I'm a commentator, I can still be in that world."

Landon placed his hands on Xavier's shoulders and gently shook him. He looked into his eyes. "You're Xavier Stone. That's who you are. It's enough. I promise you. You're enough."

He didn't know how to let go of one dream in order to grab hold of another one. Other than his family, football had always been his soft place to fall. It had given him validation, respect, admiration, and a lifestyle beyond his wildest dreams. Letting go meant failure. He was used to going the distance. He had always been a fighter.

But now he was at a crossroads. True meant the world to him. Losing her would be devastating. He knew in the weeks and months ahead, he would be grieving the fact that she was no longer in his life. And it would be excruciating. He loved this woman with every part of his being, and these feelings weren't going anywhere.

"I don't want to be like Red, always running away from life," he muttered.

It suddenly dawned on him that True had been right, despite the fact that he hadn't wanted to accept it at the time. He was on the verge of repeating his father's pattern. Running away from difficult situations. Wasn't that what he was doing by trying to leave Moose Falls? Hadn't Hattie told him that it was Red's way of dealing with life? Xavier didn't want to be that way in his own life. He wanted to push past his fears and be present for the people he loved.

He jumped up from his seat and headed toward the door. While Xavier was deep in thought, Landon had just left his office, and he needed him to come back. In reality, Xavier needed Caleb and Hattie, as well as Red. He needed his family's help so he could make things right with True.

"Landon!" he called out after seeing his brother in the corridor. "I need your help! I've got to fix things with True. Grab Caleb too."

Landon grinned at him and flashed him a thumbs-up sign.

Xavier went back into his office and sat down. His breathing was heavy, and his pulse was racing like a thoroughbred at the Kentucky Derby. He was existing on pure adrenaline, and his mind was racing with a hundred different thoughts.

He wasn't going to California. Gordon would just have to understand that it wasn't the right move for Xavier. He would always love football, but he'd found something else he loved more. True. And his life here in Moose Falls was pretty amazing. He still had work to do on his relationship with his father. And Hattie wanted him here for her final days. Xavier couldn't bear to leave the grandmother he'd grown to love.

He was going to head over to Northern Exposure so he could get his girl back. And if luck was on his side, she wouldn't slam the tavern door in his face.

🌲

"Just say the word, True, and I'll head over to Yukon Cider and give that weasel a kick in the pants." Bonnie had issued various statements like this all morning, and although True appreciated her fierce loyalty, it wasn't helping True feel any better.

"I love you, Bonnie, but violence is never the answer." She sent Bonnie a pointed look. "There will be no contact with Xavier. Understood?"

Bonnie folded her arms across her chest and made a huffing sound. "All right, if you insist, but as far as I'm concerned, good riddance. He's too pretty for my liking anyway. If you'd ended up together, he would probably hog the mirror."

True's lips twitched. "Oh, really? Because you've been drooling over him ever since he came to town." True let loose with a throaty chuckle at the outraged expression on Bonnie's face. It felt really nice to laugh.

"I'm going to ignore that comment since I'm needed in the kitchen," Bonnie said in a sassy tone as she sashayed out of True's office.

Friends didn't come any more loyal than Bonnie. True was so happy for her and Tucker. A few days ago, she had shown up for work with a sparkly diamond on her finger. Bonnie had agreed to marry Tucker after he showered her with a fancy proposal. Turns out Bonnie realized that she'd met her other half in Tucker and she didn't want to lose him. "Why not tie him down?" she'd said, laughing wildly.

Although she was excited for her friend, True couldn't help but think about what the future might have held for her and Xavier if things hadn't crashed and burned. How could their love story be ending when it had barely started? She shook off the feelings of sadness, knowing that thoughts of Xavier would only serve as a huge distraction from work. And she had lots of events to plan, vendors to call, menus to discuss with the chef, along with a host of other responsibilities.

A sudden knock on her door caused her to let out a groan. What was it now? With all these interruptions, she would never get all her work done.

"Come in," she called out, trying not to sound as annoyed as she felt.

The sight of Red and Hattie standing in the doorway caused True to let out a gasp. What were they doing here? She stood up so quickly, some of her paperwork fell to the floor. "Hattie! Red! I wasn't expecting to see you." She let out a nervous laugh. "Did I forget about a meeting or something?"

"Sorry to barge in on you, True, but my son and I have something important to discuss with you." Hattie pointed to a chair and said, "Red, pull that chair out for me. I would like to sit down." Red quickly pulled out the chair, then helped his mother sit down before grabbing another seat for himself.

A panicky feeling threatened to swallow True up whole. What was going on? Was she *being fired*? All she could fathom was that Red had decided to assume his role as owner of the tavern and she was being kicked out on her rear end. She sank back into her chair as a feeling of unease washed over her.

When it rains, it pours. Why did all the bad things have to pop up at once? She could barely handle being dumped by Xavier, and now this!

"Just get it over with," she said abruptly, leaning across the table and locking eyes with Hattie. "Am I being let go?"

Hattie let out a rich chuckle. "What in the world, True? You're not being fired, my sweet child. Your dream of owning the tavern is about to come true."

"Huh?" True asked as she swung her gaze between Hattie and Red. They were both grinning at her, their faces radiating pure joy.

"A little birdie told me that you wanted to buy Northern Exposure, and although I appreciate my mother's gesture in leaving it to me, owning a tavern has never been on my bucket list," Red explained. "I have other dreams I'd like to explore."

Hattie reached over and squeezed his hand. "Dreams are important."

"You're selling the tavern to me?" True asked. For a moment she felt breathless. Was this really happening? After all the years of hoping and dreaming, her wish was finally coming true.

"I am," Red said with a nod. "We can work something out with the payments and structure them in a way that works for you. Whatever it takes, True. We believe in you."

Tears were falling freely now, and this time they were born of joy. She almost couldn't believe her good fortune. She lightly pinched her arm, half expecting to wake up and find out this had all been a dream.

"So do you want to buy the tavern?" Red asked, wiggling his eyebrows.

"Of course I do," she shouted. "Thank you so much," she said, hugging him tightly. "The two of you have changed my life in ways you can't imagine." She leaned down and kissed Hattie on the cheek before pulling her in for a hug.

Hattie and Red exchanged a furtive glance.

"What was that look about?" True asked. The expressions etched on their faces hinted at them withholding something from her. "Spill it," she said, her hands on hips.

"You're going to have to thank Xavier, if you're still speaking to him," Hattie said. "He's the one who put all the pieces together and made it possible."

"He did," Red confirmed. "Based on something I'd said to him weeks ago, Xavier realized that the tavern might not be of interest to me. Then he told me how owning Northern Exposure was your heart's desire."

"What? I wonder why he did that," she said, feeling confused. Why would Xavier care if her dream was realized? He had shown her that she didn't matter to him at the bowling alley. She had received the message loud and clear.

"That's not for us to say, True. Only Xavier can give you that answer," Hattie said, a sweet smile playing around her lips. She turned toward Red. "And on that note, give me a hand. I think there's someone else waiting to see the new owner of Northern Exposure."

Before she could think of a response, they had sailed out of her office, leaving the door wide open. Suddenly, Xavier was standing there, looking a little rough around the edges.

He was still handsome, but his eyes looked tired, as if he hadn't gotten much sleep last night. The petty part of her thought it was just desserts for ending things with her. *Rise above it*, a little voice told her. *He's still a good guy.*

"Hi, True," he said, shoving his hands in his pockets.

"Hi, Xavier. Come on in," she said, her heart thumping as he brushed by her, their bodies having slight contact in the process. She closed the door behind him and turned to face him. She drew in a deep breath. All she really wanted to do was melt into his arms.

"Congratulations," he said. "Dreams do come true."

"I heard you had a big hand in it. Thank you. For everything," she said, tearing up. "It was really generous of you." *Don't cry. Please don't cry.*

He leaned back on the arm of the chair. "My father and I hashed things out a few days ago about the past, and it really allowed me to see him through a different lens. And although there are still issues we need to work through, we're in a much better place now. That allowed me to approach him about Northern Exposure."

He was gazing at her with such an intense look, True didn't know what to do with herself. Locking eyes with him made her feel vulnerable, as if he would see every single emotion in their depths. He had made it very clear he didn't want her love.

"That's good," she said. "I think it's important for the two of you to have a decent relationship." She wasn't going to say anything else. Xavier's personal life was no longer any of her business.

Xavier stood up and closed the distance between them. "I've been a fool," he said. "There was only one thing that I truly needed to tell you last night. I love you, True Everett. And I cut you off before you could tell me, but I think you love me too."

This was everything she wanted to hear from him, but it didn't erase everything he had said to her or the pain he'd caused. "You thought I was using you," she said, taking a step backward, away from him. "I wasn't. I never would." Emotion clogged her throat. "I can't get your words out of my head."

"Forgive me for being short-sighted and idiotic and ridiculous," Xavier said in a tender voice, his eyes never veering away from her own.

She folded her arms across her chest and scowled at him. "I could add a few more adjectives."

Xavier took another step toward her. "I let my past mess with me. My ex, Heather, got married to my friend Chazz. It made me feel like I'd been used and abused." His jaw clenched. "They portrayed me as a laughingstock. That hurt, True. But it doesn't excuse my lashing out at you."

He once again closed the distance between them and

reached out to cup her face between his hands. "I know you didn't use me. And I'm so sorry for the things I said." He winced. "I allowed pain from the past to mess with my head, and I'll always regret that. I love you, baby."

He loved her. Xavier hadn't just said it once. Hope blossomed inside her, threatening to sprout wings and fly away.

"What about California?" she asked. "Isn't that your chance to get back into pro football?"

"I'm not going to California," he said, running his hand alongside her cheek. "I'm not running away like my father did. And everything I've been chasing is right here in Moose Falls. I don't need to prove anything, True. I'm enough as I am."

"You are enough, Xavier," she said softly. "More than enough." And he was.

He dipped his head down and rained kisses all over her face. Tender kisses that spoke of his love for her and his deep remorse. "Forgive me. I'm still a work in progress."

"Oh, Xavier, I love you too. And that makes it easier to forgive you, because I want this to work out between us. I want you." She didn't know where things would lead, but she wanted to be with him. Love him. Build a life with him. Combined with ownership of Northern Exposure, she couldn't think of anything more wonderful.

"That's music to my ears," he said, closing his eyes. She rested against his chest, then wrapped her arms around his waist.

"You're mine, hotshot," she said, her voice a bit muffled.

She felt Xavier's body shake as his rumbly laughter filled the room. "And you're mine. Now and forever."

# EPILOGUE

A few weeks later, Xavier, True, Coach Lisa, and the entire Mavericks team were celebrating their first win of the season. Pizza and root beer were plentiful, and spirits were high. Xavier couldn't have been any prouder of his team and how hard they'd worked. Jaylen was now officially an athlete and a scholar, having earned a gold medal at the state spelling bee. He was an incredible kid with a brilliant future awaiting him. And Xavier wanted to play a role in his life, if True let him.

After the team's celebration came to a close, True, Xavier, and Jaylen headed back to her house. As they rounded the last curve in the road before entering True's driveway, she let out a gasp at the sight of the mountains lit up by the moon's luminescent glow. It was one of those moments when the beauty of her surroundings left her speechless.

"If I wasn't here, this could really be a romantic moment for the two of you," Jaylen piped up from the back seat. Both True and Xavier cracked up laughing at his comment. Her little brother and Xavier were developing a tight bond, one that Jaylen needed with a male figure.

"I'm not sure I'll ever get used to feeling as if I can reach out and touch the mountains, but I'm grateful to be here in Moose Falls," Xavier said, squeezing her hand after he parked the truck.

"We're happy you're here too," True said. She could no longer imagine her life without this incredible man. And she knew Hattie felt the same way. In the weeks and months ahead as Hattie's condition declined, they would be with her, providing love, companionship, and support.

Once they headed inside, Xavier packed up Jaylen's school lunch while True attempted to supervise Jaylen as he worked on math problems. There wasn't much she could help him with, but simply being there was important. He would always have shoulders to lean on.

Jaylen went to bed at a relatively early hour, exhausted after finishing all his homework. True loved the fact that he worked equally hard at football and academics. He was so well-adjusted despite all he'd lost. Xavier always told her it was largely due to her, but True believed Jaylen had been born exceptional. She had simply taught him right from wrong and loved him with all her being.

Loving and being loved in return by the people who mattered most to her were the two most important things in her world. Finding a man like Xavier had truly restored her faith in romantic love. He'd erased every bad relationship she had ever had.

"So, what're you going to do? About the company?" True asked as they cuddled on her couch.

"Honestly, I don't know. We still have nine months to figure things out. All I know is that I want to be wherever you are. Whether it's Moose Falls or Timbuktu, I'm in this for the long haul. If you'll have me."

True cocked her head to the side. "Are you asking me to marry you?"

A look of panic crossed his face. "Umm. Wait just one second." He turned away and walked down the hall into the kitchen.

True wished she'd kept her mouth shut. His response to her question hadn't been good. She hoped that she hadn't scared him away, because she hadn't really been serious. She heard sounds as if he was rummaging around in the kitchen drawers. *What was going on with him?*

A few minutes later, Xavier came striding back into the room, breathing a bit heavily.

"Are you all right?" she asked. "You look a little… rattled."

He ran his hand over his face. "I think so. I mean, yes, I'm fine."

Before she knew what was happening, Xavier was on bended knee holding out a piece of aluminum foil. "Will you marry me? I don't have a ring or anything right now, but I have this." He held the piece of aluminum foil out.

"What?" she asked. Had he really just popped the question? Was this actually going down?

Xavier let out a groan. "Never mind. It was a stupid idea." He pulled back the aluminum foil that she now realized he'd formed in the shape of a ring.

"No, no, no. It's not stupid, Xavier." She held out her finger so he could slide it on. "It's just perfect."

A smile spread across his face as he put the stand-in ring on her finger. "It's just temporary until we can pick out a ring."

"I'm going to keep it forever." True wrapped her arms around Xavier's neck. "The answer is yes. A thousand times yes, Xavier. Nothing else matters but you and me. And Jaylen."

"I can't wait to see his reaction," Xavier said. "He's

going to be over-the-moon happy." Every time True saw Xavier with Jaylen, her heart melted at the rapport between them. He was such a strong role model, full of wisdom and encouragement.

"And Hattie's as well. Something tells me she might take credit for all this."

They both laughed at the idea of Hattie taking credit for their love story. Both of them knew it was quite likely.

"Knowing this will give her joy makes me incredibly happy," Xavier said, smiling down at True, who reached up and hooked her arms around his neck.

"Me too," True told him. "This is all happening so fast for us, but I've never believed that love has a timeline."

If someone had told her six months ago that she would be engaged to a famous athlete, on her way toward ownership of Northern Exposure, and helping Jaylen with an accelerated learning plan, she would have called them a liar. After a host of struggles, life was good. Xavier was her pot of gold at the end of the rainbow.

"I'm the luckiest man in Alaska. I wanted you from the moment you served me those fireball wings," Xavier said.

True threw back her head and chuckled. "You're never going to let me live that down, are you?"

Xavier dipped his head down and placed a tender kiss on the side of her neck. "It's something we can tell our kids someday."

"Talk about making a lasting impression," True murmured. "I'm glad you didn't write me off after that."

"Not a chance," he said, placing his arms around her waist and pulling her flush against him. "From the start you made me feel things I wasn't used to feeling. You restored my faith in love."

"Ditto," True said, her heart near to bursting at the way in which everything was coming together. She had never imagined herself as the happily-ever-after type. But Xavier had proved her wrong simply by loving her.

The future was theirs for the taking, full of promise and joy. And so many adventures with both of their families. They would support and love Hattie for the rest of her days as a family. There would be no looking back now, only forward.

# ACKNOWLEDGMENTS

Writing is a solitary endeavor, yet it takes a village to bring a book to life.

I'm indebted to my husband, Randy, and my two daughters, Sierra and Amber. Thanks, Sierra, for always listening to my story details...and remembering the plots. Grateful for Amber, who always gives me her honest assessment of my names and storylines. And Randy, for always knowing when I need a takeout night and a massage.

I'm so grateful for my agent, Jessica Alvarez, for doing the hard stuff and always having my back. I appreciate you!

For my editor, Madeleine Colavita, for all of her hard work to make this book shine. And for giving me the freedom to write this story in my own way.

I'm thankful for Grace Fischetti for all of her efforts to help launch this book.

And to the entire Forever team. You are truly awesome.

Friends are so important to this process, and I love my cheerleaders. For my retreat buddies—Dana, Lee, and Jo. Same time next year? Grateful for Tina Radcliffe, Susie Dietze, Piper Huguley, Julie Hilton Steele, Angela Anderson, and Carolyn Hector Hall (and her inspiring Barbie creations) for their support.

Don't miss another trip to Moose Falls, coming in fall 2024:

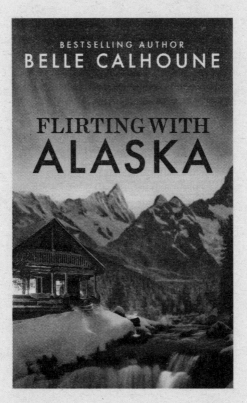

# ABOUT THE AUTHOR

**Belle Calhoune** grew up in a small town in Massachusetts as one of five children. Growing up across the street from a public library was a huge influence on her life. Married to her college sweetheart and mother to two daughters, she lives in Connecticut. A dog lover, she has a mini poodle and a black Lab.

She is a *Publishers Weekly* bestselling author as well as a member of RWA's Honor Roll. In 2019 her book *An Alaskan Christmas* was made into a movie (*Love, Alaska*) by Brain Power Studios and aired on UPTV. She is the author of more than forty novels and published by Grand Central Publishing and Harlequin Love Inspired.

*Can't get enough of that small-town charm? Forever has you covered with these heartwarming romances!*

### SUMMER ON SUNSHINE BAY
### by Debbie Mason

Lila Rosetti Sinclair returns to Sunshine Bay to share the news that she's engaged—to a man her mother has never met. Eva Rosetti is so ecstatic to have her daughter home that she wants to hide the fact that her family's restaurant, La Dolce Vita, is in trouble. With a business to save and a wedding to plan, their reunion is more than either bargained for. But with support from friends and family, it may just turn out to be the best summer of their lives.

### THE GOOD LUCK CAFÉ
### by Annie Rains

Moira Green is happy with her quiet life. Then everything goes topsy-turvy when the town council plans to demolish the site of her mother's beloved café. Moira is determined to save it, so she swallows her pride and asks Gil Ryan for help. But with Gil supporting the council's plans, Moira is forced to find another way to save Sweetie's—and it involves campaigning against Gil. As the election heats up, so does their attraction. But can these two be headed for anything but disaster?

*Discover bonus content and more on*
*read-forever.com*

**FALLING FOR ALASKA**
**by Belle Calhoune**

True Everett knows better than to let a handsome man distract her, especially when it's the same guy who stands between her and owning the tavern she manages in picturesque Moose Falls, Alaska. She didn't pour her soul into the restaurant just for former pro-football player Xavier Stone to swoop in and snatch away her dreams. But amid all the barbs—and sparks—in the air, True glimpses the man beneath the swagger. That version of Xavier, the real one, might just steal True's heart.

**SPRINGTIME IN SUGAR LAKE**
**by Marina Adair**

The last thing Glory Mann wants is to head the committee of the Miss Peach Pageant in Sugar, Georgia. Especially when her co-chairman is rugged, ripped…and barely knows she's alive. Single dad Cal McGraw already has his hands full, but he can't deny the strong chemistry he has with Glory. As squabbles threaten to blow up the contest—and the town of Sugar itself—Cal must risk everything to get a second chance at love.

**Meet your next favorite book with @ReadForeverPub on TikTok**

**CHANGE OF PLANS**
**by Dylan Newton**

When chef Bryce Weatherford is given guardianship of her three young nieces, she knows she won't have time for a life outside of managing her family and her new job. It's been years since Ryker Matthews had his below-the-knee amputation, and he's lucky to be alive. But "lucky" feels more like "cursed" to his lonely heart. When Ryker literally sweeps Bryce off her feet in the grocery store, they both feel sparks. But is falling in love one more curveball…or exactly the change of plans they need?

**FAKE IT TILL YOU MAKE IT**
**by Siera London**

When Amarie Walker leaves her life behind, she lands in a small town with no plan and no money. An opening at the animal clinic is the only gig for miles around, but the vet is a certified grump. At least his adorable dog appreciates her! When Eli Calvary took over the failing practice, he decided there was no time for social niceties. But when he needs help, it's Amarie's name that comes to his lips. Now Eli and Amarie need to hustle to save the clinic.

*Follow @ReadForeverPub on X and join the conversation using #ReadForeverPub*

### A LAKESIDE REUNION
### by C. Chilove

Reese spent every summer of her childhood in the lake town of Mount Dora, Florida, never realizing that the haven hid a divide between the haves and have-nots. Not until she fell for Duncan, a have-not. Ten years later, she's back and must come to terms with all she's missed. Mostly that Duncan is now a successful real estate developer—and time hasn't weakened the connection between them.

### AS SEEN ON TV
### by Meredith Schorr

Emerging journalist Adina Gellar is done dating in New York City. So when a real estate magnate targets tiny Pleasant Hollow for development, Adi knows it's the perfect story—one that will earn her a coveted job…and maybe even deliver her dream man. Finn Adams is not a ruthless businessman. In fact, he genuinely wants to help the small town. Only some busybody reporter is determined to mess up his plans. But he can't deny that her sense of humor and eternal optimism are a balm to his troubled past. Will following their hearts mean destroying their careers?